MARCHING TO ZION

Mary Glickman

OPEN ROAD

INTEGRATED MEDIA

NEW YORK

Cover design by Jason Gabbert

978-1-4804-3562-9

Published in 2013 by Open Road Integrated Media, Inc.
345 Hudson Street
New York, NY 10014
www.openroadmedia.com

For the lovers,
their arms around the grief of the ages

CONTENTS

FAIRER WORLDS ON HIGH
1934–1936

MARCHING TO ZION

Marching to Zion

Come, we that love the Lord,
And let our joys be known;
Join in a song with sweet accord,
And thus surround the throne.
Chorus: We're marching to Zion,
Beautiful, beautiful Zion;
We're marching upward to Zion,
The beautiful city of God.

Let those refuse to sing
Who never knew our God;
But children of the heavenly King
May speak their joys abroad.
Chorus: We're marching to Zion,
Beautiful, beautiful Zion;
We're marching upward to Zion,
The beautiful city of God.

The hill of Zion yields
A thousand sacred sweets
Before we reach the heav'nly fields,
Or walk the golden streets.
Chorus: We're marching to Zion,
Beautiful, beautiful Zion;
We're marching upward to Zion,
The beautiful city of God.

Then let our songs abound,
And ev'ry tear be dry;
We're marching thru Emanuel's ground
To fairer worlds on high.
Chorus: We're marching to Zion,
Beautiful, beautiful Zion;
We're marching upward to Zion,
The beautiful city of God.

Isaac Watts, 1707

LET THOSE REFUSE TO SING

St. Louis, Missouri, East St. Louis, Illinois,
1916–1918

I

MAGS STEPPED BACK INTO the street to see the building before her in its entirety, all five stories of it. Mags had never been inside a building that tall. She marveled that the fifth floor kept from crashing down into the first. The sight and wonder of it dropped her jaw and dried her mouth. Behind her, carriages, carts, horsemen, and motorcars raced by on urgent business, raising dust in great yellow clouds, and the dust entered her lungs through her open, dried-up mouth so that she staggered backward and set to in a coughing fit. Mags was a country gal, ignorant of city folk, their hustle and bustle, their common lack of caring about anything but their own affairs. Though not a single beating heart that passed gave two hoots she'd lost both her dignity and her respiration, she was deeply embarrassed to be seen doubled over trying to catch her breath at the side of the street, equines and vehicles swerving around her. Her lean cheeks burned hotter than if she were in a choir about to sing a new hymn without a songbook. Suddenly a strong arm went around her waist. A deep, silken voice murmured directly into her ear just loud enough for her to hear: Are you alright, darlin'? Let's get you out of the street. Would you care to set down and have a little water or somethin'?

Mags pulled away as hard as she could, startled out of her cough and into a ragged wheeze. She stood heaving, her bony back at a right angle to her knees, her head cocked to stare up with eyes wide as a bug's at the man who would expedite her fate for the next number of years, and so saw him that first time sideways, an omen for what passed between them if a sign unrecognized can be called such. What she saw was everything folk back home told her to avoid like wildfire in St. Louis—a handsome man, dandified in silks and bright cottons, a gardenia his boutonniere, a gold tooth illuminating his wide, welcoming smile. His skin and hair were as shiny black as the ebony knob of his walking stick, and his eyes were a startling, sparkling green. She heard the voice of her cousin Aurora Mae warning her. Watch yourself, Mags, with those trussed-up city men. There's ones specialize in hypnotizin' little brown rabbits like you. Exchange but a word with one of those and all your hopes and dreams will be forever gone.

Mags did nearly everything Aurora Mae told her to do. The woman was a goddess to her, despite the fact that Mags was five years older and should have been the senior cousin, dispensing advice and commands by birthright. Determined and intelligent, Mags had taught herself to read and write. Whatever humble letters Aurora Mae possessed, Mags had given her. Still, there was the matter of blood. Aurora Mae's blood was near pure African on her granddaddy's side. She was proper owner of all the land on which he'd invited the family to settle after Emancipation. Even if Aurora Mae hadn't looked the way she did—impossibly tall and lean with skin as black as a moonless, starless night with firelit eyes and a full purple mouth, all of it surrounded by a mass of rich, thick hair that had never seen scissors—Mags would have followed her into the jaws of death. She was a queen among women and men, too, a queen who knew everything the old ones did about plants and herbs, which would heal and which would kill, which bring pleasure and which bring pain. If it hadn't been for her cousin's encouragement, Mags never would have had the nerve to go to the big city by herself. Yet here she was on a Monday morning facing opportunity and danger at every crossroads.

The man smiling at her was from boots to stickpin exactly the demon she'd imagined when Aurora Mae cautioned her. Mags straightened up. She tried to speak. Her voice, which she intended to be cold and haughty, came out in a croak. I am just fine on my own, sir, she said, and then fell to coughing worse than before. Back went his arm around her, and this time there was no strength left in her to disengage. Out of necessity, she leaned into him and let him guide her out of the gutter and up the front stoop of the five-story building she'd sought since daybreak when she'd arrived on the wrong side of town after traveling half the night knocking between canisters in the back of a milk wagon.

He ushered her into the vestibule and deposited her on a wooden bench set against a wall between two fluted posts. Now, you just set here, he said. He whipped out a keychain from his left pocket and stuck a key in the door opposite her seat. He disappeared for half a minute. Came back with a glass of water, which she took and sipped slowly as it burned going down.

There, isn't that better? the fancy man said.

She raised her eyes above the rim of the glass and nodded. Thank you, she managed in a raspy whisper.

He chuckled. It was a low, rolling sound he made, reminding Mags of a daddy cooing over his newborn child, and she thought, How could a man who laughs in such a manner be a bother to a girl? It made her feel familiar to him, protected. Besides all that, he'd gone and helped her when she was suffering in a roadway, in danger of being trampled by man, beast, and machine. Mags considered then thought to extend a little trust. She straightened up, holding the water glass primly in her lap, and addressed him using the most formal constructions of language she knew to be on the safe side.

Mister, you've been very kind but might I ask you for a bit more help? I am new to this place and require confirmation of important facts before I affect the business I came here to find.

He chuckled again in another warm wave of paternal amusement, which gave her gooseflesh for no reason poor Mags could establish. The man sidled onto the bench next to her. Well, first I think introductions are in order, he said. I am Magnus Bailey, at your service.

Mags nearly lost her breath again, this time from shock. Magnus Bailey? she asked. In truth? She shoved a hand into the little bundle she carried and pulled out a worn handbill folded over four times even. She quickly unfolded it and waved it around a bit for emphasis. This Magnus Bailey?

The handbill was headed up by a drawing of twenty-two ten-dollar bills fanned out, beneath which was printed:

MY MONEY.
IT AIN'T FREE, BUT IT AIN'T HARD TO GET.
STOP BY 343 CHANCE STREET FOR A LUCKY ONE OF YOUR OWN.
~MAGNUS 'DON'T-TURN-NOBODY-DOWN-NO-HOW-NO-WAY' BAILEY~

My oh my, Bailey said. Where'd you find that old thing?

Mags opened her mouth to speak, then froze. She wasn't sure she should tell him she'd found the paper in an outhouse where it awaited standard use. She stretched things a bit.

In back of a store where I had some day work, she said. But

you're him? This moneyman what don't-turn-nobody-down-no-how-no-way?

Without knowing she was doing it, Mags gave Magnus Bailey a most fetching look. Her well-lashed black eyes went wide, the delicate nostrils of her straight, prim nose flared, and her lips, thin on the top, full on the bottom, remained parted when she was done speaking. Her lower lip trembled a little and her tongue ran over it, then disappeared.

Magnus Bailey appeared to take a breath before speech, but what he really did was succumb to a tiny gasp, a pure failure in his attempt to cover the pang of desire she planted at the root of him. Luckily for him, Mags did not have the experience to recognize his predicament.

Well, yes, that man used to be me, he said in a voice softer and deeper yet. It might be again.

She took a gulp of water for courage and put on her business voice.

Might we go into your office there, then? To discuss a matter of great importance to me?

He was on his feet steering her through his door before she had time to tuck the handbill back in her bundle. The paper fluttered to the floor and floated on the sweep of their movements to a spot under the bench on which they'd sat making acquaintance. Mags turned her head and looked down. Water sloshed over the rim of her glass to puddle on the floor.

As if they were lovers of some standing, Magnus anticipated her gesture. Don't go after that now, darlin', he said. Someone will get it later.

They were in his office alone with the door shut. As far as Mags knew, there was no one else on their floor or the whole building for that matter. He brushed behind her so that their bodies grazed. He put a hot hand on her elbow to guide her to one of two upholstered chairs across from his desk. She sunk into it. It was softer than her bed back home. Once he had her seated, he sat himself, put his feet up on his desk, and asked her polite questions about her origins and trip to town, so that she began to relax, chatting amiably, running off at the mouth a little the way country gals will do when they try to avoid sounding sullen or stupid. He listened and nodded then got up from the great oak desk, a grand affair scrolled at every corner and slick as ice on the top. He walked around, plunked himself down in the unoccupied chair, put his long heavy arm against the back of hers, and leaned in to speak.

Now, what was it you wanted that brought you from your people's piney woods and pleasant fields to this dusty metropolis in search of my money? he asked her.

She twisted in her seat and pointed her bony knees toward him. Lifting her chin to give him what she fancied was her most sophisticated, most solemn expression, Mags said, I wish to start a business, a beauty salon for colored women. Do you realize there simply are none in the colored parts of most towns? I know this because I live in the middle of nowhere, and people come to my home from far, far off just for waves and plaits. Now, I'm thinkin' I could offer 'em skin and nail treatments, eyebrow pluckin' and the like, if only I had the know-how. Because I believe with all my heart that our women deserve to look just as finished-up as the white women in the magazines. And it don't matter how hard times are, a single woman will pay for nice hair and hands on every holiday you can name if she can git 'em for not too much. She'll find the money somewhere.

She didn't tell him the single woman she was talking about was herself or that she had no knowledge of how other single women of her class and race felt. She was still young enough to think that if she felt a thing strongly, everyone else must too. She went on telling him about the extraordinary lengths she would go to if it meant achieving her goal. At last, she got to the meat of it.

I'm lookin' for you to make me a loan of one hundred dollars for my purpose, Mr. Bailey. With part of that hundred dollars, I will contrive to stay in the city and apprentice myself and with the other part, I'll buy all the supplies I need to start a salon up and git 'em on back home when I'm learned enough.

Magnus smiled and leaned in a little closer, which meant very close indeed, close enough for her to smell what his shirt was laundered in, a thing of violets and sunshine, entirely agreeable. She fought the urge to let her mind drift away on that scent by calling up Cousin Aurora Mae's warning voice. You're a good gal, Aurora Mae said inside her head, but you let yourself get distracted all the time. Keep your head on straight and you'll be alright. Mags used the voice to stick a metal rod up her spine. Her neck stiffened, which kept her mind alert.

And what are you going to give me in return, darlin'? Magnus asked.

She took a deep breath and squared her shoulders. All the ride into town she'd practiced her proposal. This was the glory part she'd figured would drive the deal home. She answered with enthusiasm.

Why, ten percent of my profits until it is paid back and then six month more at ten percent of my profits for gratitude!

Bailey rubbed his chin with the hand that formerly balanced itself on the back of her chair. This was an easy thing for him to do, not requiring so much as a good stretch. He'd moved in that close.

I hardly think that would be enough when there is such risk involved, he said.

He tilted his head and with a professional, critical air, touched her hair, then took up her hands to study their nails.

These are nice, he said slowly. If that's the kind of work you do, I'm feelin' better.

He had both her hands in the firm grip of one of his own and moved the one that rested on the back of her chair to a position that just grazed her far shoulder. If he wanted to, he could push her against him in a heartbeat.

She hesitated just a second or two. Her mouth screwed up as she wondered what he might do next. Maybe he was having a joke at her expense. His lips were curled in a tiny smile, but his eyes were serious, his gaze deep and steady. Danger, she thought, I am in terrible danger. She yelped, jerked her hands back, and jumped up from her chair, banging a knee on the scrolled corner of his enormous desk. She bent down quickly to retrieve the bundle she'd laid at her feet just as Bailey stooped to get it for her, and their heads knocked together. Mags yelped again, and this time banged her ankle on a leg of the desk as she scurried to the door.

Oh, dear, dear, dear, Bailey said, rubbing his forehead. We're getting off on the wrong foot, aren't we?

Laughing softly at his own wit, he went back behind his desk and sat. He gestured for her to return to a chair opposing him.

Don't mind me, child. A man has to try, doesn't he? And now I've done so. You'll have no more foolishness from me.

She stood, straight-backed, in front of the office door, with one hand on the doorknob behind her while the other clutched her bundle against her chest like a shield.

I came here to talk business, she said. We can either talk it with me here and you there or I'll be gone.

Magnus Bailey's game stopped short. She was mighty brave, he saw, an innocent ready to face the perils of masculine strength and casual corruption. He had no shortage of women friends. There was no need in him to toy with this one. He felt a touch of shame that he'd teased her and reconsidered her proposition.

When she emerged from the office an hour later, Mags was flushed but her honor remained intact. In one hand, she clutched a scrap of paper on which was written the address of a rooming house for ladies run by a close friend of Magnus Bailey himself. Deep in her skirt pocket, stuffed in as safe a place as she had to store it, was a ten-dollar bill Magnus gave her on loan to help her settle into life in the city. He would not give her the hundred dollars she wanted, but he was prepared to help her stay and find a city job. That way, she could earn the money on her own.

She hit the streets of St. Louis elated, energized, poised for battle against all the evils of which she had been forewarned as well as those she had already witnessed. She felt supremely confident that she had survived—no, conquered—the first challenge of life as a free woman, as a woman alone in the world, a woman away from home. She had resisted the seductions of Magnus Bailey and got a ten-dollar loan besides. Her senses felt sharp, her sensibility refined by experience. She assessed the streets and people around her, making mental notes for the letter she would write to Aurora Mae when she had the chance. St. Louis is jam-packed with rich Negroes, she'd write, and I will soon be one of them. Her judgment, of course, was framed by the poverty in which she'd been raised and against which the meanest circumstances seemed luxurious. Men in threadbare jackets and tattered shirts raised worn caps to her as she passed and she thought, Yes, I surely will be rich one day and marry a gent like one of them. Her spirits were boundless.

To celebrate her success, she stopped at a Negro café for sweet tea and a slice of sugar cake. She lingered over her treat as if she were a lady of leisure with all the time in the world to spare instead of a country bumpkin in search of a rooming house before night fell. She sat at a table by the window to watch the swells go by. She listened hard to the other customers, trying to decipher their citified speech. They spoke of snootfuls and pitch-ins and chewing rags. By the time she stepped back into the street, she felt she might have been in Europe or Asia. Every detail of life was exotic to her. Faced with diversions everywhere, she found it difficult to pay attention to the route she'd been told to take. Two or three times, she got lost.

At such a pace, it was several hours' walk to the new bridge over the river into East St. Louis and with all the sights and people to see there, Mags took another half hour to cross over. It wasn't until she reached the desired address that her high-flying confidence collapsed. The first indication she might have fallen into a pot of trouble was when a blond-headed white woman wrapped in a flimsy duster of some kind answered the door, a tired-looking woman with paint smudges under her eyes, plenty of powder, and twin red splotches on her cheeks. She greeted Mags as if she were the coal man or a rag picker. My front door? she barked. What are you doin' at my front door! Go to the back, you. 'Fore I boot you down these steps.

The door slammed in Mags's face. Heat came to her cheeks as she trudged around the back with her head down. She muttered to herself. The neighborhood hadn't looked like it changed from Negro to white by any means. What'd that Magnus Bailey do? Send her to the very edge of the color line 'round here? It plain didn't make sense. A rooming house that didn't house her kind. Why would he lend her good money then send her on a fool's errand? Maybe he'd writ the address wrong? With no place else to go and darkness coming, she knocked on the rear door, then backed down two steps in case an angry man or a mad dog jumped out. The same washed-out blond-headed woman answered. This time she smiled and asked what could she do for Mags, sweet as you please, as if their previous encounter had never occurred.

Magnus Bailey sent me here, Mags said, looking up at her with features guarded by suspicion. I hear you got lodgin'.

Maybe it was the name Magnus Bailey that worked the charm.

Well, why didn't you say so? Come in, come in, the woman said in a sugary voice, holding open the screen door for her.

Mags trudged up the stairs slowly, hugging her belongings to her chest. She still half expected someone to pop out at her, steal her bundle and her ten-dollar bill, then send her back down the stairs with a well-placed foot. She entered a large kitchen with a pantry and buttery both at the back. She did not know what to call either room and wondered at their purpose. There was a large six-burner, gas-powered stove with the gas bottle attached to its side by a web of iron fittings, along with a cast-iron drawer that allowed the additional fuel of coal or wood. Mags couldn't smell which. An ice chest marshaled the space to the left, and a sink with a pump-handle graced the right. The remainder of the kitchen was taken up by a long dining table, large enough to sit fourteen people, the chairs of which were occupied by ten women of a class and style similar to the blond-headed one, except that they were Negroes like Mags, women of a variety of ages and shapes, in hues ranging from pitch-black to butterscotch brown. Though it was late in the afternoon, they also wore dusters or silk robes. Their feet were in slippers or bare, and they drank coffee and pecked at plates of eggs like so many disinterested birds.

Mags'd learned plenty from the old handbills, newspapers, and penny dreadfuls she scavenged wherever she could, so that the scene before her caused her no small distress. Lord, o Lord, o Lord, she thought, I am landed in a bawdy house. She turned to run out the door, but it was blocked by the smiling blond woman. Trapped, she thought, I am trapped. Her eyes welled.

What's your name, gal?

Afraid to meet the gaze of whoever asked the question, Mags kept her head down. Her voice went soft. Margaret Preacher, she near whispered. Back home they call me Mags.

Well then howdy-do, Mags Preacher. I'm thinkin' you're a Bible thumper's child with a name like that. Must be, must be. I'm Char-lene, called Charly, and this here is Bethany, called Tawny because, well, look at her, and you'll know. Come on, child, pick up your head, we're friendly here.

Obedient by nature, Mags kept her head down but peeped up at the assembled open-eyed as each recited her proper name followed by a moniker won by physical nature or personality. It wouldn't be difficult to remember the nicknames, as they seemed particularly well chosen. Bobsy had hair tamed into a pile of ringlets on her crown that jigged and jumped with her every move. The shape of Cat's eyes was decidedly feline. Legs was very tall. The corners of Rain's mouth and eyes had a downward slant, so that she looked perpetually sad, even when laughing, and so on. By the time the women were done introducing themselves, Mags had to admit they were a kindly, welcoming bunch given to sweet gestures and gentle jests among them, reminding her of the cousins back home when they all got together for Sunday supper after church. Against her better judgment, she began to relax.

The woman at the table's end, a big woman, one of the darkest in skin, a woman with breasts like bed pillows, soft, high, and large, a woman called, with little poetry, Chesty, patted the empty seat next to her and said, Sit, gal. You look hungry and tired. Miss Emily will get you somethin', won't you, Miss Emily?

The blond woman took a thick slice of bread from an enamel breadbox, dropped it in a skillet greasy with the afternoon's scrambled eggs, and broke a couple fresh ones that hit the iron surface sizzling.

Hunger and exhaustion have a way of rendering even suspect surroundings appeal. Making the most of things, Mags thanked Chesty and the blond woman called Miss Emily, took a seat next to the former, and ate greedily with her hands. The half-dressed city women sitting around the table raised amused eyebrows and nudged one another with powdered elbows. Chesty draped an arm around the back of her chair much as Magnus Bailey had done back at his office.

Child, you remind me of a baby sister of mine, Chesty said, her tone as warm as the heat that radiated from her considerable mass.

You got the same round eyes, and she was a skinny li'l thing, just like you. That's right, you just eat up. Then Miss Emily'll show you a room, see if it's to your likin'.

While Mags ate, various of her tablemates stretched, yawned, and announced it was time to get ready for work. Watching them leave the kitchen one by one, Mags ate faster, thinking that if the house was one of ill-repute, she'd best fill her belly and get the heck out. Better to find an alleyway or a lonely stoop to sleep on than a place that might catch her in an everlasting trap. Miss Emily, whom she saw now was not white but a much-diluted black with dyed hair, filled her plate a second time. Mags found herself perched on the horns of a practical dilemma. Should she push away her plate and leave rather than risk degradation and indenture, or consume as much as she could when tomorrow's bread might be too dear for her to manage? Determined to eat very, very fast, she set to. After she finished, she accepted another cup of coffee thinking she needed it. A night without a roof over her head would be long indeed. Then one by one, the ladies of the table reappeared, dressed for work, and her mind took a turn.

Most were in uniforms with thin wraps thrown over. Each uniform was different in some way, either in color or cut. Judging from their attire, a woman more knowledgeable than Mags would see night-shift kitchen help, waitresses, hospital drudges, and hotel maids. Mags did the best she could with new information and fancied they might be costumed actresses in a theatrical revue as she'd read about on privy paper similar to the one that led her to St. Louis and Magnus Bailey. She was relieved that at least her housemates were not employed at the same address as the one where they slept. She hoped they kept whatever indiscretions they might commit private and out of the realm of monetary enterprise. This is the city, she reminded herself. I need to open up my mind.

After she finished eating, Miss Emily showed her a small, narrow room without a window. A radiator spit steam just outside in the hallway. Miss Emily vowed its proximity would keep her warm during the worst of winter. The room was furnished with a made-up bed and a washbasin on a stand, which looked like opulence to country eyes. Mags gladly gave Miss Emily a dollar from her ten, counting the change twice to be absolutely sure she had it right. The dollar bought her a week of room and board, a fair price as far as she knew. While the proprietress showed her the communal convenience, Mags thought to ask her where she might find work, mentioning her desire to train at a beauty salon for ladies. Miss Emily said she'd have an overnight think on it and let her know where her best bets for employment might be in the morning.

All in all, Mags figured she'd done real well for a first day in the wide world. Well fed and tuckered out, she slept sound as you please, never hearing the shouts and screams, the wail of sirens that sparked the quiet dark around her, night music as natural to East St. Louis as the shriek of bobcat and the howls of wolves in her own backyard.

II

MAGS'S SECOND DAY IN the wide world told a different tale. Miss Emily sent her around to a variety of establishments looking for hired help. Mags had trouble figuring what any of them had to do with her ambitions. There was a chemist who informed her with winks and riddles the dimmest of hicks could comprehend that he specialized in helping women set down burdens they did not wish to carry and restoring their spirits thereafter. He needed someone to sterilize his bottles, mix his potions according to his recipes, and clean up the surgery he used whenever he came across a lady who was potion-defiant. The only connection Mags could make between that man and a beauty salon was the array of suffering females in his waiting room, each of them cinched in, pushed up, and lacquered over.

The second place Miss Emily sent her was indeed a beauty salon but cross-river in a white neighborhood where Mags stuck out like a blackbird in winter for not being dressed in any kind of livery. The salon wanted part-time help cleaning and sweeping up. The proprietress told Mags straight out she wouldn't be allowed in the front part of the shop until after everyone else had left for the day. Mags couldn't see how she'd learn anything there except the workings of the indoor toilet and the washtub. With waning hopes, she headed back to the colored district and the final address Miss Emily had provided. Along the way, she endured the hostile stares and incomprehensible epithets of white people as down and out as any she'd seen in the heart of negritude. Their language was unknown to her, but their hateful spirit was familiar. Every step she took away from their enclave and closer to her own eased her.

The signpost pitched in the rolling garden of her destination read FISHBEIN'S FUNERAL HOME. Fishbein's Funeral Home was a rambling gray structure bordered by four-story tenements with no yards at all. It was half hewn stone and half wood, with enough gables and porches to accommodate a nation of ghosts. For the second time in two days, Mags stepped back into the street to stare at a building in drop-jawed amazement. The house was as grand as any she'd admired in the deeply white part of town. She looked up at the roof with three chimneys and double-, then triple-checked the address. Finally she acknowledged she had the right place although she questioned the words 'funeral home.' She did not understand their meaning. Where she came from, people waked their dead as soon as a passel of relatives washed and dressed the one gone. They waked them in the parlor if they had one, the kitchen if they had not. If time permitted, loved ones were buried in homemade coffins in the backyard, as the closest church was a distance and only easy to get to on a fair-weather Sunday. If the ground was about to freeze and time was of the essence, the dead were buried in sheets wound up tight. If times were especially hard, flour sacks stitched together sufficed. If winter made the ground unyielding to spade or shovel, the dead waited on ice until the first thaw. The idea that some poor soul without rest should have a home before flying off to the belly of hell or the bosom of Jesus struck her as so fantastical that Mags determined that 'funeral home' meant something of which she was completely unaware.

Hoping for the best interpretation, she followed the signs for the service entrance around the back, climbed three steps, and knocked on the door. No answer. She rang the bell. Same thing. She knocked and rang together. Waited a bit. Turned to leave. Then, with a great creak and crash of noise, the right side of the bulkhead door to the left of the bottom step abruptly swung open, landing on the surrounding gravel bed in a rattling thump. Half a lean brown man in a spattered white smock and big black rubber gloves popped out the opening. His color was much like her own, a caramel just this side of burnt. His face was an assembly of hard, smooth planes. He didn't have a nose so much as a beak. His brow looked as if a rectangular metal plate had been sewn beneath a scant layer of flesh that stretched over it so tight it seemed the skin would bust open if he chanced to frown. His cheeks were like two downward-pointing arrows, his black eyes bright but small, and his lips no more than straight lines colored a slightly redder hue than the rest of him. His hair was a close-cut helmet of black wool. He was a good ten years older than Mags, maybe more.

You the one causin' a ruckus, gal? he asked, clearly annoyed at the interruption of her presence. What is it that you want?

Mags said, simply, A job.

Goodness gracious me. Then come on in. If you don't mind, come on in down here. Doin' so will skip the niceties some'at but will prepare you for the employment on offer.

Mags hesitated.

The man said, If you're not brave, then go on home. I need a helper not a child to train in life's realities.

She didn't know how brave she was, but there was command in his voice, and Mags was accustomed to doing what people wanted her to do. Aurora Mae was not the only person in her ken who wore power like a cloak. She approached the bulkhead to walk down the stairs.

No, no, the man said, not like that. Turn around and come down like you was on a ladder. Hold on to the wall there.

She did as she was told and descended backward into the cold dark. Turning about, she found herself in an antechamber of the dead, a dim basement foyer lit by a single gas lamp flickering over a damp stone wall.

My name's George McCallum, the man said, holding up a gloved hand. He waved it around in exaggerated motion as apology for not shaking hers. She nodded and gave him her name and a pleased-to-meet-you with her eyes steady on his to convince him there was courage in her. For some reason she did not comprehend, it had become essential to her, vital even, from the moment her feet hit the floor, that George McCallum approve of her and offer her employment. Her chest heaved twice with determination as she struggled to combat a competing notion to flee.

He nodded back, sharply, in acknowledgment. As a further test, the small, bright eyes bored into her in a manner that dared her to look away. She did not. He reached in a pocket of his smock, handed her two cotton balls molded into plug shapes, and stepped aside.

Now brace yourself, gal.

She did. He opened the door.

The stench hit her nose like a fist. Sour, sweet, foul, choking. Her eyes teared from the sting of it. George McCallum tapped her shoulder and demonstrated the use of the cotton plugs by pushing two up his nose. She did the same and wiped her eyes with the back of her hand. McCallum grinned encouragement and gestured for her to follow along a corridor lined by many rooms, each with a closed door sentried by silence.

It's not always this bad, he said, but there was a terrible accident last week. Roof caved in on a family of five. All dead. I'm waitin' on the relatives to arrive from Arkansas for the finalities, which should occur tomorrow or the day after. Normally, I don't advise waitin' for the plantin'. Put 'em in the ground or ship 'em out, I always say, but these folks insisted. I'm workin' on the mama and the baby girl together at present as they got the same skin tones and all. I don't have to mix the face paints but once.

They reached an open space with walls dominated by cabinets pushed up against cold, beaded stone. Many had drawers or doors open. There were tables on wheels rolled under them for convenience, and on the tables and in the cabinets were a multitude of bottles holding chemicals and powders, brushes, pens, and combs. There were full wigs and partial ones in a host of colors and textures hanging from hooks like dried fish.

Finally, Mags knew what kept her putting one foot before the other when half her mind wanted to cut and run. There in the middle of the floor were two stretchers with dead bodies laid out upon them, draped mostly, but naked enough for her to recognize a woman fully grown, fat and loose like a baked brown betty that had not quite set, and a girl, a young girl, perhaps eight or ten, with long black braids that dangled over the table's edge. The young girl was sewn and painted so skillfully that she looked, not alive or merely sleeping the way people sometimes said the laid-out looked, but like a china doll, the kind Mags always admired in magazines. She was an angel, a vision of peace and grace, more beautiful in her shiny nutmeg skin than any corpse had a right to be. Her appearance was almost an insult to death itself and certainly one to life. Her mama, on the other hand, had needles with weighted threads dangling from all over her contorted features.

You see, that's the first step to how we do it, George McCallum said, explaining how he'd labored to craft the daughter's peaceful expression out of the agony that was the mama's death throes.

Amazed, Mags gestured from the girl to the woman and blurted out, You made this from that?

McCallum smiled. I did, he said.

Oh my, oh my, thought Mags. If such miracles could be worked on the dead, what splendors might be worked upon the living! Can you learn me how? she asked him.

George McCallum sized her up once more in a long, slow glance from her toes to the top of her head. He didn't run into people like Mags every day, a pretty young gal about ready to drop from excitement over learning how to care for the cold and gone. He struggled to keep his delight buried until they could work out the details of her pay.

Well, most times a body's got to be born to the death trade to study it proper, he told her while scratching his chin with the back of a rubber glove. But I suppose I could teach you if you were willing to work especially hard.

Oh yessir. I will work day and night to get me such skills. I promise you that.

He gave her a tour of the rest of the funeral home, educating her about how city folk with enough coin in their pockets buried their dead, about the rooms for laying out, the rooms for grieving, and the rooms for receiving condolences. He showed her the chapel, a kitchen, a showroom for coffins, and an office. Up on the second floor were living quarters, he told her, but these were off-limits.

When they were through and had come to agreement on salary and hours, Mags felt as if she herself had died and been resurrected. She walked on a heavenly cloud back to Miss Emily's rooming house, buoyed by hope and accomplishment. She felt exceedingly proud of herself. Only two days in the city, and already she had a loan, a home, and a job that would prepare her for the future of her dreams. Later, she announced her success to the night-crawling residents of Miss Emily's as they gathered for breakfast at six p.m. She was unconcerned at first when Chesty gasped and Bobsy shrieked, when Rain knocked every piece of wood in the room, when Cat closed her eyes up tight and pushed her nostrils up in disgust. Miss Emily, stirring a pot on the boil, frowned with one half of her mouth.

Fishbein's. Fishbein's. She's goin' to Fishbein's, Chesty said in a voice halfway between speech and prayer. She swayed back and forth the way mourners keen.

The women echoed her, murmuring the name Fishbein like a chant. Rain threw salt over her shoulders, right and left, then admonished Mags to reconsider her decision carefully as the Angel of Death did not appreciate being made light of, not at all. And that Fishbein, well, he had a reputation is all. He was a Jew, to begin with, a Jew who buried coloreds for a livin', Rain finished up. Now, that alone is odd enough to lend belief to everythin' they say about him.

It never occurred to me to ask about the owner, Mags told them. George McCallum is the boss over there.

If you say so, child, Chesty said.

Now, look you all, that's just about enough, Miss Emily added. It was me sent her over. It's not as if she ran there blind like a calf skitterin' home to its ma.

Mags had no idea what any of them meant, but she was grateful Miss Emily's words shut the others up as they shrugged or sniffed and changed the subject. One thing was certain. City people were peculiar about death. Let them try living in the country with farm animals, wild things, babies and old folk, young men in their prime, all of them dying by the barrel full in every rough season. They'd soon get over their superstitions. As she dipped her bread in coffee and chewed on a crisp stick of bacon, she felt superior to all of them, at least until the conversation turned toward public transportation and she demonstrated some fresh ignorance about the frequency of stops on the trolley line. The others laughed and teased her relentlessly the rest of the meal.

It wasn't until later that night when everyone but Miss Emily had gone to work and she lay in her bed reviewing the day, telling it all to Aurora Mae in her mind, that Mags wondered who and where this Fishbein was. There'd been no sign of him at the home. The third floor had been as quiet as a tomb. She puzzled over her housemates' reaction to his very name and decided that it was natural a man who owned such a business might be considered fearsome. By the time she found out more about him, a half dozen lives gone had been readied for the earth under her hands.

Certainly George McCallum didn't offer much information. He never so much as referred to the owner of the funeral home by name. He was the Man Upstairs. Given the way death and mourning and the consolations of prayer inhabited the house like hot air in summer, Mags thought for a while he was referring to God.

Don't be draggin' that chair 'crost the floor, he told her the first time she helped him set up the reception hall for a crowd. The Man Upstairs don't like that. He can hear you, don't you forget it. He can hear every little thing goes on in this old house.

Amen, brother, Mags said, as if they were in church and the Divine had been summoned. Amen.

God's ear, she thought, was much occupied. The house was full of sound all the time, from one end to the other, upstairs and down. It creaked, it moaned. It gave off sudden loud pops and hums as if whatever currents of energy that kept it going blocked up then belched. There were voices, too. Male and female whispers sometimes in response to each other, sometimes in chorus, sometimes repeating themselves over and over as if issuing ignored commands in plaintive tones. Mags suffered a shivering fit when she first heard them. For her, they were like nothing so much as the complaints of the dead.

George McCallum laughed when she told him her thoughts and said, The Man Upstairs had visitors today, don't you know.

She did not find the image he provided comforting. It took a fresh little dip in her well of resolve to get to work the next morning. She summoned Aurora Mae's voice telling her before she left home, Anything worth doing is worth doing two weeks to see if it takes. You feelin' unsure after that, you quit.

It was good advice. After several weeks, Mags got used to things the way they were. She was learning a lot and saw there was much more she could learn from George McCallum. She took to making lunch for them both in the kitchen on the first floor of the main house. She'd tired of stale bread and the odd slice of cold meat Miss Emily gave her wrapped in newspaper to take with, and George McCallum offered to provide the fixins if she'd provide the cookin'. It was good to get out of the basement every day for a bit, when she could take the cotton from her nose and give her throat a rest. The air was always sweet from flowers and scented candles in the next rooms, especially so when no waiting corpse accompanied them. Sometimes, it gave her a bit of a faint when the first blast of ripe, cloying air hit her, but it felt nice in a strange way, reminding her of walking into Aurora Mae's house when that woman was deep in boiling or grinding up roots and whatnot for her mustards and draughts. If a day came when all was well, when the newly dead were old and died in peace, an event more common than ever she knew, the association made her warm inside, happy. On other days, when a child came into the basement morgue or a woman hideously beaten, when the faces of the dead were fixed in the worst horror or pain, it made her dreadful homesick.

It was one of the former days. She'd put up rice then sautéed collards with onion and garlic in fatback to toss in the rice when it was done. She'd bought the fatback on the way to work, a special purchase to celebrate her first full month working at Fishbein's Funeral Home and in residence in the bustling city of East St. Louis. It was also a way to do something nice for George McCallum, who was growin' on her. They didn't talk together much beyond the necessaries during the training he gave her, but what he did say was always interesting, sometimes humorously so, other times downright wise. He was a kind man, she thought, and respectful. Besides that, she felt he liked her. So she stirred her tribute lunch and hummed an old song her daddy sang on Sundays and Wednesdays after prayer meeting. Little sparks went off in her chest as she pictured George McCallum settin' down to such a feast when a great chorus of heavy steps came clattering down the service staircase at the back of the kitchen, a staircase that had offered nothing but silence in all the days and weeks she'd been at Fishbein's Funeral Home. She jumped and spun around, dropping a spatula on the floor. The door to the staircase swung open fiercely to hit the wall with a bang.

There, on the bottom step, was Magnus Bailey.

Mr. Bailey? Mags asked, not that she was uncertain of his identity but rather of his purpose. Why was he here? Why now? Was it to collect from her? She'd given a dollar already to Miss Emily to give to Magnus Bailey as she claimed to see him regular. Had her landlady cheated her? Why else would he pose on the edge of that step in his three-piece pinstripe suit with watch fob, a bowler hat on his head, his gloved hands bracing his form on either side of the wall to keep himself balanced on feet housed in sparkling spectators?

It was the briefest moment that he did so, but she remained perplexed even after he completed his movements in a graceful landing remarkable for its lightness. He went to her, took her by both arms to set her aside from her pots, removed the skillet from the burner, and dumped its contents in the sink. When he spoke, his words were exasperated, but the tone he employed caressed, as Magnus Bailey's voice always did.

Never, he said, never use fatback in this house. The scent of it makes the Man Upstairs ill.

Startled as she was by her creditor's appearance, Mags's mind boggled at the idea that fatback enfeebled the Almighty. Then she realized her misapprehension.

You meanin' Mr. Fishbein?

Who else? Magnus Bailey rolled his green eyes at her.

You were with Mr. Fishbein?

On business.

She couldn't help herself. What business? she asked. Whatever his business was, she figured, it had nothing to do with grief or loss.

Magnus Bailey arched an eyebrow and pursed his lips, raised a finger at her and wagged it. His business was no business of hers, that eyebrow said. Bailey tamped his bowler down on his head and left by the back door off the kitchen.

From that day, Mags spent a considerable amount of time speculating about Mr. Fishbein. When she asked George McCallum why the smell of fatback made the Man Upstairs sick, he told her Jews ate peculiar sometimes. He had no idea why. Mags knew nothing about Jews except that they killed the Lord Jesus Christ. She was often lost in confounding conjecture. Whenever she was in the kitchen, she'd pause now and again, hold her breath, her ears cocked to listen for any sign of his existence. Although that old house continued to knock and wheeze, she had no way of knowing which noises were that of Mr. Fishbein, which of ghosts, and which of the house itself. George McCallum insisted the last was generally responsible. It was another month before she learned anything new.

Fishbein! Fishbein! Fishbein!

From the third floor, the forbidden floor, came an angry feminine voice followed by a crash of porcelain or glass. Mags and George

McCallum stopped the arrangement of floral tributes in the viewing room and stared wide-eyed at the ceiling. A woman's sobs muffled by the wood and plaster between them followed, then thumps made by the knocking about of heavier objects or perhaps the woman herself hurled into a wall.

Mags put a hand on George McCallum's arm.

Should we go upstairs?

No. No, I don't think so.

Another crash. Another thump. Mags's heart sank, imagining a woman in extreme distress. Her hand tightened, she stepped a tiny bit behind him for protection.

I disagree, George.

She'd never used his given name to address him before. He inclined his head toward her, more fascinated by her voice uttering his name than the commotion going on above them.

Someone's in trouble up there, George.

She saw his chest swell, felt the heat come up from him to envelop her. He set his jaw with determination and pulled apart from her, patting the hand that remained on his arm.

I'll go now. I'll go.

There followed ten long, torturous minutes of waiting. When George returned to the reception hall, he was shaking his head, in confusion, in surprise, in thoughtfulness.

He wants to see you.

Mags's jaw dropped.

Me?

Yes.

What do I do?

Go.

Alright, she said, alright. And wiping her hands on her skirt, she ascended the kitchen staircase humming that old Sunday song her daddy sang for courage.

III

⚜

THE SONG WORKED. MAGS achieved her destination filled with the spirit and feared no evil nor Jew. The landing was large, its floor covered by a rich carpet patterned in swirling reds and golds. Before her were double doors of a rich, dark wood with two brass knobs. Potted plants and stained-glass windows flanked the doors. Shafts of light poured in through the windows' green-and-blue glass to give the place an eerie, sacral air. It was a world apart from downstairs. Despite its chapel and the calls upon Jesus' name whenever a corpse made it up from the basement and into the parlor for a short stay of celebration, that place was a universe of rankest flesh. It was as if a different, second house was plunked down directly on top the first, a habitation where the rippling murmurs and woeful moans of the bereaved below were snuffed out.

Mags paused to inhale deeply, twice. She put her hands on the two knobs and pushed. The doors swung forward, leaving her standing with her arms outstretched, a hand on each knob, her neck elongated, and her head tilted up to help her keep her balance against the doors' unexpected swing. She looked like an actress making a grand entrance onstage, an actress meant to embody all that was proud and privileged instead of resembling what she was, the cautious servant of betters like Aurora Mae, Miss Emily, George McCallum, and now this Mr. Fishbein. Her eyes swept the room, looking for an injured or cowering female or broken glassware or pots or broken anything that could have made the commotion that led to her summons. She found none. What she found was Mr. Fishbein, the saddest man in all the world.

Before she came to work at a house of the dead, Mags had witnessed plenty of heartache. She'd known women whose babies died at birth, young men whose brides were taken away by fever before the honeymoon sheets had time to grow cool, let alone cold. She had a cousin who saw the face of his little girl, a beautiful child, mauled by a pack of wild dogs. She'd seen motherless children, fresh from putting their mama in the ground, shuffle through a storm of sorrow. But never had she seen a man, woman, or child with anguish so etched into his features, his posture, that it was more an expression of what dwelt within. It was his very essence.

Fishbein's eyes were large and heavy-lidded, the whites of them entirely red, brimming with unspilled tears. Deep grooves led from the eyes down his cheeks, as if carved there by a constant weeping. His mouth had a downward cast that made her sad-sack housemate Rain's look cheerful. His thick, wild eyebrows and salt-and-pepper hair were wiry, the latter poking out in all directions from beneath a tasseled cap as if long ignored or torn at constantly by despairing hands. His shoulders were stooped. Wearing a belted dressing gown and pinstripe trousers, he sat at a great rolltop desk covered in papers. His long, thin legs were pressed tightly together. His hands were folded fast in his lap so that the knuckles went white and the fingertips red. He looked to be trying to keep a raging torment still in his gut, to carry it in silent sufferance. Mags thought that if a man who looked like that tried to laugh, it would come out in a groan or a sob.

It was hard to look at him. What's more, her life's training instructed her not to look directly at a white man too long. Her gaze left him and studied the room instead. Everything around her was rich and exotic, from the crystal chandeliers to the dark paintings of stags at mountain waterfalls to the collection of silver animals that crowded the mantelpiece. Mags took it all in while struggling to hide her fascination. Fishbein spoke, startling her.

You are George's Mags? he asked.

Mags was not aware she was George's Mags, but she warmed unexpectedly at the sound of it. Since a month or two in the city, even a month or two in company with the naked dead, does not remove the shyness in a country gal, her cheeks went hot as she nodded her bowed head.

I hear you are doing very well down the stairs. George tells me you have a talent for our work.

Fishbein had an odd accent, spoken in a wet rasp as if his words had drowned in wretchedness. She knew that people far downriver spoke differently from those up north. She thought maybe that's the way they speak downriver, very far down. Even more far than Memphis, maybe, she thought, as if she knew such things.

Thank you, sir.

He coughed, clearing his throat, but the wet rasp was not gone. I am also hearing that what goes on here earlier disturbs you.

Mags chewed her lip. What was she supposed to say to that?

It is my daughter, he said. She is not well, and sometimes not herself.

Mags remained mute, unsure of what she was supposed to say. She was stuck on the question of why a daughter would call out to her daddy by their family name. Counting on the fact that white people, even Jew white people, she assumed, expected Negroes to be of wandering mind, her glance searched the room again, looking for this Fishbein gal. There were two corridors off the room in which she stood, and the daughter was likely down one of those, in an equally strange room, quiet now and with any luck returned to herself. At last she managed to say, I am sorry for that, sir. She meant she was sorry he had a daughter who was sometimes not well, because she judged this misfortune to be the reason for all his trouble. He took her differently.

Do not apologize, he said. There is a terrible rumpus, I agree. Of course you concern yourself. But all is well, this I promise you.

The more he talked, the greater Mags's discomfort grew. By the time he dismissed her, her head ached from the dozens of uncommon ways in which she'd had to stretch her experience to figure out what it was this woeful white man wanted from her, why she was standing in front of him confronting the wobble of social boundaries she'd lived with all her life through. One thing was certain. She did not want to suffer another such interview anytime soon, which she told George McCallum the second she returned to their basement workshop.

I don't understand nothin' about Jews! she said. Except that I'm beginnin' to know why folks keep away from 'em much as they can do.

George surprised her. Now, now, he said. That's right harsh. Mr. Fishbein just wanted to get a look at you after I told him how fine you were workin' out.

Caught between pleasure at his compliment and the bit of pique she'd worked herself up to, Mags floundered and changed the subject.

You know this daughter of his?

I've seen her.

What's wrong with her anyway?

George McCallum's back was to her as he bent over his table to remove the shoes of a poor, mangled boy who'd been caught in the street between a motorcar and a team of horses pulling a fire wagon.

She's small and redheaded and angry, he said. I don't know why. Maybe because her daddy put her to live in a house of the dead. It was none of his family's business. He came to town ten year ago, and he bought it from my auntie, whose husband, the man what trained me, passed. He knew nothin' about the work. He asked me to run things, and I stayed on. Miss Minnie weren't much more than a squallin' redheaded baby mess in those times. I apologize I didn't tell about her before, but you know, she's been quiet a long time these days. I thought maybe she's cured of whatever it is ails her. I need your help here to straighten this poor chappie's arm.

It was a longer speech and more information than Mags had ever had from George McCallum at one spill. She fell to helping him without question. Her mind drifted to her interview upstairs, where the sad man called her George's Mags. Thinking on it lent a certain spice to their activities. She got gooseflesh when George McCallum stood up tight next to her as they bore down to break the poor chappie's bones then lay them down neat inside the shirt and jacket of his Sunday suit. George either noticed her condition or shared it, because after they were done and gone upstairs to cull the fading blossoms from the fresh out of the vases in the viewing room, he took a yellow rose just starting to brown at the tips of its outermost petals and stuck it in her hair on the right side, where her thick plaits would hold it in good. They both smiled, and he kissed her.

They liked each other. There was nothing standing in their way. In that day, folk didn't hem and haw about such matters. Within weeks, they decided to marry at the end of the month, knowing each other pretty well in some ways and not at all in others. George lived at the funeral home, in the back, in the two great rooms off the right side of the kitchen. He had a small porch of his own with a rocking chair. There was a little strip of green before the alleyways took over where he grew cooking herbs in a box. He bought another rocking chair for Mags and a little table to put between the rockers as an engagement present. He paid off her remaining debt to Magnus Bailey as well. He did all of this with few words and fewer gestures. There were no more kisses in the workrooms, which they decided was beyond improper, but each day when their labors were over, she made them a supper then carried it on a tray to the porch as the season permitted such. They ate with the little table between them in a warm glow of waiting for what George called 'the big day.' When they were done eating, George would tell her to rest while he did the cleaning up. Later, they sat and watched the moon rise over buildings so tall Mags thought she'd never get used to them. They held hands over the tabletop until she'd start to yawn, at which time George would walk her home. Still holding her hand, he'd take her all the way to Miss Emily's front door, where he'd kiss her good night three times, once on the forehead, once on her cheek, and last on her lips.

Mags had reason beyond romance to be grateful for his company. The first two blocks of her walk home were not the safest, limned as they were by plain, crowded apartment buildings inhabited by foreign factory workers, white ones from Poland and Germany, her future husband told her. Their children loitered on stoops and called out to her in their mamas' tongues things she did not understand. Until George McCallum started looking after her, she thought they were calling to one another. Once he was at her side nightly, she saw how he kept between her and them, stiffening his body, alert with tension. His grip on her hand was tight until they turned the corner two blocks up and walked deep into a territory of wooden shacks and the dark, familiar faces of home where he loosed his hold on her in a manner as telling as a sigh. She would have thought about it more, but she'd grown up expecting both the condescension and enmity of white people. It might've helped her to know racial tensions in East St. Louis approached a boiling point. At many of the factories, white union workers were on strike. The scabs the bosses hired were Negroes fresh off the train from down south, where recruiters painted rosy pictures of generous wages and freedom from Jim Crow up north—paid their fare, too. They arrived, many of them, shoeless and poor in the Missouri winter, shackled as much by need to their place on the line as they had been by law and custom back home. They lived stuffed into miserable tenements at inflated rents, their wages a fraction of what a white man, even a half-literate immigrant, might earn at the same job, and they faced daily the seething hatred of those they had replaced.

Mags knew none of this. Her life had taken on such a burnish of light and love, her mind turned away from common unpleasantries and toward all that was George McCallum and the future he promised. It was not as if copies of the *Chicago Defender,* the Negro newspaper that reported on civil unrest and such, piled up on her doorstep. Nothing of her neighbors' hostility seemed out of the ordinary to her.

They had the wedding in Miss Emily's parlor. Neither of them wanted a party, really. They were reserved people who kept their feelings close. But Miss Emily insisted. All of the girls were there—Chesty, Rain, Charly, Bobsy, Tawny, and the rest—and Magnus Bailey, too, along with the three blood relatives George McCallum had in the world, his old aunt Lily and cousins Sam and Jack, both of whom came with wives. Aurora Mae and her brother, Horace, traveled up for the occasion, along with cousins Alice and Jefferson. George was in his best black suit, the one he wore for funerals of the most important people Fishbein's had to bury. Mags wore a home-made bridal costume, created with the help of her fellow boarders. Cream-colored, it had a closely tailored bodice, long lace-edged sleeves, and a gently flowing skirt with a handkerchief hem around which was sewn a double row of teardrop beads of shimmering nacre to match those sewn on her smartly conceived headband with its stylish short veil. The couple dressed early and received their guests together as they arrived. Before long, Miss Emily's parlor was full of warm greetings and merry voices when two white faces appeared among the black and brown. There was quiet, confusion, and then George said, Mr. Fishbein! And Miss Minnie! How good of you to come! Ignoring the watchful silence around them, he took Mags by the hand and brought her to the Fishbeins' side for an introduction to his employer's daughter, whom she had not yet had occasion to meet.

Minerva Fishbein was a slender, wild-eyed girl with a shoulder-length mane of curly red hair. She was not quite so little as George had led his bride to believe, more like a ripe fourteen or even sixteen. She wore a fitted green dress and gray jacket molding high, round breasts that had just begun to bud. She was on the short side, coming up to Mags's shoulder, and Mags herself was not especially tall. Fishbein was dressed in an undertaker's black suit with an old-fashioned swatch of black silk tied in a loose, loopy bow at his neck. He wore a top hat too, and carried a walking stick with a gold knob. He stood behind his girl, hovering over her, as if in protection.

How kind of you, George, to invite us, Fishbein said as soon as introductions were accomplished. He reached inside his suit jacket and presented Mags with an envelope. With our best wishes, he said, executing a courtly little bow of his head.

Mags's cheeks warmed. She thanked him. George did too, then beckoned to Miss Emily that he might introduce their hostess as well. The room slowly returned to its genial hubbub. Minerva fidgeted at her father's side, uninterested in either the bride or groom. Her eyes darted about the parlor until Magnus Bailey came in from the kitchen bearing a tray of glasses he set upon a side table. The girl caught her breath and held it until he noticed her. He waved a greeting, at which her high, round chest exhaled in a thin stream as if she'd been punctured there by a sharp instrument. Mags found this curious but assumed the girl was nervous to be in a Negro rooming house, and the sight of a familiar face calmed her. Anyway, the bride had much more on her mind and did not pause long about it.

They had tea sandwiches, hard lemonade, and honey cake after the ceremony. Chesty had a little too much of the drink and began to sing hymns in a loud, happy voice. That turned out alright, because it was a good voice overall. Somewhere along the way, the hymns turned to love songs both gay and sorry. The rug got rolled up, a harmonica and a squeeze box were produced, and people started in to dance, even Miss Minnie with her hands raised up high to sit on the shoulders of Magnus Bailey, who shook the floor with his fast-moving feet tapping and sweeping in time to the tune. Her daddy looked on with a kind of somber longing. After Minnie, Magnus gave Aurora Mae a turn. That was a sight to see, the dandy and the goddess half a head taller than him giving it a go. Magnus was done up in silks and cottons more costly than the bridal costume. Aurora Mae wore a plain clean dress the color of butter. It was the best she owned, and against her black skin it took on the look of gold. She danced with pride and ineffable grace while her hair snaked down her back and bounced about like a thing alive. After their dance, Fishbein's daughter went straight up to Bailey and tugged his jacket for another round.

Aurora Mae and Mags went off to have the talk her mother would have given her had she been alive. Aurora Mae, who was virginal as far as the bride knew, gave her what wisdom she possessed from listening to the complaints of wives who came to her for something to start their bleeding or something to stop it, for draughts that might renew their husband's interest or for others that might keep him away. Be careful how you start out, she told her. Men don't like change. How you start out is how you'll end.

Once evening fell, Mags and George stood in the doorway about to leave. She threw her bouquet. It hit Tawny in the chest, bounced off, and fell into old Aunt Lily's lap as she sat nearby, a wallflower sitting all by herself nodding her head. Everyone laughed. The party went on long after the bridal couple left.

That first night, Aurora Mae's words of advice echoed in Mags's head. They cautioned her as she undressed behind the closet door and put on the nightgown the ladies of Miss Emily's had given her, the sum of her trousseau. The words rattled her as she fiddled with its straps, trying to get the thing to hang right so that her small breasts weren't swamped in satin and lace. The words burned into her with a roiling heat as George McCallum took his time to open her up and ready her. They paled to a whisper as their lovemaking became a joining of two who wished to please each other, not just the one eager male making it up as he went along, loving trial by gentle error. Then Aurora Mae's words came crashing back when the screams of Fishbein! Fishbein! Fishbein! started, followed by the sounds of smashing and breaking, the great knocking of toppled furniture and hurled objects upstairs. How you start is how you'll end, the rhythm of splintered wood and shattered glass warned above the ruckus. How you start is how you'll end.

Alarmed, George and Mags McCallum stopped and held each other, gasping for breath and staring at the ceiling, waiting for the clamor to cease, which it did soon enough. They murmured a decision to ignore the girl's tantrums from now on, and they finished what they'd set out to do, although Mags McCallum was some distracted, thinking again and again, how you start is how you end. She wondered what kind of omen Miss Minnie's fit had delivered, but she did not want to hurt her husband's feelings, so she kept her worries to herself.

Despite Miss Minnie's outburst, the marriage got off to a good start. They spent their days at work, the evenings were full of tenderness. They had no visitors. Fishbein's was not a place people visited by choice, which was just fine with the McCallums. They were getting to know each other and found, as luck was with them, that a loving life was as easy to achieve as falling off a log. Their nights and times off were a mirror image of the workday. They did everything together, the cleaning, the shopping, the cooking, the laundry. If she picked up a dust rag, he picked up a broom. If she broke an egg of a morning, he pulled out the coffee. When Mags tried to make George just sit and let her do for him, he'd say, I don't want to be away from you. And she'd think she was the luckiest woman alive. For a while, she was.

Until the United States plodded its way into the Great War, the only blot on their lives was Minerva Fishbein. While her eruptions were few and far between, she found occasion to unnerve them regularly. Sometimes, while they sat on their little porch, rocking, devoted to low, loving conversation, an odd snuffling noise from the balcony above disturbed them. They knew it was Miss Minnie, eavesdropping. Another time, they'd be making their dinner and the patter of Miss Minnie running down the kitchen steps and throwing open the door would startle them. She never said hello, just nodded while she went to the ice chest to grab a bite of whatever appealed, or opened the breadbox to pilfer something there. And it was pilfering. Fishbein had his own kitchen up there on the second floor and no victuals kept on the first belonged to him or his daughter. Following her husband's example on such occasion, Mags would smile and say, Why good day, Miss Minnie, although there was never more response than a grunt before the girl went back upstairs, her footsteps as heavy and plodding in ascent as they'd been rapid and light on the way down.

Minnie had tutors coming and going every day but the Fishbein Sabbath and on that day, Saturdays, they would often hear her wail with boredom or frustration. Come winter, she began music lessons.

On Wednesdays they could count on listening to Miss Minnie attack a piano as if it had murdered her mother and she sought annihilating vengeance. On such occasions, George McCallum would say to his wife, That child's not right. And Mags would say, What do you think it is? George would only shake his head and return to helping her do. Over time, Mags learned to accept Miss Minnie's mercurial presence in her life the way she accepted the unexpected arrival of thunder and lightning or a snow squall.

As for the girl's daddy, she never saw him at all nor heard him anymore for that matter. George went up to the second floor weekly to collect their wages and report on the business below. How's Mr. Fishbein? Mags asked afterward. And George would say, The same. She'd picture that sad face, the hunched shoulders, the spindly arms, crossed as if protecting his wounded, bleeding heart, and ask no more.

Every once in a while, George McCallum was required to go to the rail station to pick up special-order coffins, chemical supplies, maybe the bones of a son of East St. Louis who'd sought his fortune elsewhere. Mags went with him whenever their schedule permitted. Her interest in the feminine arts had not waned since life had taken her talents in an unexpected direction. She enjoyed watching the people on the platform. She studied the hairstyles and costumes of the ladies from far-off cities as they disembarked and regarded critically the careful toilettes of women who paced the waiting room searching with darting eyes the arrival of a lover, son, or husband. When she went home from such expeditions, she'd rearrange her hair and sew onto her sleeve or bodice a gewgaw, a ribbon, a dime-store bauble she thought echoed the new fashion she'd observed. She kept a modest store of such treasures in a cigar box under the bed that allowed her imagination to soar. Once satisfied, she'd parade her transformation in front of George for a man's opinion. He nearly always praised her. When he did not and she pressed him, he talked in a roundabout way so as not to hurt her feelings.

The train was late one day toward the end of March 1917, barely a week before war was declared. A high wind came in from the river. The colored waiting room, a place established by routine rather than law as it was elsewhere, was cold and uncommonly crowded. Negroes pressed up against one another on every square inch of space. The ones who couldn't fit were outside, shivering and stamping their feet. George was outside. He was not the sort who would take a woman's spot to avoid the elements. Mags watched him blow on his hands and tap-dance, then duck his angular head inside his jacket when the wind came up. She felt proud, and she felt happy.

On the way home that day, she thought about the scene on the platform, especially when the train arrived and the passenger cars emptied. Did you notice, she asked George, how many colored men got into town today? There musta been a hundred of 'em gettin' out of that one car, poor boys in cotton shirts and no jackets luggin' bundles tied in string. It's been like that for a while. There's twice as many of 'em comin' as before. What's it all about, do you think?

She looked up at her husband in the way she had, full of admiration and trust. It seared his heart when she looked at him that way. On occasion, he gave detailed opinion on subjects he barely knew about, because he could not bear to disappoint her and risk lowering himself in her eyes. This time, he was sure of his answer.

It's a lot a things. Boys been comin' up here in droves since the Delta flood last year, for one. Between the flood and the weevil, there just ain't the work what used to be. I told you about them factories sendin' train cars south and offerin' the cousins free passage north to streets paved with gold. Life got so desperate down there, more boys 'n ever fall for that one. But mostly, it's that war 'crost the ocean. We're goin' to be in it very soon now, they say, the way those Germans keep sinkin' our ships for no good reason but meanness. And it's no lie there's new jobs 'round here with the factories gettin' ready for war. Good jobs, white men's jobs, at near white men's wages. Lots of them Germans and Poles used to work 'em went back home to fight their war. The ones that stay are angry folk, always strikin', always complainin'. The bosses don't mind replacin' them with folk who'll work for less and be grateful for it. Why shouldn't the cousins come up here for work? Sure beats pickin' beans and cotton while the boss plagues your wife and the babies starve. Why I heard there's more'n a thousand a week come up t' here.

Mags shook her head and told him how lucky she was to have a well-established husband whose boss took no unseemly interest in her. Our baby will never starve, she said.

George McCallum pulled up the rented wagon loaded with chemical bins. What baby? he asked.

Why, our baby, she said, smiling and patting her belly. While cars honked and horses whipped into speed dashed around them, George, being the kind of man he was, embraced her there in the street and wept.

Remembering that day and telling her daughter, Sara Kate, about it years later, Mags would say if it wasn't for the war, life would have gone on from there like a happy dream. But she didn't mean the war across the sea. She meant the one waged in chaos and blood on the streets of East St. Louis.

IV

WAR, EVEN A WAR fought on the other side of the world, intensifies life on the home front. Every dawn brings anxiety, an expectation of no one knows what. The hours that follow are spent in heightened awareness, that sharp mental state in which every gesture, every word may harbor a clue of what comes next. Significance is attached to routine events if only to dispel the constant, fretful waiting for sirens, for telegrams, for howls in the night, for betrayals, for pronouncement, for orders, for release. After such a day, sleep is either rock solid or agitated by spidered dreams. At first light, suspense begins again.

For Mags, pregnancy exaggerated everything. One day she was lighthearted, celebrating her news with George, the next she was heavy with anxious anticipation, imagining all the things that could go wrong when a woman is in such a condition at such a time. The morning St. Louis held its draft registration, she awoke to the sounds of church bells, train whistles, brass bands, cannon shot calling all men to the registry. A terror filled her that never quite left, even after George was rejected due to the miracle of her pregnancy, while so many of the able-bodied Negro men she knew were snatched up quick as you please and eager they were too for the job of soldier. George said they wanted to prove they were as brave and patriotic as white men.

The Army needs cooks and ditch diggers as much as pilots and sharpshooters, he said. So there they are, lining up for the chance to face cannon with a dishrag in their hands.

He spit off the porch railing, grumbling that none of them remembered the Spanish War, so why should anyone remember the Indian Wars? What happened both times was bound to occur again.

Remind me, George, what happened then, Mags said with her gaze averted, embarrassed by her ignorance.

Oh, well, darlin', of course they put the colored men at the front wherever the fightin' was the most hopeless and let the enemy use up their ammunition on 'em. Like them buffalo soldiers comin' up Kettle Hill over to San Juan. Nothin' but fodder they were. Then the white boys rode over the dead and dying to fair advantage.

Mags worried that if the war got worse, they might start taking anybody they could find, including those with dependent wives and children. For sure, they'd start with the Negro fathers and exhaust them before the whites were chosen. That was the way things always went when there was a hard, dangerous job to do, wasn't it?

In the month of May, there was trouble—big, ugly trouble. Rumor had it that black men and white women had fraternized at a union meeting of workers badgering Aluminum Ore Company and American Steel. Soon enough, a mob of white men gathered downtown looking for Negroes to rob of life and treasure. No one much cared if the local boys beat up a few blacks, but when they set to destroying buildings, the authorities were called in. Peace was restored, but it was a shaky one.

June came and went. It was hot. Mags was six months along, showing now, confined to Fishbein's Funeral Home at the insistence of George McCallum. He did not want her on the streets, especially their street, because there was more than one kind of heat, he told her, and both of them together made fire. He didn't have to say more. She knew what he meant. She didn't have to go so far as the curb in front of Fishbein's to feel the burn. When she swept the front porch, the eyes across the street were on her, Polish eyes, German eyes, all of 'em blazing eyes, cutting into her back like brands. Men and boys jabbered in words she could not understand, but their message was clear, spitting sparks of hate into the scorched air as June melted into July.

Like the calm before a storm, business got quiet around the same time. It wasn't, George said, that people stopped dyin' or all the Negroes had packed up and moved away. Thanks to the war jobs, the town was bustin' at the seams. People lived on top of one another. Everyone you met had a new-arrived relative or two stickin' out of their side pocket. There were more coloreds in East St. Louis than there ever were. But folk were taking care of their dead in the old way, in the country way, rather than come to Fishbein's, where things just didn't feel right that close to the color line. Everyone on both sides of that line waited for something awful to happen, for the match to strike the tinderbox, for the fire to start, and then as it had to, as it was destined to, it did.

For the rest of her life Mags wondered what would have happened if she'd gone with George to the train station that day. She'd been cooped up so long without much to do, she was about to tear her hair. She tried everything she could to get him to take her. She cajoled, she pouted, she pushed out her belly and stroked the baby while peeping up at him with her big eyes pleading. Nothing worked. In the end, she would never be able to say if that was a good thing or a bad one. It wasn't an hour after he was gone that the trouble started.

She sat between two open windows to catch a summer's breeze when the noise of glass shattering distracted her from her sewing. She got up slowly, with care, in the way of women heavy with child, one hand upon a table, the other at the small of her back, and lumbered over to a window where she saw them, the mob, the white mob, twenty or thirty men with sleeves rolled up and brickbats and clubs and knives, big ones that dripped something red, in their hands. They were at the top of Fishbein's street, advancing, steadily, with ruinous purpose, breaking everything they passed, yelling in that rough, piercing language she did not know. They seemed headed for Fishbein's particularly. She screamed.

The man upstairs ran down from the second floor to the parlor, Magnus Bailey and Miss Minnie quick behind him. Minnie grabbed Mags by the hand and pulled her away from the window, then all of them hurried down into the basement, where a single dressed and painted corpse awaited transport to Georgia for burial. The big black fancy man, the small redheaded young woman, and the pregnant country one stood in front of Mr. Fishbein, trying to ignore the defeat in his slumped shoulders, the helplessness of his haunted features. He was their leader. They looked to him for instruction, for wisdom, a plan, anything. They held their breath as he looked back at them from his sad eyes and shook his head. I do not know, he said. I do not know. His lips trembled. He took his daughter's hand and placed it inside the palm of Magnus Bailey. Save her, he said. Take her across the river to where is safe. I cannot.

The mob had not yet reached the funeral home, but the noise of them grew louder. Magnus moved toward the bulkhead door, pulling Minerva Fishbein roughly down the passage to their escape and grabbing onto Mags along the way. She wrested from his grasp.

No! I'm waitin' on George.

Bailey grabbed at her again. Fishbein's daughter reached out and held on to her skirt.

No! Mags twisted, wrapped her arms around a support beam that stood in the middle of the preparation room. I will not go.

Above them, a tumult began. The crashes of furniture. The voices of intruders. Cries for blood. The locked door to the basement rattled, then something rammed into it.

Suit yourself, Bailey said. With Minnie Fishbein behind him, he raced through the corridor to the bulkhead door, flung it open. The two climbed up the stairs. Without so much as a glance behind them, they disappeared into the warren of alleyways beyond George's little patch of backyard grass where herbs grew heedless as wildflowers in a meadow, ignorant of their post at the gateway to death.

Three thumps landed hard against the basement door. It cracked.

Mr. Fishbein went to the bulkhead, closed and bolted it. He put a hand on Mags's elbow. His breath was heavy in her ear. We must hide, he said. Murmuring unintelligible encouragements as one might to a child or a pet, he guided her to a storage room, where coffins of varying sizes and quality were stacked. Quilts were draped between the coffins to protect the wood from scratch and stain. Here, he said, here we will wait for George. He took her to a middle row of adult coffins and lifted the bottom quilt from a stack three coffins high. See? Is like a tent, he said in his strange accent that continued to lilt supportively though there was a tremor in it. We will pretend we are in the woods on a camping expedition. Yes?

She nodded.

The only thing Mags was sure of was that Fishbein was not murderous and that the men upstairs certainly were. She ducked under the quilt and knelt beside him to await her fate, to await her baby's fate, to wait for George. While she waited, she prayed continuously, begging Jesus to save them all, even the mad Jew beside her.

Mayhem broke out around them. The basement door split open. There were cheers. Boots ran down the stairs. A rank odor of sweat and blood and rage strong enough to obliterate the usual scent of chemicals and decay seeped through the coffin-room door. Fishbein put his arm around Mags and held her close. They shook against each other in fear. In the next room, orders were shouted. There were shrieks, bellows, the hurling of cabinets to the floor. Men burst into their sanctuary, banged on coffin lids with their bats, and left quickly. These men wanted flesh to rip. Finding none, they ran off. After a time, the house grew quiet. The two fugitives remained huddled together in the close dark, motionless, afraid to breathe. At last, Fishbein said, I think we can maybe leave.

He held up the quilt, and using his body as a steadying post, Mags drew herself up. She felt faint and leaned against the wall. Fishbein got up and began to bob from the waist, up and down to as low as his knees, muttering in a language with harsh sounds and mournful rhythms. Tears fell to his jaw, beading there while soft, deep moans escaped from his throat. Having never seen a Jew pray before, she thought he might be having some kind of a fit. She reached out to touch him, to try to help, when suddenly he stopped. Taking a handkerchief from his pants pocket, he wiped his face, blew his nose, and groaned.

Oy, mine Gott, he said. *Mine Gott.* Now we must wait. Yes? Now we must wait. For news of your husband and for news of my little girl.

They left the coffin room. They picked their way through the debris of the workroom, leaning on each other, weak from the sights they saw. Absolute carnage had been wreaked upon the place. The poor boy waiting to go home to Georgia had been ripped from his box, his clothes torn off, his body mutilated as if his violators thought a boy could die twice. When she saw him, Mags sank to her knees. Mr. Fishbein lifted her up. Things were no better on the first floor or in the living quarters on the second. The devastation could not have been worse had a bomb gone off. When the smoke and smell of gunshot came to them through the broken places, they realized they had been lucky.

Whatever control of emotion Mags had managed that day out of the need to survive melted. No, no, no, she wept, as she paced through the parlor over sharp bits of debris that cut into the thin soles of her shoes. Fishbein watched her helplessly. He trembled and slapped his hands against his cheeks in a slow, steady rhythm.

What is happening? Mags asked the walls, the smoke blowing through the ruined house. Guns went off not too far away. Oh, George, where are you? Where?

Fishbein moaned and swayed and slapped his cheeks.

There was an explosion somewhere nearby. The sound shattered the jagged glass that remained in the windows of the first floor. Screams came to them. Not the screams of the terrified but the screams of the tortured, the kind of screams that pierce the ears like needles, rip the spine, and rattle teeth.

Hearing them, Fishbein returned to himself. He took Mags to the bedroom off the kitchen. The covers of her marriage bed were full of shards. He tore the linens off. He turned the mattress and sat her on its edge and begged her to lie down, to rest. That he did this in his own tongue made no difference. She understood him and complied. She lay on her back, stared at the ceiling while holding her belly.

What is happening? she asked again.

A pogrom, Fishbein said.

What is a pogrom?

A festival of evil.

She shuddered. Her mouth was very dry. It was difficult to speak. She coughed. Fishbein left the room and returned with water in a teacup. She drank.

What do we do?

What we are doing. We hide. We wait. They will go forwards, they will not come back. This is what we must believe and hope. To pray also wouldn't hurt.

He lay in bed beside her. She reached out a hand, and he took it.

I will protect you with mine own life, he said.

Why would you do that? she asked, mystified by the idea that a white man would endanger himself for her. For George?

Yes, for George. Of course, for George. But more than him and more than you and more than the child you carry, I will do it for mine dead.

Mags was confounded. His dead? Those who stopped at Fishbein Funeral Home on their way to the cold ground? For them? It made no sense. So she asked, What dead?

He exhaled in the weary sigh of a man who lays down a burden he has carried too long. He muttered in cadences that rose and fell as if he were deciding whether to bend and take the burden up again. *Nu,* he muttered, but to whom it was impossible to tell. *Nu,* I shall tell, why not? There may be no more chances. Here is a good woman with child, who is much beloved. Who better to absolve me?

Mags listened, perplexed. Finally, he clapped his free hand over the one that held hers as if shaking it.

Once, he said, I have a wife whom I love.

Miss Minnie's mother?

He pushed out his lower lip and shrugged.

My little girl is the child of storm and fire. If she has a mother, Sonya is it. But before that, Sonya is my wife. We married under a chuppah when I am twenty and she is sixteen. I met her the month before we were to marry. Until the wedding, we are not together for even a few minutes alone. From the first, I adore her. She is a miracle of intelligence, of delicacy in form and spirit. It is another miracle that I am matched with her. I am a nothing, an apprentice jeweler to my father, dependent entirely upon his fortunes and with none of my own. Her father is a goldsmith, so our match makes sense somewhere in the universe but hardly to mine own mind. I spend the month of our engagement in astonishment that I, a boy who prays only when he must, who lives in a world without challenge to his soul, protected from every evil either through his ignorance or by the walls of our neighborhood, have somehow won such favor from the Divine that this marvel is given to me. To me! I have such respect for her that when our wedding night comes, I can do no more than kiss her hands. Rather than spoil her and win only her disgust, I cut my hand to stain the sheets so the old women who comes later to inspect them find virgin blood. In the end, it is she who guides me through the gates of pleasure where we stay locked together, a holy treasure nestled in a strongbox, far away from all the world.

He paused, resting in the most pleasant place of his history. The wind had changed direction. The clouds of smoke were thinner now, though an odor that stung the eyes lingered within them. It was the odor of burning flesh. The sound of gunshot was less frequent, and the screams as well. With that smell in the air, the relative quiet eased neither's anxiety. Mags pressed Fishbein's hand to tell him to continue. To lie there waiting for whatever might come next was excruciating. The distraction of his voice was her sole relief. The sensibilities he described and the words he chose to describe them were exotic, nearly incomprehensible to her except for the love in them. The love she understood. He continued.

If only we could have stayed in that moment, in that box. If only the world does not visit us on an afternoon when I am not at home. That day, my father sends me to the central post office to inquire about the delivery of an order for display cards. He prefers a certain type of card, collapsible, designed of wood and velvet, which can only be obtained from the capital. It is the only card he would use. He goes to travel the next week to trade in Riga and is anxious about their delivery, and *nu,* I must go. When I say good-bye to Sonya that day, it is with the usual reluctance. Even though I do not expect to be apart from her for more than a handful of hours, I hate to leave her on any day and at that time. She is like you, with child. We had three years of bliss together before the child is coming. In that time, my mother often complains that there are no grandchildren from us. Once, thank Gott not in Sonya's presence, she dares to remind me that if together we cannot fulfill the obligation to be fruitful and multiply, our law permits and even encourages divorce. I am enraged by her suggestion. I berate her without mercy. I am ashame to say it is the only time in my life I almost strike a woman, and my own mother! You know the Ten Commandments, Mags McCallum? Of course you do. Honor thy father and mother is the fifth of these. The first four commandments deal with what we must do for Gott, the fifth is the first that tells us what we must do for each other. This is how important it is to honor thy father and mother. But on the day my mother proposes to me I abandon Sonya, I discover I can hate her who bore me. We continues, all of us, to live together although I nurse a hot seed of resentment towards my mother from that day on and often wish her ill. When finally Sonya is with child, my mother dotes on her, but for me it is too little, too late. In the time since, I often thought perhaps the hardness of my heart is why the Holy One, blessed be He, punishes me. But this is selfish, isn't it? To think that a world of suffering rains down on a multitude because of my sin. Yes, pure selfishness.

Fishbein fell silent. The rat-a-tat-tat of gunshot replaced his voice as the only sound in the room. It sounded even farther away than before. Mags forced herself to believe it came from a direction that was not the rail station where George had gone on Fishbein's errand. She imagined her husband holed-up, safe, waiting for things to die down or the police to arrive before he came to her. This image began to fade as soon as she achieved it. She knew what kind of man her George was and knew he was trying with everything he had to get home that very minute. She saw him face mortal danger at every turn, desperate with fear for her, for the baby. A shivering sweat went through her. Fishbein took off his jacket and covered her as best he could. Though her teeth chattered, Mags managed to ask Fishbein to continue his story. Listening to him speak was better than lying there terrorized by images of George hurt or worse.

Yes. Of course. I am saying good-bye to Sonya, no? Yes. She is beautiful as ever, her eyes sparkle. She teases me, I recall. She said, You are so afraid to leave me even for half a day? Such a clever man my husband is! You finds me out! Yes, I shall run away with the butcher's boy as soon as you turn a corner. Her time is close, very close, but it's not our way to mention fears about such things or the angels and demons who listen to every human word might bring our fears to life. So I smile and kiss her and goes my way.

I don't get so far. Not ten blocks from our neighborhood, I am beset upon by thugs. They tear my pockets and pull the hair from my head. They hit me with clubs, and I am unconscious in the street. When I awake, night is fallen. At first, I don't know where it is I am or what happens to me. I stumble about. There are sounds in the night, a clamor of chaos and cruelty, but I am drunk with confusion. I cannot determine what it is going on. Suddenly, I realize. It is a pogrom. A pogrom. The one no one thinks will come to our city, because the *goyim* they are so friendly, we think they love us. From the capital of our province, newspapers incite hatred against the Jews for a long time, but that is the capital. In our quiet town, a place people come to vacation, to take the waters and listen to concerts, people are genteel, we think, or too content, too lazy to read, to act. But a pogrom it is. And I know what means a pogrom. I must gets home.

What can I tell you? Without the grace of Gott, nothing is easy. It takes me until the dawn's light to get home. Or what is left of

home. I find there a shambles. First the murderers and then the looters have come. Like here, everything is smashed, destroyed, or if it is
of value, it is taken away. My father is hung from a rafter, with his
pants pulled off, and my mother is in the corner of the kitchen with
her skirts up, her body stained with the refuse of her pots, which
are strewn all over. She bleeds from every orifice and from her chest.
You know, a son—especially a guilty, angry son—should never see
such things, but it is not the worst sight for me. The worst is my
Sonya, with her skirts also up and her breasts exposed, and her
belly, her belly rent in two, as if she is a fish they have gutted, and
my child, a boy, a little boy, lying next to her, strangled by the cord
that keeps him attached to her forever, in life and in death. Count
them. There are four. These are my dead. For whose sake I shall
protect you, Mags McCallum, with my life.

He stopped, finished with speaking for now. Immediately, he
wondered whether he should have spoken at all. His own heart was
queerly relieved yet innervated, unexpectedly so. Mags wiped tears
from her eyes with one hand, pressed his with her other, and her
chest and belly heaved. Fishbein was appalled by his own insensitiv-
ity. In setting down his burden, he had handed her one to carry. He
struck his breast three times with his free hand while petitioning her
clemency.

Forgive me, forgive me, forgive me, he said. As I tell you, I am a
stupid, selfish man. I see my unhappy tale gives you fresh heartache.
Believe me, I will let no one harm you as my Sonya was. The mystics
teach us that under the eye of Gott, all opposites achieve balance. I
am sure, I am confident this very room is the place where today the
Holy One, blessed be He, will create perfect harmony out of turmoil. On one side of the scale is the murder of my loved ones. *Nu?*
On the other is your safety. My suffering assures your future joy.
Why not? Is there a reason on Gott's green earth why this should
not be so?

In spite of herself, Mags's heart swelled with hope. Yes, she said, why not?

Quiet can be as strong a bond between two people as a thousand heartfelt words. After several silent minutes, she felt comfortable enough to ask a question that on any other day would not cross her lips for its assumption of intimacy, but this question nagged at her.

And Miss Minnie? If she's not your wife's child, where did she come from?

Ah! My little girl. She is a foundling, of course. When I goes home that day to find, well, you know what, I spend the first nights alone with my dead. I take my father down from where he is hung, and I wash and wrap him in a sheet. My mother and my wife and child, I also wash and bind. I find candles and lights them and mourn by them without cease. The world around me does not exist. The czar's army can storm into our house and I would not hear them approach. Yet on the fourth day, I am staring at my child, my boy, whose tiny body has grown stiff, whose tiny face peeking out of his shroud I watch turn blue, then black while I weep over him. For four days, I am imagining for him the life he will never know, and suddenly, I hear him cry. Can you know what a shock that is? I jump up. The cry sounds again only now I hear it comes from behind me. I turn and there, in the doorway, is another child, a red-headed girl child of maybe three or four years, and she is naked, covered in blood. She is crying in my doorway, first in little bleats like a lamb led to slaughter and then when she sees she gets my attention, louder and louder in the wails of a woman. I take her in. In the weeks that follow, I cannot find who she is or from where she comes. I decide she is sent from Gott to be mine. For me, she is a reason to live. For her, I am life itself.

Time went by, he told her, and he realized he could not continue to live in his town, amid the destruction there and his memories. As it happened, the looters had not got everything after all. His father took a certain jacket on his trips. In its hems his mother stitched the jewels he would carry to trade that they might be safe on the road and in the common houses where he slept. For the trip he was to make to Riga days after his murder, his father wanted only his best stock. The hems of his jacket were full of precious stones. The looters did not think to steal that worn jacket, which gave Fishbein a fortune to stake out a new life. He left the Black Sea behind him. After a time, he and his little girl found themselves in America. He looked things over and disliked the similarities between Saint Petersburg and New York. He traveled up and down the Great River looking for a home, and settled in East St. Louis.

But why here?

We are here when Minerva grows tired and announces she wishes to go no farther.

And why this business?

Fishbein smiled an odd smile, a smile with anguish in it.

I prefer the company of the dead to that of the living, he said. It is where my heart lays.

The second night of the riots, they tried to sleep lying side by side. Each woke a dozen times, half a breath after sleep claimed them, either from the bloody chaos outside or from the nightmares that rim exhaustion. It was hard to tell which was which. Just after first light, there was a commotion at the front door, one neither distant nor imaginary. Mags gasped. Mr. Fishbein leapt up to stand in front of her, a human shield, holding a weapon in each raised hand. From out of nowhere Mags could determine, he'd produced a ten-inch butcher's knife and a chair leg with a great nail sticking out of its carved haunch.

Under the bed, he whispered to her, under the bed. Please.

She moved to roll off the bed to hide beneath it when Magnus Bailey appeared at the doorway.

The man's face was slick with sweat, his fine clothes torn and foul. River mud covered his boots to his ankles.

Before Fishbein could ask, he said, Miss Minnie is safe. I put her in a good place 'crost river. I need water. Have you got water? They gave it to him, and he told them what was what in the world outside.

It started when some white men drove through the colored town and shot some boys just standin' in the street, talkin' 'bout their own business, he said, who knows why. The police came in an unmarked car, all of 'em totin' rifles pointin' out the windows the way they do. There's colored folk had armed themselves by then. Not knowin' who was in the car, they opened fire afore they'd get shot themselves. It was the police wound up dead. Next thing you know, thousands of white men are in the streets, screamin' for vengeance, raidin' the colored homes, burnin' and killin' any poor black man, woman, or child they find.

Bailey buried his head in his hands for a moment, remembering. Mags noticed that his hands trembled against his face. When he took them away, he wrung them together. He kept wringing them throughout his report, except when he balled a fist and smacked his palm, either for emphasis or to achieve control, she could not tell which.

The things I saw last night, the things I saw. Them little houses and stores south of city hall? Burnt down to the ground. And while they're burnin', whole families runnin' out of 'em. Oh, those poor babies! Gettin' shot by white men loungin' around with their backs against walls, calm as you please, just waitin' for targets to come out of a house afire. They'd shoot a body down, then pick 'em up and toss 'em back in to burn alive. Cut the fire hoses, too. The soldiers got called in, but they don't do nothin' but march around in their tight columns more concerned with protectin' themselves than restorin' the peace. I don't expect they know what to do. It is the Apocalypse.

By the free bridge and even by the Eads, there's a stream of people hurryin' acrost with whatever they can carry, colored folk meanin' to find rescue over there in Missouri. There must be ten thousand of 'em and where are they going to go? Who's goin' to have 'em? It's quite a sight. The orange sky, the smoke, the fire trucks with no hoses and trucks with soldiers racin' around not knowin' where to go or what to do once they get there, the people leavin', the dead burnin' or hung from the lampposts and set on fire while they're still twitchin' with life.

For a moment, Bailey's throat closed, he could not speak. He smacked his palm with a balled-up fist twice. Then he spoke in a rush of words as if anxious to get his story out and over with so that he could begin to digest it.

It's the unions, mostly, he said. They out to kill Negroes, calling 'em the ones who drive down wages for everybody, foreigners and native boys alike. Truth don't seem to matter to any of 'em. They're out for blood. There's white gals on the loose, pointin' out women and children for their men to take down and if the men's too slow, they're doin' it themselves. I saw a colored gang or two on the way over here. They're beatin' back the whites, and they don't care if they're fightin' murderers or bystanders or their neighbors from two blocks over. So if you ask me, things gonna go from bad to plain evil on our side as well. It's the worst thing I've ever seen, and I've seen some.

George? Do you know where George is?

No, ma'am. I don't. But that's one man I'm not worried about. He'll turn up, I'm sure. He's a smart man, your George. He wouldn'a rode straight into hell without a backward look. We'll find him. Don't you worry. More likely, he'll find you.

Mags wanted to say, Yes! He would! He'd ride straight into hell at high noon to get to me! He would in a heartbeat! But if he'd done that, he'd have been home before Magnus Bailey crawled back. So she didn't say it, in fear that the saying might curse herself and George and the baby altogether. Each hour that passed without her husband turning up brought her closer to despair.

Two days later, it was all over. An eerie peace settled over East St. Louis while officials and newsmen sorted out a version of the truth. Whole blocks smoldered while people searched for the missing and dead. Mr. Fishbein went to the stockyards, where recovered corpses lay under tarps awaiting identification. He went with little hope of finding George, even if George were dead. There were thirty-nine dead Negroes lined up on the ground, but hundreds of colored men and women were unaccounted-for. There was no way to tell if those lost souls were burnt beyond recognition of ever having been human to begin with, if their mangled bodies had been tossed in the river, or if they were alive but had fled. Thirty-nine was a pitiful number out of so many, but George McCallum was among them. How he died exactly was uncertain. There were ligatures around his neck, and his lower body had been burned. Although the cart he'd ridden to the railways was never found, the horse that pulled it returned to the barn of his owner a week later, three-legged lame. The liveryman put him down.

Magnus Bailey offered, but it was Mr. Fishbein who broke the news to George McCallum's widow. He did the best he could to break it gently. He went to Miss Emily's, where he had installed her until the funeral home could achieve proper repair. Miss Emily was glad to have her. Her establishment had escaped the carnage, but most of her other boarders were either out of work, unable to pay, or had moved on in the days just after the riots.

Fishbein sat in the parlor where the wedding had been, his walking stick between his legs. His hands rested on its knob and his chin on his hands as he muttered to himself, trying to find the words required. I should say I am so very sorry, he muttered. No, she'll know right away. First I should tell her she looks so well and ask for the baby. Oh, dear me, I shall have to smile, then, won't I? *Oy. Mine Gott,* can I do that? And it was while he was practicing a stupid, pleasant smile that would fool no one that Mags came in with Miss

Emily at her elbow, saw him, and shrieked. Luckily, Miss Emily kept her from falling hard to the floor in grief, protecting her unborn child from any harm.

The Widow McCallum had her child in her bed at Miss Emily's. Chesty and Miss Emily performed as midwives. For them, bringing into the world little Sara Kate, named for George's mama, who had passed decades before, was a great holiday. For the widow, it was an unfathomable sadness.

Look at that little face, Chesty cooed at her. Just like her daddy. Ain't it a miracle?

And it was true; Sara Kate had the same sharp nose, the same dark caramel skin, the same small black eyes. Only her mouth, plump and pouting, was her own. Otherwise, George McCallum was stamped all over her, down to her quiet, steely temperament. Even as an infant, the child rarely cried. Her small fist with its long, thin fingers gripped whatever it could with uncommon strength. All of which broke her mother's heart.

Take her away, please, I can't look at her, Mags said whenever they brought the child to her. The women tried to change her mind, telling her she was just tired from the birth, and once the healing and the pain was over and done, she'd come to want the baby at her teat. They put the girl directly on her mama's chest. Look at her, they said, look how cunnin' she is. Mags pushed her off.

She's like him, just like him, and that makes her a plague to me, she said. Tears ran down her cheeks and her voice was flat cold. Why would he visit me like this? As a tiny, squirmin', helpless little thing? I don't want her. I don't want her.

A few months later when her blood settled, Mags warmed up to the child, but by then it was too late. The damage was done. Sara Kate grew up reserved, suspicious always, looking without respite for a love that could fill the deep loneliness she felt from the cradle on.

MARCHING THRU EMANUEL'S GROUND

The Road to Memphis, 1918–1924

V

NO MATTER WHAT SHE went through later on in life, and there was plenty, Aurora Mae always said that one of the strangest sights she ever saw was the caravan that brought Mags Preacher McCallum and little Sara Kate home to the family colony at the old plantation south of St. Louis. It was getting on in the day. The light had begun to fade. Aurora Mae rocked on the porch of the big house, watching shadows gambol at the edge of the dark wood. She was wrapped in a quilt, as the air got crisp that time of year soon as the sun made a fare-thee-well. All at once, before she saw or heard a thing, the three mongrel dogs that kept her company took off and yelped down the road with hell on their heels. She knew those three well enough to get to her feet and watch for whatever approached. The big house, where the Stanton siblings lived, was set at the top of a hill bordered by cultivated fruit trees and, beyond them, dense thicket on three sides. The Stanton home was the vanguard of the family colony and its first line of both welcome and defense.

Horace, you best come quick, she called out to her brother. And bring the shotgun. I don't know what-all this is a-comin'.

On the bottom road, churning up an enormous amount of dust, was a covered mule-drawn cart, a gypsy caravan. From each end of its cab, long poles crowned by flickering lanterns swayed back and forth casting yellow beams of quivering light. The mules' fittings were of wildly colored wool braided with leather from which flowed a rainbow's worth of streamers. A more sedate ornament, the tall black plume of a funeral cortege, fluttered at their polls. Driving the team of two was a big black man in a striped suit and tall beaver hat, a man who looked somewhat familiar, and beside him sat a young, redheaded white woman in a long heavy coat. She wore a pale-blue feather boa around her neck. Two such humans together was a strange enough sight in those parts in that time, with or without their remarkable conveyance. The mules walked up the lawn and stopped twenty or so feet away from the front porch. Now that it was close by, Aurora Mae realized who was come for a visit. Her brother descended the porch stairs to shake the hand of Magnus Bailey, who'd already disembarked from the wagon to assist Miss Minnie. Aurora Mae waved them toward her and moved to enter the house to get a pitcher of sweet tea ready, as the two looked severely parched, when it occurred that the dogs were still barking. She looked back to the road. Another vehicle approached, a motorcar.

A motorcar on that lonesome country road in that day was as rare as a mixed-race gypsy caravan, but this car would have turned heads on the streets of any city between New Orleans and Chicago. It was a Packard funeral bus, built to house a coffin, pallbearers, and up to twenty mourners. Its exterior was of wood carved with bas relief columns alternating with archangels, heads bowed and leaning on their swords. Statues of kneeling seraphim sprang from its roof. There were large side windows, but these were draped in a heavy gold cloth hung to shield the dead and their loved ones from the turmoil of the living world. Aurora Mae and Horace could not see who drove the bus, except that a stooped creature was hunched over the cab's wheel. Then it hit them both.

Lord, Cousin Mags and the baby are in there, ain't they, Horace said to his sister.

Yes, Magnus Bailey said, they are.

Aurora Mae ran down the steps and to the car, her long legs closing the distance between in remarkable time. The car stopped or it would have run into her. She leaned over on the passenger's side seeking with little hope a breathing Cousin Mags, but the mother was in the back nursing her child. All her gaze met was the perpetually despondent expression of Mr. Fishbein. They'd not got up that close at the wedding. Aurora Mae could not recall sharing more than a word or two with him. She remembered him the way she might a brown wren in a flock of bluebirds. Now she saw the pain in his eyes, which sent a shock through her chest—a small one, but sharp. Terrible things flew to her mind. Her fists pounded against the window.

Where are they? What have you done with them?

By now she was certain Cousin Mags and the baby were laid out in there. The Spanish fever was all over East St. Louis, folk said. In the next moment, Mags reached forward from the back to give Sara Kate to Mr. Fishbein so she could come out and embrace her cousin. The sight of the saddest man in all the world holding the squirming child struck Aurora Mae dumb, which was not a common occurrence. Then Mags's arms were around her. They held on as tightly to each other as they had the day Mags left home two years before.

Miss Minnie had already entered the house to look it over without so much as a by-your-leave, but the scene on the lawn held the attention of the others, and no one noticed. From the porch where he stood with Horace, Bailey said, Well, that's a picture, ain't it?

Horace shook his head. It was true. Delicate, brown Mags looked like a child pressed against the bosom of a deity. Aurora Mae was a woman tall as their warrior ancestors. Her glorious, impossible hair was loose. It sprang out all around her and to the backs of her knees. Her limbs were lean and fierce, her face a queen's image carved from obsidian, harmonious and severe. Her eyes were laced in happy tears that caught the light to grace them with sparks of fire.

Watching her, Bailey thought, Someday, I will have me some of that.

Horace caught the scent of his ambitions and did what he could to break the mood. 'Rora Mae finds most of her love with family women, he said, as if his sister's emotional life was a common subject. Big as she is, she's young yet. I believe she would break in two the man who tried to take her afore she's ready.

Aurora Mae and Mags got to fixing a supper together of pole beans and rice cooked with onion, peppers, and chicken livers, as Mags said Mr. Fishbein would not eat the pork. While they washed beans and chopped peppers, they talked old times and caught up with the new. More than a few times, they spoke of George McCallum, and stopped to weep awhile in each other's arms.

Meanwhile, Minerva Fishbein took a nap with the baby in Aurora Mae's bed, and the men sat on the porch. Bailey let Horace in on all their plans, all the war news, and the state of the city since the riots, confirming that yes, the Spanish fever had arrived, which made Horace wonder why Mr. Fishbein would choose to leave town just when business should be hopping good. Horace was an uncomplicated man with the good manners of country folk, unaccustomed to the company of white men of substance. He worried if he did not do or say the correct thing that things could turn ugly on a pauper's dime. Curiosity got the better of him. With such cautious deference he might as well have held a hat to his chest and gazed at his feet, he asked, Is this true, Mr. Fishbein, you're moving to Memphis?

I am.

That's a ways downriver, ain't it?

Yes.

There was a long pause while Horace determined whether he could ask a more personal question of the man tasting the night air on his porch, whose daughter slept in his sister's bed.

And what do you find recommends it?

Nothing. Nothing special.

Despite his concerns, Horace could not help himself. He leaned in close to Mr. Fishbein as he might with Magnus Bailey or any other of his own when he wished to determine the sincerity of a speaker who had just said an astonishing thing.

Then why are you goin' there?

Fishbein sighed. The drawn-out, ragged sound bore the ruin of a horde of troubles.

Several matters impel me, my friend. The first is that George McCallum is dead. I cannot manage my business without him. I am feeling aggrieved enough by his murder not to hire another to take his place. And aggrieved enough to want to leave the town that has caused this fresh sorrow both to a woman—your cousin, of whom I am most fond—and to myself, who has had enough of sorrow altogether. I would start over elsewheres doing somethings new.

Yes, but why Memphis? Why there?

Why not? I am a wanderer, Mr. Stanton. Do you know where I have wandered?

No.

I've wandered through the desert with Moses . . .

Fishbein extended his hand in a languid gesture as if he held a baton and conducted an orchestra. Horace was enthralled by his guest's manner of speaking, his lilting phrases executed in an accent that forced him to listen closely. It didn't matter that Fishbein made no sense. He followed the graceful arc of the man's movements while unexpectedly his chest swelled with pleasant feeling.

. . . through Babylon and all of Europe, through the Russias, and through America.

And now to Memphis? Horace asked, just to keep him talking.

Yes, now to Memphis. A place, I am told, with much difference from East St. Louis. It has not the factories spewing smoke, not the railroads everywhere with crowds constantly coming and going, and I am hoping not the brutes.

Well, I wish you good fortune there, Horace said without telling him he considered there were likely brutes in equal number everywhere. The man's long, riven cheeks and red-rimmed eyes informed him his guest already knew.

I thank you.

What Fishbein did not say was that he had chosen Memphis on the recommendation of Magnus Bailey, who had his own reasons for traveling there. They were a strange couple, those two, bonded since the day, years before, when Fishbein disembarked at St. Louis from a riverboat carrying the child Minerva, all of five years old, who slept in his arms. The girl's knees pressed against the right side of his chest and her head nestled against his heart. Her red hair fell in long, tangled waves over the crook of his arm. Fishbein looked so thin and bent, his burden appeared bigger than she was. Bailey worked the dock nearby, making book for a swarm of dockhands on a coming horse race of consuming local interest. He stood surrounded by calloused black hands clutching banknotes when Fishbein stumbled, falling to his knees, nearly dropping the child just a few feet from the spot where Bailey traded notes for chits. The dockhands stepped back. Maybe they feared being charged with making a white man carrying a child fall, Bailey didn't know, but he saw a need and stepped forward to offer the man assistance, tipping his hat with one hand, placing the other around the man's waist, slender as a woman's, to help him up. Fishbein ascendant was dazed. He swayed on his feet. The girl, only half drawn from that impervious sleep children enjoy, looked in peril of her father falling yet again, so Bailey did the sensible thing. He took her from her father's arms and bore her himself down the few remaining steps of the gangway. Minerva blinked and studied him with intense curiosity. Her little hands wound about his big, thick neck to bring her face closer to his that she might regard him more thoroughly. *Der shvartser has grine oygn,* she said. The blackie has green eyes. Fishbein steadied himself on the gangway's ropes. *Der mensch has grine oygn, mine kind,* he replied, indicating she must call this helpful Negro a good man to show respect. Bailey had no idea what they were talking about or what language they employed, but the way the girl grabbed the hair of his head and boldly kissed his cheek, giggling, *A mensch, a mensch!* made him smile and cradle her with a sweeter grip.

Where are you going? Bailey asked.

The Clairmont Hotel.

And your luggage?

Already it's been sent.

The Clairmont was not far from the river, claiming water views from nearly every room. Bailey led the way there, carrying the child, while Fishbein walked behind. The docks and streets were crowded. Heads turned in their direction as they passed. Hostile, suspicious glances followed them. Bailey guessed they thought he had stolen the child or that Fishbein had sold her. He fought an old anger rising up in his throat.

When they arrived at the Clairmont, Fishbein said, *Gevalt.* My luggage, it is outside the door. Why is this?

Light and swift as a bug, he grabbed his bags, stuck them inside the door, then made directly for the front desk. Bailey followed behind, carrying the girl. He stood at a discreet distance while Fish-bein puffed himself up with indignation to demand of the clerk why his luggage was left outside the door where any thief might make off with it. This required an explanation or he would not remain with this establishment another minute.

The desk clerk, a short, red-faced bald man with shiny apple cheeks, looked up from his work, his mouth tight and twisting. What he was about to do was not his favorite duty, but rules were rules.

I regret to inform you we do not take your kind here. Please leave without a fuss.

Magnus Bailey put the child down. With difficulty, he smiled and tipped his hat while his heart pounded.

I'm sorry, he said. The two small words seared his throat. I was just helpin' the man. I wasn't stayin' on.

Not you, the clerk said. Well of course you, but what I meant was them. There's been a misunderstanding. They will have to leave.

Bailey was perplexed. Flamboyant, slick, at twenty-two a man of the world to whom others came for practical advice, Bailey was not by nature bold outside his own community. There were lessons a black man in 1906 America learned almost from the cradle. He'd learned his painfully at as young an age as any. But the child and her father were clearly white and moneyed. This was new social territory for him, and he meant to understand it before strolling on.

What type is that? he asked.

His question flustered the clerk. He jabbed his pen in Fishbein's direction.

Jews, he said. Jews like him.

Fishbein's chest deflated. Without another word, he turned about, took his daughter's hand, and headed toward the door.

Now what we are going to do, he muttered to his luggage.

Again, Bailey saved the day. He told the two to wait while he made arrangements and soon enough brought them by cab to a hotel that catered to all types, no questions asked. Fishbein was grateful. The three dined together that night at a place Bailey knew, where Fishbein ordered wine and fish. His tongue loosened, Fishbein told the man that in the year he had been in the United States of America, this was only the third time he'd come across a hotel that did not take Jews. In the end, this was a remarkable circumstance rather than a thorny one.

So it's true? Bailey asked. Jews is the type you are?

Oh, yes.

Well, I'll be.

They both laughed then and ate and drank together long after little Minerva fell asleep in her dining chair. They discussed the city of St. Louis, what a savvy man like Bailey knew of the ins and outs of the place, and where some seed money might in its season come to glorious flower. It was the birth of a working relationship between them, one that constantly evolved, depending on what business they conducted together. First there was the loan business, then the livery. There was the bottle business, the ice truck, and the medical supplies. A handful of years and twenty different investments went by before Fishbein realized he had not a secretary, a contractor, or a go-between in Bailey but a partner with whom he was inextricably entangled. There was another facet to their association that for Fishbein would have been enough to endear him, to bring Bailey close, regardless of their business dealings. Minerva loved the man.

Her love for Bailey was a lonely ray of light in her dark and troubled world. Minerva was high-strung. Minerva was rarely happy. From the first, Fishbein watched her struggle to control everything about her so that she could simply breathe. A day without sunshine, a wrinkle in her dress, a chop too well done, a book with the corner of a single page turned down was enough to throw her into a fit of temper. When she was five, he bought her a bag of marbles to amuse her. For Minerva, the bag was not a common child's toy but a problem she must immediately solve. Frowning, she sorted the contents by color and size, scrutinizing each one with care, holding them up to the light, revolving them between her small fingers slowly, slowly until she was satisfied she'd inspected every swirl, every dot and bubble. When she was done, she took a piece of string and knotted it so that she could measure a distance of about three inches. Then she created a ring of marbles grouped by color on the floor, each three inches apart, sorting them also by size and design. When she was done, she sat inside the ring, happy for the moment that she might gaze all around her and view order, conformity, perfection. She sighed with contentment, a sound as rare from her as birdsong in the dead of a Russian winter. Fishbein would never forget what happened next. She lay down inside her magic marble ring where nothing could harm her and slept a sleep so deep, so unusual for his little girl, that he sat outside the ring and wept. An hour later, her foot shot out as she dreamt, sending agates spinning all over the room. She woke and screamed for half the night.

When Magnus Bailey came into their lives, something shifted in her, at least on Bailey's account. One day, Minerva was in the midst of a fit or brewing to pitch one. Her little face collapsed in on itself, scrunched up, her hands reached into her hair, her back hunched. Fishbein watched her in growing panic. Once the muttering started, there was no turning back. Helpless, he danced around her, a hopping crow circling the coalescence of a cyclone. Her feet tapped. A low, terrifying hum emanated from somewhere in her chest. Tears sprung to Fishbein's eyes. He braced himself, holding his breath in anticipation of the inevitable burst of rage. Then Bailey's footsteps were heard on the stairs. Immediately, there was a hissing sound as the hot, wretched air of Minerva's torment dissipated through her clenched teeth. Bailey was at their door, in their living room, and she opened up like a Chinese toy suddenly unwound. Just like that. Magic.

It took time, it took years, really, but eventually Fishbein figured out what it was about Bailey that enchanted her, why his very presence gave her islands of peace, and why his departures often threw her into a fragile state, ready to explode once again at the first disordered object or event in her path. First of all, he was a natty man, unlike her rumpled father, with not a hair out of place, never a spot or stain on his shirt, jacket, pants, or shoes. Every word out of his mouth was considered. Not that he was slow of speech. He was a master of seductive patter, of persuasion, of salesmanship, capable of communicating double meanings or vague truths with such flair, such charm his listeners were enchanted and went willingly wherever his words sent them. He was big, and when he chose to be, intimidating. He was the soul of calculation. In every endeavor, he sought his main chance and exploited it. This bred an aura of power about him, which, her father saw, Minerva recognized and clung to. Being in his company gave her a sense of protection, a sense Fishbein for all his riches could not supply. Life had taught Fishbein to mistrust the plans of men. He had long ago abandoned himself to fate, though he did not expect fate to be kind. Magnus Bailey found the courage to forge his destiny in a world devoted to his subjugation. How he did this was a mystery. Fishbein marveled but didn't care. It was enough, in the beginning, that Minerva loved him.

Her nickname, Minnie, came from Bailey. He gave her lessons in life Fishbein had never learned. He taught her to be brave and take what she wanted, because, he told her, the world was not going to give her anything without a fight. He taught her to keep her thoughts to herself, to refuse others admission to the intimate workings of her mind. He taught her style. When Fishbein took her shopping, he came along posing, as he always did, as their manservant. He gave little signals over her father's head of what was flattering and what was not, surreptitious lessons in how to dress with panache. He taught her street slang and the haughty phrases of society both. When she turned fifteen, he saw the way men on the street watched her walk in her pretty clothes, with her red hair floating on the river's breeze. Neither Fishbein nor his daughter seemed to notice their attentions, which struck him as perilous. It had come time for someone to talk to Miss Minnie about the facts of life, or at least those concerning the wiles of men. He knew Fishbein would not do it, so he took on the job himself.

The fact of the matter was that Magnus Bailey loved Minerva Fishbein right back. He told himself his love was that of an uncle or an elder brother or, given their age difference, perhaps that of a second father. Like most men devoted to an existence that eschews domestic ties, he longed for them in spite of himself. The women he chose were light o' loves, good-hearted creatures of adventurous spirit or sidekicks in the scheme of the day. They came, they went, and if they were slow to go, he helped them along. Still, he was a man, he'd been a boy once; he had his longings. Rather than bind himself to wife, lover, or child, he fostered the bond he shared with Miss Minnie, the daughter of his business partner, from the day he carried her down the gangway, and this was enough for Bailey for a long time.

The afternoon that changed everything was in late summer. He'd dropped by Fishbein's Funeral Home with the week's receipts for the bail bondsman outfit Bailey had talked his partner into three months earlier. Minerva opened the door to the private quarters on the second floor with her eyes downcast. Seeing the soft leather spats with brass buttons no one else wore anymore but which Bailey favored for their undeniable elegance, she lit up and raised her face to meet his. Magnus! She jumped up a bit to hug him. They shared an outburst of tenderness, then separated. He felt an emptiness at the spot she'd pressed against, but it was warm and entirely pleasant. She led him to the parlor.

Well, Miss Minnie, he said. Where's your daddy?

At the *mikvah*. Did you forget? Tonight begins Tisha B'Av.

Over the years, Bailey had come to know about Jews. He knew
the *mikvah* was a ritual bath and that Fishbein always went there
before a solemn holiday, and especially on this day of mourning
for the destruction of their temple in Jerusalem and by extension
all calamities that had befallen Jews ever since. Forget about New
Year's and Pesach, thought Bailey. For Fishbein, Tisha B'Av was the
holiest day of the year. His mind tsk-tsked. Poor little Minnie, born
to all that sadness. What good did her father's perpetual grief do
her? Bailey didn't fixate on his own people's miseries from the day
they were captured in Africa and sold into slavery. He figured there
was enough misery around day to day. Why wallow in the past? But
Jews. If Fishbein were anything to go by, the past was their world
entire.

Do you want tea? Minerva asked. Although he did not, she
looked so eager to do something for him, he said yes. She left him
alone for a bit, during which time he thumbed idly through papers
on Fishbein's desk to see what he could see. She returned carrying
a heavy silver tray with teapot and glasses that sat inside holders
of filigreed silver, along with lemon slices, sugar cubes, and hard
cookies studded with almonds on china plates embossed with gold.
He smiled. She'd brought out the best to him, a teenager playing
grown-up lady, biting her lower lip with concentration as she laid
the tray down on the mahogany table between them. She held her
breath and knit her brow until her task was accomplished without rattling glasses or sloshing tea out of the pot, after which she
plopped down on her father's humpbacked velvet couch. Relieved
and happy, she sat back and slowly let the air out of her chest.

Sweet Jesus, Bailey thought. She has no idea how fetching she
is. Another man, a white man, would be on her side of that table
in a heartbeat, sitting close by for the joy of watching her heat rise

until, poor little firecracker, she exploded in his waiting arms. As if
to confirm his fears, she served them both then took a cube of sugar
between her pretty teeth and sipped tea through it with her lips
parted. When she'd finished, the tip of her tongue darted out to take
the rest of the sugar into her rosebud of a mouth. Her eyes sparkled
with merriment. Bailey grew flustered, surprising himself.

You cannot do that, Miss Minnie.

Why, what, Bailey?

It was impossible, but a rush of temper roiled his stomach. He
spoke with an anger toward her, one he had no idea lived inside
him.

How can you not know? How can you not? Surely you know
the world of men is selfish and vile, devoted to the spoilin' of young
gals like you. And you, my dear redheaded child, are a torment and
a torture designed to plague the masculine world until it can ravage
you. You must learn to disguise your heart or men will pluck it from
you and eat it for breakfast.

He found himself leaning forward, slapping his thigh for emphasis.

You must, you must! Or you will be ruined. Think what that
would do to your daddy, child. Think on it for a time.

He fell back in his chair. His breath came hard. Minerva Fishbein looked at him without expression. Her chin tucked inward, her
red hair fell over her brow, and her eyes bored into him like flame.
The silence between them grew thick. Magnus Bailey squirmed,
finding himself in the rare and uncomfortable position of not knowing what would come next. The timely miracle of Fishbein's return
home saved them all.

The Jew's face beamed with the purity of the ritually cleansed.
His presence charged the room with light, dispelling the dark, restless mood that had sprung up over the tea service like a lightning
bolt chasing a demon. Magnus Bailey concluded his business and
left, feeling saved from he dared not think what.

After that day, everything between Bailey and the Fishbeins changed. Minerva's looks to him went limpid. She quieted in his presence. She stared at him from shadowed corners. He would think her gone from the room, then, on quitting her father, turn to find her just behind him, speechless, staring. It was terrifying. He blamed himself, his arrogance in thinking he shared a parenthood over her. Of his own fault, the tide of the child's affection toward him had irrevocably turned. How long it would be before she expressed herself openly he had no idea, but he feared her inevitable confession greatly. From that moment on, he searched for a way to disengage his fortunes from that of the Fishbeins. Then, like a gift from the devil, the riots came and gave him one.

Of course, no one but he knew what was in his mind or how he intended to accomplish his goal. Bailey sat there rocking on Horace and Aurora Mae's porch with Fishbein, who was in as playful a mood as ever he saw him, while his daughter, Bailey's nemesis, slept soundly inside. Magnus Bailey counted the remaining steps of his plan to escape from the imbroglio that was the curse of a white woman's passion for a colored man in America and was calmed.

VI

At dinner, Aurora Mae sat closest to the stove by the head of the table, with Horace facing her at the other end. Mags and Fishbein flanked Aurora Mae on the right side of the table. The baby lay on blankets set in a wood box near her mother. Magnus Bailey and Minerva sat together on the opposite side. How he and the girl wound up next to each other was none of Bailey's doing or desire, but there she was anyway. When they'd started their exodus from East St. Louis, Mags rode in the caravan with Bailey, her baby at the breast, while the Fishbeins drove behind in the funeral car. Once they were out from under the city's gaze and in the wilderness that lay between that place and the Stanton farm, positions got switched about in a way that Bailey could not recount for love or money. It was the same with the dinner table.

After a time, Mags took up Sara Kate and retired with her to Aurora Mae's room. The others drank wildflower tea. The hostess chatted with Magnus Bailey, showing him the grace any woman shows a guest at her elbow and nothing more, but her attentions unsettled Fishbein's daughter. Her feet tapped under the table, she fidgeted noisily with her plate. Bailey, unable to hear when her father spoke, put his hand over hers to still it.

I will leave the hearse with your cousin Mags, Fishbein told the Stanton siblings. I am done with that business. She can sell it or not, I don't care. All of the goods in it are hers. To the furnishings from the house, I have added what she mights need from the kitchen. There are also some of the things from the workshop that George tells me long ago she is interested in.

Horace found the use of a gypsy wagon a near inconceivable choice of vehicle for a white man of means. He wanted to ask why Fishbein traveled by such a method rather than by motorcar or even an old-fashioned coach but didn't dare be so forward. Instead, he asked, How'd you come by that caravan?

Ah, it's an interesting story, Mr. Stanton.

Horace smiled. He just loved the way the man talked. He settled back in his chair, holding his teacup at his chest, ready for a good one.

When we decided to embark on our travels . . .

You all's wanderin'.

Yes, our wanderings. First I am making some decisions about what to take with us and what to leave, how we might ferry Mags McCallum and Sara Kate back to her people along with their belongings. I'll tell you this now, because she isn't here to stops me. Mags McCallum has only seen the hearse in use twice. There are not too many bereaveds who wish to pay the fee for it, a fee which I've had to make high. The costs of the petrol alone!

He raised his eyes to heaven for emphasis, then tilted his head and shrugged. Horace mimicked him in response. When they were both done, Fishbein continued.

I see you understand. Now both those two times, I watch her from my rooms when the bus is loaded with the peoples and the flowers and the dead, and George McCallum, so splendid in his black suit and top hat flowing with crepe, gets behind the wheel to drive to the cemetery. She is proud like a mama when her boy is bar mitzvah. Beaming! *Nu*. The first decision is I will give it to her. I don't care what she does with it. She can saw off the angels and use them to decorate her yard. She can sells it. It means nothing to me anymore. And I think it might mean a little bit to her.

Now, if we are going to Memphis, I am thinking how is the best way to get there. You will see, Mr. Stanton, that I am a widowed Jew with a beautiful young daughter and our companion is a Negro who is not, shall we say, shy. On the railway, on the big roads, this could attract problems to us, no? So we decide to find some kind of carriage and make a camping expedition of our way to Memphis. I send Magnus Bailey to the livery to make a list for me what there is we mights buy. When he tells me I have the option of this magnificent wagon as I have not seen since I left Europe, I am immediately against it. It is common. It is garish. But my daughter is enchanted by it. She will have no other. What can I say? I am a papa who indulges his girl, who is no longer little.

Alright. The next thing is to negotiate a price with its owner. *O mine Gott*. You would not believe the creature who comes to us for this purpose. He is a dark little man with bulging black eyes, in a threadbare suit and an orange shirt, his scarf purple and red. He is wearing gold hoops in his ears and on his fingers rings of every metal you can name, each one carved into fantastical shapes or set with bright stones I can see are merely glass. Oh, and on his head there is a black hat with a feather that screams 'The mountains of south of Europe is my home, if home I had.' He walks into my house with such swagger, I am thinking any minute he will begin to dance.

Fishbein raised his arms above his head, waved them from side to side, and snapped his fingers to demonstrate. Horace thought he might get up and dance himself. That, he thought, would be quite a sight. But the man stayed in his seat, shrugged, and continued.

I offer him schnapps. He takes, and we drink. He tries to rob me, but we make a fair price in the end, which I make up later in a contract for Bailey to bring to the livery with the payment. Then just before the gypsy is leaving, he stops on his way to the door and shudders. Truly, from head to toe, he shakes like leaves in the wind. I help him to a seat. With great emotion, he tells me it is his habit to speak to the dead, and the voices in my house are so very many they are shouting inside his head. What's more, they have news for me. Oh, I am thinking this man is a trickster who sees perhaps the grief which has lived in me many years. I brace myself, ready to deny him. How could he, a man from nowhere, hear my beloveds when I cannot? But what he says has nothing to do with my own. He tells me the voices are telling him that a stranger in my house will lose the most cherished thing and then find it again after a long time, but there will be hearts broken all along the way, most especially at the end. Now I know he is a trickster. There are no strangers in my house. And if there were, what kind of thing is this to predict? It is the story of every life! So I thanks him and let him go.

A ridiculous person, no? But an interesting one. I have thought many times about him, what his life musts be like, what maybe did he do with the price of his wagon. During our travel so far, you know, Minerva has told me of queer trinkets made of sticks and leaves and little bundles of hair tied with string she finds stuffed in the caravan's floorboards and walls. If he left them there to protect or to curse us, I cannot say.

Horace, who had been listening, enraptured, stirred in his chair. He was happy to have something to offer his guest, something useful.

My sister here's an expert in old-time remedies and such. Maybe she can figure out what those objects are for, if you give her a look.

Aurora Mae nodded. I can try.

All three turned to Minerva to ask her to fetch the things, but she had fallen asleep against Magnus Bailey's shoulder, her hands wound tight around his biceps. The Stantons gave Bailey a look of no small concern while Fishbein appeared completely unaware that an important protocol had been breached.

In the morning, Bailey and the Fishbeins left after tender fare-wells, with hugs and handshakes all 'round. For Mags Preacher McCallum, it was a most solemn occasion, signifying the true end of her life with George. From now on, there would be no one around her who had really known him, no one who had touched him or knew his voice or appreciated his kindness and honesty. No one to whom she could say, Remember the time George did this or laughed at that? No one among the cousins of the family plantation could do that, not even Aurora Mae and Horace, whose meetings with George were limited to the wedding. Not the way the Fishbeins and Magnus Bailey could. As the gypsy caravan rolled down the lawn and into the road below, she stood on the porch of Aurora Mae's house holding Sara Kate, waving good-bye, heartsore, with tears in her eyes. She felt she would see none of them ever again and indeed, it was ten years before she did.

Bailey drove the mules. Fishbein sat next to him, and Minerva rode in the wagon, placid, happy to have her men to herself again. Things were well set up in the back. There were mattresses, bottles of water, and a chest stocked with food so they could eat and sleep on the road in comfort. There were oil lamps and a brazier designed for cooking. They had blankets and linens and a washboard and tub. They passed the bridge at Thebes marveling at its splendor from a distance. When they came to Cairo from the wild western banks of the great river, they decided to stop and resupply before going farther. Magnus Bailey walked into town to bring back what they needed rather than expose them all to unpredictable judgments in an unknown town. He took a knapsack and was gone for two days. When he returned to their encampment, the knapsack was gone, his face was bruised, a patch of his hair had been pulled out, and the sleeve was torn from his jacket. Minerva took one look at him, groaned, and fell to her knees next to the cold cook fire. She wept and piled ashes on her head as if to say Kaddish for him, which broke his heart.

That's a mean place, Magnus Bailey said, but look, I'm back in one piece.

He put his hand on top of Minerva's hair and shook the ash from it.

Minnie, Minnie, I'm alright.

He crouched next to her and raised her chin with his hand.

Look at me, gal. I'm alright.

He pulled from his pockets the goods those who had set upon him did not acquire and lay them before her as a lover might blossoms picked in a field. A bit of candy, coffee, a bar of soap, two tins of sardines and a packet of dried herring wrapped in cloth, three short, thick candles. She barely looked at them. Her eyes brimming with tears, she studied his face, finding the last forty-eight hours in its depths. Stabbed to the core by what she saw, she collapsed shivering against his chest, where he rocked her until she quieted. He looked over her head at her father, who spread his arms, palms up, his features set in the same grim expression he wore daily, as if her state of desolation was just a variation of her usual tantrums. A thousand sentiments pounded through Magnus Bailey's blood and the last of these was, How sweetly her heart beats against mine, which terrified him.

That night, they slept under the stars on the mattresses they'd brought, each of them fully dressed, covered by a thick blanket to pro-

vide the warmth the fading fire would not. It was a clear night with a
half moon and swarms of stars. A rustling in the brush woke Magnus
Bailey from fitful dreams, or perhaps it was the flutter of Fishbein's
snores or the pain at his spine from the beating he'd sustained.

As if she'd been awake the whole time waiting for him to stir,
Minerva's voice called softly. Magnus.

Yes, child?

Why are we going to Memphis again?

It's a city of opportunity, and we need a change. All of us.

I don't.

How can you say that? Do I have to remind you of the night
we fled the riots? The horrors we saw, the terror, the hatred everywhere? Child. George McCallum was slaughtered.

I'm sorry about that, of course. But.

But what?

It was the most wonderful night of my life.

Before she could tell him why, Bailey got up muttering about a
call to nature. He leaned against a tree a good distance apart from
the Fishbeins and considered running immediately, in any direction, without even his boots. Behind him, a woman's voice sounded,
growing louder as the woman advanced, step by step.

We were together, alone, beneath the bridge, the voice said, and
he knew it was Minerva Fishbein's voice, but it didn't sound like her;
it sounded like no one he knew, a voice made of molten honey and
fire. The sound of it did not so much fall upon his ears as enter them
to inhabit the inside of his head, where it would haunt him forever.
If he'd known the term, he would have said it was the voice of a
dybbuk. He broke into a sweat. As much as he wanted to flee barefoot into the night, he was held fast by the voice and could not move.

You held me against you. I buried my mouth in your neck. I
tasted the salt of you, I could smell your fear but also your courage,
your devotion. Though hell was all around, I knew I was safe.

She was directly behind him. One arm went around his waist. He did not know where the other would land. He could not move. He could not move. Emotion he'd never acknowledged, a lover's longings, hot, white, pure, rose up in his throat and threatened to choke him. An exultation made his limbs, his head, light, robbing him of any defense against her. But there was terror, too. For the first time since childhood, his eyes filled with helpless tears. Then Jesus saved him. Fishbein awoke to their absence.

Bailey? Minerva? What is goings on? Where are you? Minerva? Bailey?

Minerva's arm slowly slipped away from him. The spell broken, Magnus Bailey pushed her aside and pointed in a westerly direction. He pushed her a second time and with more force to signal she must hurry over to the west that they may appear to approach the campfire from two directions. She gave him a pouting, angry look but did as he suggested.

I'm right here, Bailey said from his position.

I'm coming, Papa, Minerva said from hers.

By the grace of God, it rained the next two days. The three slept in the caravan in close quarters, which made any monkey business Minerva had up her sleeve impossible. By the third day, they were nearly to Memphis. Once again, Magnus Bailey went ahead to make arrangements for their accommodations. It did not escape her father's notice that his daughter either moped about their campsite or paced anxiously to the road and back, watching for the first sign of his return. He attempted to soothe her.

Our friend will be fine, he said. He was born near Memphis. This is not like his last excursion, *mine kind,* where he was among strangers. You need not worry.

It didn't help. Minerva became increasingly troubled as the hours passed without sight of Bailey. On the second day, she was near inconsolable. She sat on a boulder near the road's edge with a face as long and miserable as Fishbein's. By noon, the sun beat down upon her, making her hair a cap of bright, wet ringlets. Her dress clung to her breasts and waist. Her father brought her water, which she refused to drink. When the night came and with it a crisp, cool breeze, she began to shiver off and on as if a dark terror seized her intermittently and shook her nerves. Fishbein draped her in a blanket. She did not appear to notice. Minerva was locked in her thoughts and her father could not raise her from them. By dawn, he himself was pacing. At last, he stood over her, ready to strike to see what good a shock might do, but he hesitated. His hand went up, then froze in midair; he bit his lip, and tears ran down his face as he summoned his resolve, when, without warning, she blinked three times, got up of her own accord, and disappeared inside the caravan, reemerging some minutes later dressed in a pair of her father's pants, a plain white shirt, an old jacket, and her sturdiest shoes. Her hair was tucked up under one of Magnus Bailey's bowler hats.

He must live, she said. Or I would be dead. I will go to the town and find him.

Nothing Fishbein said could dissuade her. He put his hands on her, but she was the stronger and easily evaded him. He slapped his cheeks with two hands, whimpered, begged.

Suddenly there he was, Bailey, striding down the road, hands in his pockets, his hat tipped to the back of his head, his step light, jaunty you might say. With him was another man, shorter, rounder, brown as a coffee bean, and as smartly attired as ever Magnus Bailey himself was. The man swung a walking stick in a wide and winsome arc, his gait that of a man without a care in the world out for a day's stroll. Minerva Fishbein took off running toward them. The bowler fell off and rolled in the dirt. Her hair cascaded to her shoulders like flame. She knocked against Bailey with a fearsome force, nearly throwing him off balance. She hugged him and kissed his cheeks, one after the other in a kind of frenzy. His companion's eyebrows raised in surprise at her display, his chin tucked. His gaze went to Fishbein, who'd hurried behind. What is this? the stranger seemed to ask of Minerva's father.

He shrugged and replied, Magnus Bailey is with us since she is a baby.

With some difficulty, Bailey detached himself from her. In order to make what had happened less scandalous in the mind of his companion, he went to her father and embraced him, clapping that frail man on the back as if dramatic moments of physical affection were common between them. Startled, Fishbein coughed and was released.

The four stood in the middle of the road smiling at one another with varying degrees of sincerity.

Ah, I am forgetting myself, Magnus Bailey said at last. This is my cousin, Thomas DeGrace. Thomas, the Fishbeins of whom I've told you much.

They all nodded, shook hands, and dispensed pleasantries.

Thomas has agreed to help us.

With what? Minerva asked, an edge to her voice.

Taking a deep breath, puffing himself up, Magnus Bailey laid the foundation of his grand plan.

As luck would have it, child, when I got to town, I found my mother in difficulty. Her health fails. Her home is in need of repair. There are legal problems. Financial ones. I'm afraid I must devote myself to her welfare from now on.

He turned toward her father.

But of course I would never leave you all high and dry. My cousin Thomas here can take over my duties with you. He's a hand in many businesses you'll find interesting. His energy is boundless.

Thomas DeGrace took Fishbein's arm and led him away from the other two, bending his ear about the opportunities that lay ahead. Once they were gone, Bailey's chest deflated. He could not look at

Minerva. He feared her reaction to what had just happened. He had taken the first step toward abandoning her. Part of him wanted to take her in his arms and tell her that in another world, another time, he would have loved her, taken care of her for the rest of her natural life, and found heaven on earth in doing so. Except we are in this time, in this world, he would have said. Yes, he would have said it, but he knew if she protested, he would be lost. Instead, he walked apart with his head down, ashamed, dejected. He muttered to her that he would get a towel and bathe in the creek nearby and then sleep. The dust of the road had near done him in. Her heavy silence behind him pierced his back and went straight through his heart.

During the next weeks, Thomas DeGrace proved a useful fellow. In short order, he found them a furnished house on a pleasant street, a house modeled on the old Gayoso Hotel with the same wrought-iron balconies and views of the river as that legendary establishment. He took the gypsy caravan off their hands and acquired on their behalf a modest motorcar in which he drove them around wearing a dark suit and a chauffeur's cap. Once they were settled, he found tutors for Minerva that she might continue her education. He introduced the Fishbeins to the Loebs, the Ottenheims, the Goldsmiths, and the Levys through the good offices of their help, ensuring Minerva's chances of entering Memphis's highest stratum of Jewish society. Of the many projects he brought Fishbein, there were only two or three that captured the man's halfhearted interest. From these he selected just one—a concern that supplied essential tools for the lumber mills, such as ropes, chains, saw blades, and the like. The investment was more thank-you to DeGrace for services rendered than a hope for significant return. His experience in East St. Louis had changed him. He had little interest now in making more money. He was, in the wisdom of the Talmud, a rich man. He felt he had enough. He intended to spend what remained of his life in study and prayer. His only tie to the world was his daughter, and materially, at least, her life was secure. Minerva's temperament remained problematic. A new listlessness had overtaken her. She neither brooded nor exploded with frustration, but her common occupation was to stand at a window watching the street, anticipating he knew not what. Even on Sundays, when Magnus Bailey paid them a short visit, she remained dull, barely responding to his questions and ripostes. On one visit, she spoke but once.

Fishbein inquired after the health of Bailey's mother.

She's doin' better, but weak, Bailey said.

I would like to visit her, Minerva announced in a voice oddly loud, strident even.

You cannot, child, Bailey answered.

His features took on a guarded cast while his voice went as mild, as warm, as hers had been everything opposite.

She's in Orange Mound, and Orange Mound's not a place for the likes of you, Miss Minnie. You'd be better off strollin' down Beale Street in the dead of night. But I'll tell her the prettiest little white gal I ever knew has been askin' for her.

She made a soft snort in response and said no more.

The following Sunday, Bailey did not come. Neither did he come the Sunday after that. On the third Sunday, Thomas DeGrace came in his place and told them Magnus Bailey's mother had passed on. Bailey had gone downriver to bring her home. Minerva walked up to him and grabbed DeGrace with two hands by his lapels. Where is that? she demanded. Where? Startled, he answered her. A small town a ways away. Tulips End.

Tulips End, Tulips End, she said over and over, and the next morning she was gone.

VII

MINERVA WAS BUT A single night into her journey, headed on foot by an ill-used road to a town she did not know, when a ragtag band of men, desperate and cruel, came upon her, dragged her screaming to the bushes, and took from her everything she had, including a small velvet bag containing three gemstones she'd stolen from her daddy's hiding place. Their leader, a bearded, burly man of indiscriminate race, could not believe his good fortune in coming across such treasure in the middle of nowhere. Pickings that easy had never fallen to him before. He could only imagine that this redheaded vagabond was some kind of good-luck charm to him. He stopped his boys just as they were getting up for a round of fun and put her under his personal protection, which did not sit well with them except that they feared him. Although they'd been on their way to rob flatboats and ferries operating along less-traveled points of the river, there seemed no point chasing nickels and dimes after the capture of Minerva Fishbein. They returned to their camp, a dismal spot tucked away in the backwoods of Arkansas. Without horses or a motorcar, it took a night or two to get there. She would never recall which, as her mind was driven into darkness by the rigorous and intimate service her captor demanded once it got dark and they were alone inside his bedroll. At his first rough touch, she descended into a pit in which a part of her remained until her last breath.

There were women at the camp and a handful of dirty children, huts made of scavenged planks of wood and hunks of rusted metal. As soon as the women saw the captive, her delicate hands and flawless face, her wild eyes and flame-colored hair, saw her tied by the wrists and tethered to the boss, they determined to be rid of her. They got their men stone drunk, and while the thieves slept wherever they had fallen, the women cut Minerva loose, then beat her with sticks in the direction of the same road on which she'd met her great misfortune. When she was free of them, she ran helter-skelter into the pitch-black night without a sense of where she was or in what direction she was headed. She fell into stones and puddles. She ran until her feet bled inside her shoes.

When she collapsed at last, she lay in the mud on a patch of river grass and thanked God for it. She could hear the river flow nearby and the birds waking to song. She slept a little, then found a secluded spot on the riverbank. She took off her shoes and immersed her feet, swollen and cut, in a place where the tide pooled. Removing all but her underclothes, she washed herself and her dress, spreading the latter out on a rock to dry in the dawning sun. She lay nearby with her eyes closed and tried, very hard, to order her thoughts and emotions. The hardest effort she put to ignoring the burning pain between her legs, which hindered her from stuffing the memory of what caused it into an irretrievable place. It stayed there at the fringes of her consciousness, threatening to rush back to the forefront and overwhelm her senses. She slept some more. When she awoke, a ravenous hunger afflicted her, but she had no knowledge of what there was that grew or hopped or swam around her that she might safely eat, and so she put her dress back on, tied her shoes by their laces to wear them about her neck, and went back to the road hoping that she might encounter someone who would help her. Wiser now, she kept her eyes and ears alert to any sight or sound of approach, planning to hide by the side of the road until she could determine whether the passersby looked kindly.

It was hours before anyone at all came down that stretch of dirt. By then, she was so hungry and miserable, she stood in the middle of the path waving her arms at an encroaching cloud of dust as if it were Elijah's chariot descendant from heaven to rescue her. Just as good luck often follows bad, the dust cloud turned out to be a motorcar driven by an elderly white man in company with a middle-aged woman and three half-grown children, all of them on their way to a potluck Sunday dinner at their church. He stopped and picked her up out of Christian charity, taking her to the House of God Triumphant, where a flock of well-meaning women fluttered about tending her wounded feet and feeding her sundry victuals from all their kitchens, dishes of crab and shrimp and pork, none of which had she tasted in all her short life. They asked her who she was and where she was going. She told them she was Minnie Bailey and that she was headed toward Tulips End in search of family. None had heard of such a place. When she told them it was a small town just downriver of Memphis, Tennessee, a clucking of tongues erupted. Why, you are in Mississippi, they told her. Memphis is up thataway, they said, pointing north.

The congregation drew lots to find who would have the honor of taking their guest home for the night. By a curious piece of destiny, the winner was the same man who'd picked her up in his car, a planter by name of Mr. Deacon Brown. Brown and his wife took her back home. At sunset, they put her to bed between their daughters, two sweet girls not much younger than she. By nine o'clock, she was out of bed with her head stuck out the window, vomiting most of what she'd eaten that afternoon.

Deacon Brown's wife heard the ruckus and went to see what was going on. She put her arm around Minerva Fishbein's waist and guided her to the kitchen, where she washed her face and gave her cool well water to drink.

What's makin' you sick? she asked the girl. You don't seem to carry a fever.

That food wasn't regular for me, she answered. Her voice box rasped from exertion. I never ate things like that before.

This was unbelievable to a child of the Mississippi. Mrs. Brown looked doubtful she heard right.

What? No pork, no shrimp? Ever?

Never ever.

Deacon Brown had got up too by now and stood in the kitchen doorway in long johns and bathrobe, a shotgun in his hands, just in case.

Why in Jesus' good name not? he asked.

My papa never let me have it. We're Jews, you see.

There were gasps from both the Browns and then a heavy silence. At last, the couple exchanged a look of agreement as if they'd heard each other's thoughts. Deacon Brown laid down the law.

Alright, then. I cannot harbor a daughter of the demon Lilith under my roof, much less have her lay her head between those of my innocent baby girls. You can finish out the night in the barn, but be on your way at daybreak.

Yessir, Minerva said, I'm going and I thank you for what you've done for me already. But can you tell me, please, which way is north again?

She spent the night on a bed of straw with what livestock the Browns kept, leaving at the crack of dawn after raiding the henhouse of eggs, which she stored in a stolen feed sack. She headed north, keeping to the cover of bramble and hedge at the side of the road, avoiding others, rationing her eggs and eating them raw. After a few days, she came upon a clearing where a quartet of lovers, two young men and their honey-haired sweethearts, picnicked under the trees. They ate fried chicken from a wicker basket, tossing their refuse into the bushes where Minerva hid, watching them. She scrambled after chicken bones with plenty of meat still on them and ate while she watched. One of the young women, reclining in her lover's arms, enjoying his every warm caress while gazing at the gently rolling hills beyond, said, Someone is watchin' us.

The other young woman said, I was thinkin' the same thing, sister.

The young men chided them at first, sweetly, using pet names and other intimate phrases so that for all Minnie knew they spoke a foreign language. But the women insisted. The men got up to police the perimeters of their hideaway and in short order produced a struggling Minerva Fishbein, who, despite her writhings and determination to be freed, clung to a gnawed-up chicken breast in one hand and a gnawed-up chicken thigh in the other, because that's how very hungry she was at the time. The women instantly saw her extremity and ordered their men to let her go, after which they petted her and fed her as if she was a big old doll they played with, cooing and ahhing until she told them she was on her way to Tulips End to be reunited with her family. Tulips End? they asked, surprised. That's not much farther, the boys can take you there, but it's a colored town, you know. Are you sure that's where you're meant to go?

Minerva wiped the grease from her chin with the back of her hand.

I'm meeting a man from Memphis at Tulips End who will take me to my papa, she said.

The women studied her then as if she were some strange child of nature who'd grown up under a rock. Neither would venture into a colored town without male protection if their own mothers were tied to stakes and burning in the public square. They backed away and stood, collecting their blankets and drinking cups, putting them away in the wicker basket, instructing the young men first to drive them home and then transport Minerva to Tulips End. They wished her good luck but ceased more familiar attentions straightaway.

After they dropped the girls at their daddy's farm, the young men took Minerva to a place some distance down the road before turning off it. She feared they might be planning to abuse her, that they figured she owed them something for interrupting their love-making and taking them out of their way. But either their minds were not quite so vile or the posture she took—arms locked across her chest, her knees pressed tightly together, her face a storm of aggression about to erupt—put them off. They shoved her out the car and into the dirt without a care, joking about her destination, the local nigger town, as they called it, and clapped each other on the back, full of themselves, telling her as they sped off that Tulips End was not more than a quarter mile away. They hoped she'd find as good a time there as they'd just shown their gals, although they doubted such was possible.

She knelt in the dirt where they had cast her, wept awhile, then filled her spirit with the thought of seeing Magnus Bailey again. If only they could be together, she thought, all her troubles would melt away. Tired and hungry as she was, this was the idea that saved her, that kept her going, that leapt to her mind over and over. He is near.

It was dusk by the time she took to the road again. Soon enough, before night had time to take hold of the world, two Negro women emerged from a hidden path some distance ahead of her, walking arm in arm, their heads together. Their voices came to her soft as a river breeze on a calm, summer day. They murmured then laughed or gestured with their free arms in a way that bespoke amusement or surprise. Everything about them looked gentle and affectionate. Minerva took a chance and ran up to them, tugged on the back of their clothes. They jumped and turned about.

Who? What? they said, looking behind and beyond her in every direction wondering where this weird white child came from and who might be with her, following in secret.

Begging their pardon for startling them, Minerva told she was on urgent business to find a Magnus Bailey from Tulips End. Did they know it and could they help her find him?

They took her to a plain, unremarkable cabin with two goats tethered in the yard under the shade of a gum tree. Standing there on the porch, her eyes teared, she chewed her lip. Her chest felt as if white-hot nails were implanted between her breasts, searing her insides with every breath. Calling upon the great love within her heart to give her courage, she knocked on the door and waited. A shuffle of footsteps from within nearly put her into a faint. The door creaked open and on the other side was an old black woman, hair pulled back in an unassuming bun, her bony frame draped in a loose flowered dress. She was barefoot. She wore glasses.

Good evening, ma'am, Minerva said, bowing her head a little to show respect and that she meant no harm. I apologize for disturbing a house of mourning. I'm looking for Magnus Bailey. Is he here?

Who's that, Mama?

The voice of her beloved sent such a blaze of joy through Minerva Fishbein she did not hear how he'd addressed the very-much-alive-and-well woman before her.

Magnus Bailey! she cried out, and he came to her and he was all she could see. The old woman faded from her vision so that she might have been a ghost after all.

Bailey was as she'd never seen him, dressed in overalls and a broadcloth shirt, his feet as bare as his mother's. His hair, bereft of pomade, sprung up around his head in a thicket of curls. But it was Bailey, it was him, and she threw her arms around his neck and dissolved into a shivering fit of happy tears against his chest. His own eyes welled. He held her close, stroking her back, rocking her as one would any hysterical child, saying: Shhh, shhh. Hush now, my Minnie, hush.

How did you come here? he asked when she'd calmed enough to be led to a deep couch set before a stone fireplace. Does your daddy know you're here?

In fits and starts she told him the story of her flight from her father's house, leaving out nothing. When she came to the worst bits, he groaned and held her close again.

Oh, why did you do this? he asked, his voice tortured and raw. Why? Why have you done this to yourself? To your father? Lord, even to me?

She pulled away from him and took his big, black face in her small, white hands.

I've lived all my life motherless, she said. It's a pain I've never stopped feeling. There's a place inside where my mother's absence eats at me every day of my life. I can't imagine what a sorrow it is to have a mother, have her always, then watch her grow ill and die. To bury her. I love you too much, Magnus, to let you suffer that alone. I had to come. To look after you as you've looked after papa and me for as long as I can remember. And for all that's happened, I'd do it again. I would.

When she was done, she dropped her hands and looked to her lap. She blushed and smiled, realizing that she'd just confessed her love to the object of her long-suffering, silent passion. She'd seen in his eyes the pain her story caused him and decided he loved her, too, in exactly the way she'd hoped. Then a voice rang through the room, ruining everything.

I'm dead now, am I?

It was the woman who'd opened the door. Minerva Fishbein had forgotten her. The sight, the smell, the touch of Magnus Bailey had driven the woman clear out of her mind. At the sound of her words, Minerva's back went straight, her ears pricked.

My oh my, son. So this is the mischief you've been up to in town. Who is this crazy, ragamuffin child you've drug into my house? No wonder you came home to hide out a spell. If you think she's stayin' here, you're as crazy as she is. She needs to leave. Before the people 'crost the hollow get wind of her and kill us all.

Bailey got up and patted the air with his hands.

Now, Mama . . .

Ma-ma, ma-ma. The two syllables struck Minerva Fishbein like blows. Slowly, the depth of Bailey's betrayal sunk in. He'd lied to her. And it was an awful, ugly lie. He'd lied to her. And she'd poisoned her life on account of it. She'd been an idiot. A fool. Worse. She was too stupid to live.

She got up. She walked out the door. She walked down the road. Bailey followed her, begging her to stop, to listen to him just a little. She did not answer. He went back to the cabin, put on a jacket and shoes, borrowed a horse and wagon, and took off. When he caught up with his Minnie, she would not speak to him. He blocked her way, halted the horse, and got out, telling her to get into the wagon. She remained mute, but she stood still. He put his arms around her knees and back to pick her up. Her body had no resistance. She was a dead weight, as if drained of life, which made his task difficult. He banged her feet against the buckboard and her head against the top of the seat. Once set, she slumped over, not onto him, who was beside her, but to the opposite end so that she crumpled up in a heap. While all grew dark and cold around them, he shook the reins and drove her home.

When they came to the outskirts of Memphis, Bailey took a square of canvas from the back and threw it over the girl so no one would see he carried an insensate white woman beside him. He drove first to Thomas DeGrace's house in Orange Mound, rousing the man and telling him to get in the rear of the wagon, they had urgent business to conduct. Sleepy but compliant, Thomas hastily dressed and did as he was told, not even taking the time to ask what in the world was going on. When he came awake from bouncing around in the back, he noticed his cousin was dressed in country clothes. What's more, he was unkempt and bleary and gave off a troubling scent as strong as marsh mud in August. That unusual state alone was enough to spark a man's curiosity. He reached forward and lifted a corner of canvas to see exactly what Bailey hauled in the dead of night.

Sweet Jesus! he said on catching a glimpse of the glazed eyes of Fishbein's daughter. Where'd you find her? The old man's near dead from worry.

She found me.

When they arrived at Fishbein's house, Magnus Bailey told Thomas to get Miss Minnie up and out and escort her in. While he did so and amid the great clamor of her homecoming, Bailey slunk away like Judas into the night, leaving the horse and wagon in the other man's care.

VIII

BEFORE HIS DAUGHTER RAN away, the saddest man in the world could present himself as personable, even charming, if he had to. Otherwise, how could he make business? Business required he rise from his grave of memories for the time it took to strike a deal. How else could he pray with the minyan in the Pinch? Unless he shrugged at the kind of woes that afflicted Jews everywhere, the others would ask him why he thought his troubles were so special. Before his daughter ran away, he could sometimes take pleasure in a meal, a starry night, the softness of his sheets, and thank God for them all. Afterward, everything he touched, every sight before his eyes, every morsel of food turned to ash in his mouth. He considered her absence a fresh punishment for those small pleasures he'd allowed into his grieving, guilty heart. By the time she went missing a week, a malaise fiercer than any he'd experienced in the past gripped his heart and soul in its talons and squeezed them dry. Fishbein was a shell, a husk. Whispers were as shouts to him, the fairest breeze a gale. His clothing was a suit of mail studded with thorns.

And then Thomas DeGrace brought her home.

At first, he left the door unanswered. Hope had abandoned him. There seemed no point. But DeGrace was persistent. Holding Fishbein's inert daughter in his arms, he battered the door so hard with his foot it seemed the thick oak would split. When at last the knob turned, he pushed his way in.

Fishbein staggered aside and cried out, *Mine kind! Mine kind!*

Minerva's eyes fluttered open at the sounds and smells of home. She parted her lips but no sound came forth. Fishbein wrung his hands while DeGrace carried Minerva to the parlor to lay her down on the humpbacked couch. He stood back while father and daughter were reunited in a blending of huddled, sobbing shapes.

It took a while, perhaps several days, but eventually Minerva told Fishbein everything that had happened to her, leaving out no detail of the calamities she'd met on the road. Her violation by the robber chief, her ejection from safe haven by the anti-Semite Deacon Brown, her hunger and the sufferance of all her wounds she reported flatly, as if she recited a household shopping list. To hear her tell the tale, her tribulations were no more than inconveniences. Throughout, her eyes were dull and stared ahead. Until she came to her arrival at Tulips End, Fishbein feared her experiences had numbed her completely, that she was beyond repair. Then she tried to tell him of Magnus Bailey's deceptions.

It turned out, she said, that Ma . . . Ma . . . Ma . . .

Her mouth twisted uselessly. She could not utter his name. First she swallowed her lips, then she jutted them out. She stretched out her neck. She tried again.

Ma . . . Ma . . . Ma . . .

Her hand went to her throat, where the name was trapped. Her nails clawed at her skin. Fishbein grabbed her hands and held them fast before she could draw blood.

Magnus, he said, softly. Magnus.

And she nodded vigorously. Suddenly, her eyes were on fire.

Yes! Yes, Papa. He betrayed me, he betrayed me! His mama is alive! He lied to me! He ran away!

She burst into a flood of tears, howling like a beast of the field. For a few moments, Fishbein was hopeful. If she can weep like that, he thought, perhaps she will heal. But after she stopped, she withdrew inside herself to a place so deep, she drifted through the house like a being without substance, a dark angel or a ghost.

Over the next weeks, it became increasingly doubtful whether Minerva or her father would recover from the catastrophe of her heart's compulsions. Minerva's tutors were turned away at the door. The piano gathered dust. There were no trips to the haberdasher or to the bank. Fishbein spent his days in grief. He forsook even the shul. Rather than attend the daily minyan, he sat at home, shoeless, sitting on a stool as if in mourning, reading Lamentations and the Book of Job. After a number of weeks, the rabbi and president of the Baron Hirsch Synagogue visited him to implore him to return to the fold. He did not allow them inside. Dinah, the cook Thomas DeGrace had installed in their home after a long search for a woman who'd worked in Jewish households before and could manage a kosher kitchen, was full of complaints.

Them two just don't eat! she told him. For him maybe a little soup if I ask pretty and often. For her a piece of bread from time to time. I swear she likes it best dry and old and hard as rock candy. Even on the Sabbath neither one will eat more than an egg or an itty-bitty bite of chicken. It won't be long 'fore they both keel over, and I will not have folk say that two adult human bein's in my care died from starvation! I'm tellin' you, Thomas. Either they start eatin' or I quit!

Time went by. Dinah quit.

The old man continued to provide DeGrace a weekly stipend for the management of his business, but he no longer bothered to pretend an interest in lumber supplies. DeGrace pressed Fishbein to sell the concern, making himself a healthy commission once he found a buyer, and then he quit his service also. He might have stuck around the Fishbeins for the easy cash, but the girl's glowering stares unnerved him. He was afraid she might build up enough steam to ask him one day about his cousin, Magnus Bailey, who had plain disappeared. His own mama didn't know where he was. DeGrace resented Minerva for that.

Father and daughter settled into a desolate life. They went out as little as possible. What they needed was delivered to their back door by the lackeys of tradesmen. Minerva took over from Dinah in the kitchen. Twice a week, she telephoned the grocer, the butcher, the laundry, the coalman and iceman and ordered whatever they required. Afterward, she sat at the kitchen table drinking tea, immersed in her regrets, waiting for deliveries made by Negroes whose faces and bodies she scanned for resemblance to her lost love. When one of these chanced to have the same shade of skin or shape of hand, a gold tooth, perhaps, at just that spot revealed by only the widest smiles, or best of all eyes with any green in them, she took her time telling the man where to lay his burdens down, and took more time in paying him, maneuvering her movements that she might brush against him for an instant and feel, once again, alive. Naturally, she developed a reputation amongst them of a woman to fear or to mock. Watch out for that redheaded gal, the old hands warned new hires. She's lookin' for somethin' that'll get some poor boy killed one day. Or: That skinny l'il thing is moonbat crazy. A man could blow her over with a single breath, have his way, and be out of town 'fore she opened her eyes and begged for mercy.

There was a colored man sent to fix a leak in the pipes under the kitchen sink who came close to taking advantage of her. There was not much Magnus to him, except that he spoke well and in a voice that reminded her of Bailey's rich baritone. She got up close to him while he worked, getting on her knees and peering under the sink, asking him questions about the function of wrenches and O rings, just to hear him talk. He worked on his back, glancing over at her from time to time. When his leg nudged her own, she leaned into it, and he smiled. He was reaching out to find some part of her flesh to touch when Fishbein came into the room. Minerva got up quickly before her father noticed anything. The man finished his work. He drew up a bill and she wrote a check to his boss. After he left, she discovered he'd written something in a margin of the bill. *Big Sam's Bar on Beale Street,* it said, *most any night.*

Months went by. Seasons changed. Out of the blue, Minerva started eating. She filled the house with the scents of cabbage, potatoes, and onions, groats and noodles. On Fridays, she baked challah and prepared soup glistening with chicken fat, fish salads, beef, and cinnamon dainties. Infected by her change of mood, her father ate too. One day in the middle of the week, she hired a cab and went downtown by herself, coming home with bobbed hair and a dozen boxes of dresses, hats, stockings, and shoes. Fishbein didn't know what to make of her transformation, especially the shortened skirts, the painted lips, the boldly colored flowers and feathers that sprang from her hatbands, but it strengthened his miserable heart to see her take an interest in her appearance again. He considered going back to shul, put away Lamentations, and took up Psalms.

Thomas DeGrace had gone on with his life. He filled his time and pockets with pre-Fishbein pursuits: card playing and cockfights, cadging money from rubes and dockworkers to invest in one grand scheme or another. He combed the juke joints up and down the Mississippi for the guitar pickers and blues singers he brought to Memphis, depositing them on whatever free corner Beale Street offered up that they might audition for passersby and build a reputation the bars could not ignore. Most nights after midnight, he could be found collecting his commission from their handouts.

One night he was doing just that when he heard a scuffle in an alleyway. This was nothing unusual in that neighborhood at two in the morning. He tried to ignore it rather than put his nose in where it didn't belong, as he liked his nose just where it was—on his face. But a voice called out above the thumps and grunts. At the sound of it, every hair on his neck stood up. The voice was familiar, feminine, its tone frantic. Thomas DeGrace, it said, help me!

He turned and peered down the dark depths of brick corridor stinking of booze and horse piss. Two hulking black men battled over the favors of one of the town's more adventurous whores, a white, red-haired floozy in a skirt that exposed her legs above her powdered knees. She wore black lace garters and red pumps. A lamp outside Big Sam's exit door illuminated a face painted heavily as a clown's. It was Minerva Fishbein.

Thomas! Thomas DeGrace! Help me! she said again, extending her hand. Her black-ringed eyes were beggar's eyes. He could not resist them. He grabbed her by the wrist and dragged her away. Together they ran fast as they could from men too drunk and bruised-up to follow very far. At the river walk, he shoved her inside a shack he knew that sold stolen goods during the day and kept itself quiet as a churchyard at night. Panting, trying to catch her breath, she shrunk against a wall and stared at him. He paced back and forth in front of her, trying to think up what to say. This took some time.

Does your father know what you've been up to? he blurted at the end, earning himself a short, bitter laugh in response.

How long has this been goin' on? he asked next.

She shrugged.

Oh, Miss Minnie. What would Magnus Bailey say? he tried at last.

I don't know what Magnus Bailey would say. There was a kind of poison in her tone although her eyes teared at the name.

Thomas DeGrace continued to pace. His arms slashed through the air in sharp, useless gestures.

I do. It would break his heart to see you like this. Why, he'd take you by the scruff and drag you home to lock you up.

Minerva Fishbein tossed her head. No, he wouldn't. He was a coward. I know braver men now.

He clucked his tongue and rubbed the back of his neck with one hand, wondering what to do. Her lips curled into a pout. She stepped up good and close to him. He went still.

You helped me out tonight, Thomas. Whoever won that fight would've cut me just for fun. There somethin' I can do for you? She spoke in a dark, throaty purr, which frightened him more than a bucket of spiders. Then she draped her arms around his neck.

He broke away from her. She gave him a scornful grin, smoothed her skirt, squared her shoulders, and left him there, distraught, confused, and alone.

After that night, he'd run into her plying her trade from time to time, always in the early morning hours. He kept an eye on her, although they rarely spoke. Sometime during that summer, she disappeared as thoroughly as Magnus Bailey. When he asked around for L'il Red, as she'd come to be known, no one knew where she'd gone, though many murmured her name wistfully and wished her back home to Beale Street, where she belonged.

It was a good year before she turned up, heavier, harder, and full of new angles on the flesh game. She bought a house on South Third and dressed it up in velvet curtains and chandeliers, hired an eighty-eighter, two bartenders capable of keeping the peace, and half a dozen girls fresh from the backwater and full of juice. She taught them everything she knew about men. Folk said she had a silent partner, the moneyman, a handsome degenerate from an old Memphis family with too much time on his hands. L'il Red's was a big success. Thomas DeGrace passed her establishment nearly every night on his way to his usual haunts. More than once, he considered stopping in just to see how she got on, but he didn't.

There was a barbershop downtown that catered to coloreds, Uncle Pete's, and this was a place where DeGrace took a shave and a shine whenever he was feeling flush. Since he was a good tipper, old Pete took messages for him on his telephone and allowed him to make calls for a small fee. After he'd run a particularly profitable craps game the night before, DeGrace went to Uncle Pete's for the shave deluxe that came with a neck massage. Old Pete greeted him with uncommon urgency.

Thomas! Thomas! The barber was so excited to see him, he wrapped a steaming-hot towel around a customer's face tighter than he should. The man squealed.

Sorry there, son, he apologized before addressing DeGrace again in a hurried, hot voice. Every day, twice a day for near a week, a man's been callin' here lookin' for you, and I'm gettin' so peeved I nearly sent my grandson out on the streets to find you. Thank Jesus' sweet name I did not, as that boy is too young to see the joints you visit. It's a thing neither one of us would want on our souls, exposing that dear child to the life you lead.

Given that a profitable craps game required its runner to drink more bourbon than each of its marks combined, DeGrace was assaulted by the man's words in a way that made his head hurt. What followed made his head hurt more. He took the phone number from Pete and instructed the operator to dial it straightaway. While the phone rang, he held his breath until his lungs burned.

After five rings, there was the clicking sound of a phone picked up but no voice acknowledging such. Hello, hello, hello? DeGrace spoke into his end until a voice responded that was so frail it made the very act of answering the phone seem herculean.

This is Thomas DeGrace, cousin of Magnus Bailey? it asked, as if it were impossible that any other person might chance to call.

Yes.

This is your old friend Fishbein, my dear. I have urgent needs of you.

While DeGrace raised his eyes to heaven and laid his aching head against the barbershop wall, Fishbein continued.

I needs you to bring Minerva to me. It's taken so long to find you, it's become a matter of life and death. I can tell you where she is living. Do you know this place? I am hoping not, but if you do, you will understand why I cannot see her there myself and live.

How could Thomas DeGrace refuse? Cursing his cousin for setting him up with the Fishbeins to begin with, he went directly to the house on South Third known as Li'l Red's. It was two in the afternoon, the hour bordellos begin to come awake. Windows are opened to chase out the funk, floors are swept. Little dishes of vinegar under the beds are freshened to further sweeten the air. If it's a Wednesday, the sheets are changed. Sleepy girls of no virtue at all stumble downstairs in kimonos and bare feet for their coffees and sugar treats, trading affection or insult, depending on what transpired between them the night before. A little later, bath water's drawn, hair is coiffed. Yesterday's makeup is at last washed off, the skin breathes awhile before new paints are applied. When Thomas arrived, he walked straight in through the front door. Five light-skinned colored women and one very black one lounged about the drawing room looking at beauty magazines, chiding one another for this and that. They stared at him with a bored, judgmental curiosity.

The barkeep, occupied with taking inventory of a delivery of boot-leg, did not look up from his chore.

Not open yet, bub, he said. But one of these li'l birds might be willin' to sing you a song of glory. Up to them.

I'm here to see Minerva Fishbein, Thomas said. He tried not to look at the girls, who made a game of opening and closing their legs to plague him.

L'il Red don't take no callers before five.

I'm not a caller. I got family business.

The barkeep shrugged. Lifted his chin and pointed it in the direction of the staircase.

First door on the left. If she answers it, she answers it. But don't expect her to be in a good mood this time of day.

He ascended the stairs, hat in hand. He knocked on the first door on the left. A gruff feminine voice answered him.

Who dares?

Miss Minnie, it's Thomas DeGrace, he said. I have news.

There was the rustling sound of a woman's movement, then the rapid tap-tap of her light step rushing to the door. It swung open, and there she was, L'il Red, her hair longer now, reaching her shoulders in a cascade of curls as tight as any Negro gal's and just as thick. In contrast to the sluggish disarray of her girls downstairs, she was alert, animated, dressed in a crisp navy blue dress that fell to the middle of her calves. It had a starched white collar and cuffs while a shock of white lace popped out from the bodice as sweetly as a flower marks the pure bosom of a virgin. She wore stockings of a modest hue and the thick, solid shoes of a grieving widow. She held a pen in one hand, and the fingers that held it were stained with ink.

Come in, come in, she said, and as he did, shut the door behind him. What is it you have to tell me?

Her brown eyes held a terrible intensity, which fixed itself on him, presenting a passionate challenge he did not comprehend.

Then he saw the way her chest filled up with air and stopped, all life in her suspended, waiting for his response. Oh no, he thought, his mind sensitized under the fierce light of her expectation. She thinks I come from Magnus. His tongue grew thick in his mouth.

I will slap you if you don't speak, Thomas.

He swallowed and words tumbled out.

Your daddy. A matter of life and death, he says. You must come right away.

She blinked twice, her lower lip quivered, and the air left her lungs in a short, defeated puff.

Alright, she said. She went to her desk, a large ornate piece accented by scrollwork and the claws of animals, its top covered in a sparkling sheet of glass. She put down her pen, closed her books. Take me there, she said. My driver is on an errand. Call us a cab.

Taking up the phone on her desk to do so, Thomas noticed how tidy everything was, not a paper, a clip without its place. As she went to the next room for her good cloth coat and a navy cloche, he looked around and saw that everything else in the room was sleek, structured for efficiency and order, that nothing there suggested the tangled clutter one might expect from the offices of the town's most trafficked whorehouse. For reasons he could only guess, a chill went down his spine.

Thomas sat in the front of the cab next to the driver. There was no further conversation between them. When they arrived at Fishbein's home, Minerva told both DeGrace and the driver to wait in the cab in case she had further need of them.

As soon as she'd entered the house, the driver said, L'il Red makin' house calls these days? and started to chuckle at the idea, which, however absurd, was the only explanation he could think of for this strange trip from the town's worst streets to its best.

Thomas DeGrace surprised himself by quitting the car and slamming the door in response. As he leaned against the car's rear, waiting for Miss Minnie, he pondered the startling idea that he felt a loyalty to the old Jew and his slut of a daughter. For the second time that day, he found himself cursing his cousin.

An hour passed. When at last Minerva Fishbein reappeared, her father emerged from the house as well to bid her good-bye on the veranda. He looked smaller, frailer than the last time Thomas DeGrace had seen him, which was, he figured, maybe three years before. A good gust of wind would pick him up and land him in Alabam', he thought.

Father and daughter embraced, the madam of South Third Street breaking from the man slowly, the way dancers do when the song has ended but for the last waning notes. Fishbein groaned and pulled her back, close to him, which astonished given his appearance. DeGrace would not have thought him capable of restraining a kitten, let alone that fearsome will known as L'il Red. The old man took her hands in his, raised them to his lips, and kissed them over and over. He begged her in a voice loud enough for Thomas and, indeed, the neighbors hiding behind their curtains to watch the scandalous spectacle of a pious father pleading with his infamous daughter, to hear.

Don't go back to that life. You are home now. Stay with me. We can send Thomas DeGrace over that place to settle your interests. You stay here. Stay with me. I will heal you as in days of old.

Without a word, she shook him off and left Fishbein weeping, his arms outstretched in the direction of her back. Everyone who watched and listened, covertly or openly, considered her a heartless creature without conscience or mercy.

When she got to the car, Thomas DeGrace opened the passenger door. He saw her eyes were red. Her nose ran a little. She sat down and clasped her hands together to stop their shake. She cleared her throat to ask him where she could drop him off. He gave her an address at the edge of Orange Mound. When they got there, he left the car after refusing the bills she offered him for his services. As he did, she leaned forward in her seat to give the driver a new address.

Macklin Sanatorium, she said, Broadway Avenue, West Memphis.

This was such an unexpected destination, Thomas DeGrace started, unsure he heard correctly. He turned to look back into the car, where Minerva Fishbein stared at him again with that fiery challenge he could not bear. He looked away while the car took off in a cloud of gasoline exhaust mixed with the dust of the road.

Before We Reach the Heav'nly Fields

Along the Mississippi, Before and After the Flood, 1923–1932

IX

MAGNUS BAILEY WAS ON the run for years. He would not have described his movements in terms of flight, but that didn't change a thing. He was running, alright. Away from Memphis, away from Fishbein, away from Tulips End, away from Minnie, away from danger, away from love. In his mind, he was running to something not away from it, a thought that allowed his tortured soul the balm of self-deception. If asked what it was he ran to, he'd have said freedom.

The first place he ran to was the great mother Mississippi, offering himself as a barge swab, which signified he wished to punish himself as well as hide. Within a few days, his city-boy hands were no longer smooth and soft but swollen, bloody, and, within a few weeks, hard, weathered. He looked down at them with some surprise, as if they belonged to someone else, and thought, These are not the kind of hands meant to touch the sweet skin of a lady. Then he shuddered because Minerva Fishbein was the first lady he imagined them on. The mind of man is a sewer, he told the swab next to him, who raised his wooly head to give Bailey a gap-toothed grin.

Do tell, the man said, leaning on a barge pole, ready for a story that might titillate or amuse and so break the wretched, sodden burden of every day on that deck, on that river under the eye and stanchion of a drunken pilot with a mean streak.

Magnus Bailey muttered and dropped his gaze, angry with himself for speaking out loud. Minnie lived in a private place in him, buried deep from the ken of others, buried so deep she only appeared to him unbidden in fantasies and dreams.

Most times, it plain hurt to think of her, which is why he pushed his thoughts away as soon as they surfaced. In his dreams, she would emerge from the river, dressed in dripping white. She hung on a cross, a crown of wilted lilies on her head, her hair twisting down to her waist in ropes of wet curls like so many crimson snakes. In such dreams, he would sometimes weep in awe of the miracle that she had sacrificed herself for his sins. Other times, they released within him a bottled rage that she had done so, and he scourged her with stalks of river grass plaited with thorns. He'd awake heartsore and haunted for days and drank to keep from dreaming. On rare occasions, he had a pleasant dream of her. In these, she was kept safe behind her father's walls and was no longer troubled by men. The pleasant dreams disturbed him most.

Bailey's barge went as far south as Vicksburg, Mississippi, and as far north as St. Louis, Missouri. Whenever they stopped in Memphis, the others would leave and head over to Beale Street for high times. Magnus had not the habit, preferring to hide out between boxes and bales on deck rather than risk recognition by someone from the old days. Not that he stood much of a chance of being discovered. He'd gained weight and grown a beard. He sported a scar or two from dustups he drank himself into in other towns. His eyes, once so bright and quick, had dulled. Deep, puffy bags sprang up beneath them. He still had the gold tooth but lost the tooth next to it. He might've heard of L'il Red's from the men returning to the barge after their adventures, but he never visited there and had no knowledge of how far his Minnie had fallen.

Magnus Bailey's childhood had been filled with lust for treasure and glory, courtesy of his mama's gift for storytelling. Sitting cross-legged with him on the dirt floor of their cabin, she told him of African princes directly in his bloodline, men of great wisdom and bravery, men with a dozen wives and a hundred children, all dressed in garments with threads of gold. She told him of slaves who rose up and killed their masters then escaped across the sea to live lives of luxury in the courts of kings. She told him fables of creatures of the woods who were clever and resourceful, cheating man of their hides to wear and their flesh to eat. For young Magnus every one of these tales was instruction in a life worth living. He resolved to become elegant, suave, cunning, a master of romance. His first education in the manners of swells he accomplished at eight years old as a bootblack on a Memphis street, at a corner near the wharf where the pleasure boats docked, where gamblers, hucksters, and ladies' men—rich boys on a tear—came to rid themselves of Mississippi mud before strutting their stuff down the boardwalk for all the world to admire. Quick-witted, a fast learner, Magnus mastered their speech and style by the time he was twelve. He moved up in the world, became a runner on the boats themselves, pocketing enough money in tips to gild both his life and his mama's, too. From there on in, it was just a matter of time before he became the well-heeled fancy man Fishbein and his daughter encountered on the docks of East St. Louis. It was a life that suited his nature, made the best use of his talents, none of which were engaged in his years on the run. At first he'd had to restrain himself from sweet-talking the pilot into advantage or acquiring extra cash from his mates through subterfuge. Then he got used to sweat, dirt, and deprivation. Reflecting on the ruination he'd caused Minerva Fishbein, he figured he deserved them.

He might have lived against his nature for the rest of his days were it not for the Great Flood of '27. He'd seen rough seasons on the river before that terrible year. High water, crops ruined, winds that blew a man clear off deck, fogs thick enough to chew, none of these were unknown to him. But from the fall of '26, it was obvious to every old hand that the Mississippi was getting ready to pitch one of her fits. While it was still winter, the rains stopped briefly, engendering hope in the naïve and foolish that the river might recede some before the spring melt brought more water downstream. The high-water marks of earlier floods had not yet been surpassed. Before long, the rains began again, and the cargo on Bailey's barge changed. Loads of winter crops, ginned cotton, farm equipment, and milled lumber gave way to stockpiles of sandbags, boxes of canned goods and medical supplies, then government engineers with the tools of their trade wrapped tight and stored under the rifles of guardsmen. Just before Magnus Bailey realized he liked life enough to save himself, they took on refugees from the Yazoo and Ohio Rivers, where the water was highest—whole families and all the possessions they could carry, looking for the best place to get close to high land. That alone was the dream of desperate men.

The Delta ain't never been nothin' but flat as a pancake, the pilot reminded Bailey of a Saturday night. These fools think I got someplace to land 'em where they can walk half a day and scamper up some hill, but all I got is a place to store their money until they get tired of our Lady here and beg to put their feet on dirt.

Bailey decided that's just where he wanted his two feet by March. The Mississippi had grown as dangerous as any sea. The barge, even when loaded to its maximum weight, was sometimes tossed amidst her currents like a matchbox in a whirlpool. Twice they lost mules that dragged the barge upstream from shore when the earth sank beneath their feet. The pilot cut their harness quick enough and watched them drown. The river cracked and groaned day and night; its clamor could drive a man mad. Bailey had some savings out of his miserable salary since he never spent ready money except on drink. Rather than wire his mama for bank notes from the strongbox he kept hidden in her smokehouse, he decided to put his spare coin to use. He quit the barge and disembarked at Vicksburg. He bought himself a suit of clothes and a good pair of boots. He shaved his beard, got his hair trimmed, and hopped a train to Birmingham, where he tried his hand at some of the old games. They might have worked had he not been dissolute. While he was there, the world he knew drowned wholesale. Every newspaper reported a disaster a day as the Mississippi had her way with the puny defenses of men, flooding the homes of a million before she was done. By the time the flood rushed toward Memphis, Magnus Bailey woke from dissipation and worried about folk back home. He packed up and went to Tulips End to see his mama and know how she had done.

When he arrived, he found Tulips End was gone. Tulips End and all her people. Gone. Vanished underwater a day or two before he arrived. He got there so close on the heels of disaster, bodies had not yet drifted up from underneath the rubble of homes and fences, trapping them on the floor of floodwater high enough to obscure chimney tops. White men from across the hollow told him that was because of the dynamite.

Oh yes, there'd been dynamite, they said. Just a few sticks put around Tulips End by those rascals on t'other side of the river. Them folk wanted to make sure when the floodwaters went lookin' for a levee to break through, they'd find the colored town's and not their own. It was a matter of survival, don't you know. If the coloreds had got holda dynamite, it woulda been the other way around, no doubt about it. It'd be white men, women, and children trapped beneath their homes to pop up in weeks to come, bloated so much you don't know who's who. Just the luck of the draw it was. Every one of us will pray for their immortal souls, they said.

Magnus Bailey was uncertain if they meant to intercede for those souls of Tulips End who'd been sacrificed for the welfare of their neighbors across the river or those who lit the fuse and gave the river permission to slaughter them all.

Escaping the hell that claimed his mama and all his childhood people was enough to make Magnus Bailey grateful to God and the river that he had been spared. He grieved awhile, but the fact that his life savings lay at the bottom of the river along with his dead caused him no bitterness. What was money compared to a life? He'd have given it all to get his mama back. In his sorrow, he considered going home to Memphis, as that town was the only place he'd found on earth where he felt himself and halfway whole. He thought to look up the Fishbeins to see how they'd made out, but he didn't. Instead, he went looking for a job on the Yellow Dog Railroad. The man hiring liked the mellow tone of his deep voice, claimed it made him sound as close to a gent as a colored could get, and took him on as a porter straightaway. It went alright for a while. After the barge, rail work was nothing much. He kept to himself and out of trouble. Come that summer, when Vice President Dawes and Secretary Herbert Hoover toured the flood zone to plan the relief effort, they took his train. The conductor appointed him as their personal porter on account of his no-nonsense manner. Seeing the devastation around him, the army of conscripted Negro men working at the reconstruction, sleeping in mud under the gun, perishing of starvation and disease while white men ate their fill, Magnus Bailey could only be grateful again that he was not one of them.

Once, when he carried a silver tray of coffee and sweet rolls to the presidential car, he thought, If only my Minnie could see me now at the right hand of princes. Like a thunderbolt from God sent to smite him for his pride, out of nowhere there came a pandemonium of noise such as he'd never heard before. A rumble, a crash, a screech of metal rolled over his ears like the fists of brutes. He lost his footing. The tray bobbled in his hands. There followed a small, stinging stretch of silence that made him wonder if the indefinable mayhem had deafened him. And then the crash, screech, rumble returned, only louder this time. He was hurled to the floor by a power unseen. The tea tray flew through the air and slammed against a wall. A bomb, he thought. An anarchist looking to murder the vice president and Secretary Hoover. He sat with his hands braced against the floor, dry-mouthed, trembling, waiting for what would come next.

After the dust settled, he learned that when the engineer attempted to cross a bridge against the river's wishes, the bridge collapsed. The train derailed. The engine car dangled over a cliff and the engineer was dead. Dawes and Hoover and Magnus Bailey were banged up some but survived. Soon as a new train arrived to whisk them away, Dawes and Hoover went on with the work of the relief tour. That train was fully staffed. Bailey was replaced.

Now he was truly lost. He had nowhere to go. He had no plan. His ready money was gone. He had no work. He felt cursed, driven out, an Ishmael in the wilderness. Thoughts of Minnie and his poor sainted mama haunted him. He felt that those he loved had paid for his sins, but that he himself was not nearly done doing so. He waited for the Hand of God to deliver the final blow and crush him. While he waited, he wandered. He crossed the river and wandered to Little Rock, to Dallas, to Wichita, to Des Moines. He avoided the flood zone, often traveling by night, hiding in the bush by day that he might not be kidnapped and traded to a work camp, where he would surely die. In every city, he hired himself out pushing a broom, washing windows, or hauling garbage, whatever dirty work might be had. In Des Moines, he revived his youthful skill as a street-corner bootblack for a time. He crossed the river again and went to Chicago and Indianapolis. From there he headed to where he was going all along, to St. Louis, or rather just south of there, to the home of Aurora Mae and Horace Stanton, where he hoped to find Mags Preacher McCallum and hear news of his Minnie, who had not once through all his trials and travels left that secret place in his heart where he'd stuck her like a splinter through soft and tender flesh.

Before he got to the Stanton farm, he bathed in the river and brushed the dust of the road from his one good suit of clothes. He planned how he'd speak to the Stantons so that he'd not too quickly betray the purpose of his visit. He remembered how magnificent Aurora Mae was, how he'd thought to bed her one day, and was wistful toward the man he used to be before Minerva Fishbein taught him regret. He strolled up the grassy hill that led to the Stanton front door with a swagger that belied the anxious pounding of his heart. He walked up the steps, past a pack of stretched-out, lazy dogs who barely lifted an eyelid to him, and knocked on the door with his new marble-knobbed walking stick bought especially as a prop for this occasion. Then he summoned his young rake's smile and froze it on his face. O Lord, O Lord, O Lord, he prayed, let Mags still be around here so I can find out what I come to know.

When the door opened, there she was, an answered prayer, Mags Preacher McCallum, looking exactly the same as she did ten years before when he'd left her at that very doorstep with the funeral car and her baby girl, little Sara Kate. Twin boys, maybe five years old, clung to her skirts, one on each leg. A girl child with small bright eyes and cheeks as sharp as two arrowheads stood just behind her. She peered around one of the boys, chewing her lower lip and looking like the pint-sized ghost of George McCallum himself.

Sweet Jesus, it's you, Magnus Bailey, ain't it? Mags said. She opened the door wider to give him a swift, chaste embrace before waving him in. Babies, she said, this is a man I knew years ago, a man who was kind to me when I was just a green country gal gone to the big city to make my fortune.

She invited him to sit down at the kitchen table and sent the boys to find their father in the fields and bring him back to meet their very special visitor. She put Sara Kate to heating up the stew pot and fixing some chicory brew that Magnus Bailey might refresh himself.

She's just like her daddy, Magnus said. Right down to the way she walks.

Mags sighed. She felt an uncommon need to express herself, the way people often do when the past comes up by surprise and smacks them across the face, when all the old feelings sleeping inside revive intact and strong. She spoke to Magnus Bailey as if they'd been the very best of friends and confidants those years ago when all they'd ever been was passing friendly, their sole communalities in life Miss Emily's rooming house and the Fishbeins. But time gone can burnish old acquaintances with sentiment, and Bailey was the reason, indirectly anyway, that Mags met George McCallum to begin with, which is why she leaned forward with her elbows on the table and let go.

It's true what you say. I swear she's so much like George it sometimes makes me sad just to look at her. I married again, mostly because her father made me so happy, I couldn't live alone anymore. I kept wantin' company, especially with this one sproutin' up around me, remindin' me how nice life is when you got somebody. Now, the boys' father. He's a good man alright. I wouldn't dishonor George by marryin' anybody but a good man. Still, when I look at my Sara Kate, I think of her daddy, and Lord help me, I miss him more'n a bit.

The child in question brought Magnus Bailey a hot bowl of squirrel stew with onions, yams, and collards, and he found it wasn't half bad. Mags went on while he ate, reminiscing about George's way with a needle and how much he comforted the bereaved just by standing there, looking dignified. It must have been a good twenty minutes before she mentioned the Fishbeins. For Bailey, it felt like hours.

Mr. Fishbein was good to us, very good. He'd learned some hard lessons from life in the old country, so I was told, but they never turned him cruel. Always respectful, he was, and not once did he cheat us of a dime we had comin'. And what a generous soul! Remember that big old bus he gave me? I sold it pretty fast. Know what I did with it? I put half in the bank for Sara Kate's welfare. There's enough there for all my children's future, I'm bettin'. How many of us can say that? Then I bought me some beauty supplies to add to the dead man's paints Mr. Fishbein let me have, and a great big old hair dryer, tough as a gun. It wasn't much more than a couple of trash-can lids wired to hold a bundle of lightbulbs. Why, I woulda got more heat on a lady's head if I set her down in front of an open oven door. We didn't have the electricity up here yet. I had to buy a dynamo for an old shed out back. That dynamo cost me a whopper but it made me a shop out of those four walls. It was drafty and plain. The country cousins, they flocked to me from all over anyways just to get a look at it. I did everything for 'em I told you I would in times gone. I made beauties out of good-lookin' gals and lookers out of plain ones. More than a few owe the catchin' of their husbands' eye to me. Then the chemicals got to me. I started to cough too much. I had to give it up. I never did make my fortune from that business. I guess that means you were right to deny me my hundred dollars, Mr. Magnus Don't-Turn-Nobody-Down-No-How-No-Way Bailey!

She laughed heartily. Bailey joined her, laughing with just the right measure of nostalgia, nothing too loud or harsh in his tone, although his heart raced and his mind burned for the next moment when he could bring up Minerva. Casual, he thought, it's got to be casual. He arranged his features in a simple, curious expression and opened his mouth.

I wonder how he and his daughter are these days, he began, when Mags Preacher McCallum's second husband came in the door, a good-natured smile on his broad, happy face, his big farmer's hand extended for Magnus Bailey to shake.

Joe Dunlap, he said, pleased to meet you.

Magnus Bailey, the other replied with a false smile. All hope of conversation about the Fishbeins was about to turn to dust. Desperate, he tried to steer talk back to the old days.

How is it, he asked, that you've taken over the Stanton house? I'll never forget the night we delivered you here and the hospitality we enjoyed. Come to think of it, where are Aurora Mae and Horace? Why, I can see us all dancin' at your weddin' and sittin' together at this very table as time went by. You were over there and Horace up the head and Aurora Mae facin' him. Then me here, where I am now, with Miss Minnie beside me . . .

All his machinations brought him was an excited spill of words from Mags about the curious fates of her cousins. Half of it made no sense to him, but he nodded and oohed and ahhed while she rattled on anyway.

Oh, there has been so much, so much gone on, I don't know where to start tellin' you, she said. Poor Aurora Mae. How she suffered, you know, just for bein' what she was. So big, so beautiful. No woman like that can live in peace. Not in this world. The night riders come up some year ago, while she was all alone, killed her dogs, and took her away. Why, when poor Horace got back here, she was gone without a trace, and no matter how hard he tried, he could not find her.

Bailey thought of Minnie then, of her violation on the road to Tulips End, and how her father, like Horace, searched and could not find her. His eyes stung.

They were reunited by the flood, Mags continued. Somewhere, somehow, they found each other, got a hold of money, too—piles of it. They came home awhile, and then, without warnin', they left, each their separate ways. I took the house over. Aurora Mae wound up in Memphis. I know, as we write from time to time. I don't know where Horace went off to.

The mention of Memphis gave Magnus Bailey the opportunity he needed.

I'm very sorry to hear all that, he began. We all vulnerable, ain't we? In the good times and the bad. Poor George, Aurora Mae, even I been hurt, although to a lesser degree.

He studied his hands which were rough and raw from his life on the barge and the hard labor he'd been put to after. He waved them about for her to see. Mags shrugged and shook her head.

Aurora Mae's in Memphis? She doin' alright?

Mags shrugged again.

Money heals all kinds of wounds, she said.

Yes, it does, Miss Mags. It certainly does. I wonder if she's in touch with our old boss. I haven't seen him in years.

Well, I don't know about him, Mags said. But that Minerva, that l'il redheaded devil Minerva . . .

She broke off. Bailey sucked in a great breath of air, then let it out slowly, waiting. Mags dropped her head and sighed. Her mouth twisted as she pondered how much to tell Bailey, how much to leave out. She glanced at her husband, who'd remained quiet throughout their talk. He nodded encouragement for her to continue with a seriousness that frightened their guest. He could not imagine what all this hesitation was about. Dead, he thought. A hot, hard lump throbbed in his throat. My Minnie must be dead. What he next heard made the grieving of her look good.

Aurora Mae had a terrible time with those night riders. You can imagine how they used her. When they was done with her, they took her over to Minerva Fishbein's bawdy house. L'il Red might have turned into the stone dead weight of her daddy's heart and the biggest whore in all of Tennessee, but she saved Aurora Mae from that life. Took her in, then got her out of there. I believe she got her off to be a cook somewhere. No matter what, I got to thank her for that.

At last, the coward Magnus Bailey's wait was over. His soul received its just deserts. Standing in for the Hand of God, Mags Preacher McCallum Dunlap's words bound him to the racks of hell. He spent the night at the old Stanton place, on their best feather bed, as befit an honored guest. It might have been a bed of hot coals for all the rest it gave him. He writhed the night long in a fresh agony of guilt. In the morning, he quit the hospitality of the Stanton farm for the rigors of the road to Memphis, where he resolved to journey and put things right.

X

DURING THE LONG WALK to Memphis, Magnus Bailey resurrected everything he'd forgotten about artifice and the exploitation of human weakness. This was not the halfhearted attempt at restoration he'd made in the days after he'd left the barge or even the hasty effort he made as he approached the Stanton farm. He was dry now, and his purpose that of the zealot reborn. He recalled first the simple things, those basic skills in how to convince others to do what they least wanted. He practiced the various ways he could turn his head or hunch his shoulders to provoke the desired response to a leading question posed in just the right tone of voice. While he walked down dusty roads, thrusting his walking stick forward, pulling up his thoughtful self behind, he muttered stock phrases he'd not used in years, practiced the laughter of collusion, the sigh of feigned surprise. His lips and eyes danced along the rhythm of his murmurs. With fluid grace, his body made sudden pivots and his arms grand, bold gestures either to the left or the right, depending on which side he carried his suitcase that was packed with canned goods, a bit of dried meat courtesy of Mags Preacher McCallum Dunlap, and everything else he needed to keep his suit brushed, his shoes shined, and his hair tamed. Walking down the road, he looked like nothing so much as a well-groomed, hyperkinetic lunatic. A handful of automobiles and wagons passed. None offered him a ride.

It was half a year since the flood. The flood water had long drained from the streets of Memphis, but the damage was everywhere. Homes abandoned and rotting out dotted even affluent districts. Businesses owned by families established before the Chickasaws left were gone without a trace. Downtown corners were piled high with planks of wood placed when needed across the thoroughfares to facilitate travel on roads where the mud was still thick. The air was cold but the hard frost, always a random visitor in that town, had not yet come. Everywhere Magnus stopped to pass the time of day and catch the pulse of life, folk voiced a longing for freezing temperatures that the mud might get rock hard and ease their burdens. Oh yes, he'd respond solemnly, the hard frost will come. But to himself, he said: Lordy! Hard mud on the streets of Memphis? Crunchy, maybe, long about dawn in January. But hard? And then his heart cheered thinking if folk were that desperate, his pickings might be considerable.

So far they'd been anything but. He couldn't understand what was wrong. Whenever he needed money in the past, it came to him like rust to iron. All he had to do was wait and keep his eyes open. Where his genius lay was in seizing whatever opportunity presented itself and wringing it dry of purpose. He wasn't a visionary so much as an expeditor of the ideas of others. If you had something to sell, a problem to solve, an inside chance to coax into a sure thing, Magnus Bailey was your man. But these days, folk played their cards close to their vests. The word on the street was mum. Since the disaster, no one trusted the future anymore. Old gamblers had become hoarders. Entrepreneurs minded the store and kept their dreams small. The high life had gone low and hard. Beale Street was about nothing but the blues.

Magnus Bailey needed money. He needed lots to make things right. He wasn't at all sure how he would do that. The only thing he was sure of was that he'd need to be flush. At first, the only work he could get was as a part-time doorman over to the Robert E. Lee Riverside Hotel, a place sparsely visited by parsimonious guests mean with a tip. He bided his time. He made inquiries, found out that L'il Red's was still in operation after the flood, that in fact the doors had never officially closed. When her premises went underwater, L'il Red pitched tents next to the encampment of the government- and relief-worker guards, trading her whores' services for food and medicine instead of coin. He wasn't half ready to go to her place and confront her, although he knew such a confrontation was essential, the first step toward emancipation for them both. Then the angels of forgiveness smiled upon him. He secured a second part-time job, cleaning floors and toilets at the main library two nights a week. The regular janitor was a churchman who wanted one night for prayer meeting and Saturdays for his family. That man hid copies of the *Chicago Defender* in the maintenance closet between the mops and the buckets. It was still a dangerous matter in some quarters for a colored man to be found with the *Defender* in his possession. Magnus found them and read the papers in his spare time. Between articles urging Negroes to quit the South and move north, where equality and decent jobs awaited them like ripe fruit ready to drop from the trees—argument that to Magnus Bailey, veteran of the St. Louis riots, rang false—he read stories about Josephine Baker and Langston Hughes living the white-man's life in Gay Paree, and these he swallowed whole. A dream was born. Why hadn't he thought about it before? The world was bigger than the Mississippi. There were places he could take Minnie where they could be together without fear. He assembled the texts he needed to discover where those places might be and how to get there. Soon enough, Bailey's grand design was in order. He took to dreaming about his inevitable meeting with the instrument of his redemption and the dozens of tricks he tucked up his sleeve to win her cooperation for what came next. Lack of funds kept everything in the future, a future he envisioned bathed in a rosy mist, spiked with dangerous challenge and bright with glory altogether. If ever he got the money.

He avoided contact with her father. He went by the old place at night to see what he could from the curb. The house was derelict, the paint a mess, chipped and riven with mold. One of the front windows was broken and patched over with board. The lawn was wild and full of weeds. Inside on the first floor, there were lights on, and another light glowed on the second floor where Fishbein's bedroom had been. The thin, stooped shadow of a man crossed the bedroom window. It looked enough like his old partner to soothe his mind. He's hangin' on, Magnus Bailey thought. I guess me and Minnie haven't killed him yet. Though this came as a relief, over the next few days he lay awake at night, staring at the ceiling while he adjusted his calculations to include the rescue of Minnie's daddy, for it looked to him that rescue was required.

For the time being, he stayed with Thomas DeGrace, who was about the only family he had left. He slept on a cot near the stove. Thomas lived in a shotgun house built when Orange Mound was established as a colored district nearly fifty years before. He bought the place on the cheap from an unmarried ironmonger getting ready to die, ornamenting it with scraps of Italian molding and hand painted tile he scavenged from swankier neighborhoods. That was before the flood. Afterward, everything changed. Thomas was conscripted for levee work down in Greenville just before the deluge.

While he was so bonded under the gun, unable to escape, his home was looted and stripped of everything the tides hadn't swept away. Later, the house was sold at tax auction to a white man. When the levee let him go, Thomas rented his own house from the new owner. That just about broke him.

There's no such thing as a free Negro in America, DeGrace told his cousin. I was mindin' my business, buyin' up supplies down-river to take to Tulips End. I knew the folk back home would be in trouble. My daddy and mama, my aunties. They never would leave when the river got high. I rode all over three states lookin' for what I needed. Finally, I had a cart loaded up and a mule. The day I was headin' back to Tulips End, I was stopped on the road by militia, they called themselves. Foulest, evilest-lookin' crackers you can care to imagine, ten of 'em on horseback and totin' rifles, each one pointed in my face. They took my cart and put me on the levee. Oh, dear God. What a hell. We slept in the mud with near nothin' to eat. They put tags around our neck like we was livestock. When we got sick with the dysentery and the fever, they just let us rot and waited to see who nature would save and who not. I got assigned to unloadin' the relief boats after the flood. I stole what I could, and that's the only reason I'm alive today. That and Jesus. Praise the Lord. Praise the Lord Almighty. You comin' to church?

Thomas DeGrace had got religion. He dressed like a country boy now, his home was without creature comfort, and every spare cent he got hold of he gave to the Miracle Church of God's People, the congregation set up over a storefront by the Rev. Dr. Willie Smalls, a minister arrived in Memphis just as the water receded, a man look-ing to preach penance to unworthy survivors. Though sometimes he felt he might like a taste of some old-time religion, sing a hymn or two, and pray for his mama, Magnus Bailey would rather die by lightning than stand up and clap hands under the sway of a man like

Dr. Willie—in Bailey's opinion a big-bellied, sweet-tongued fraud bleeding the poor while he danced on the graves of their dead.

Wednesday nights were for prayer meeting above McCracken's Cash Groceries, held to keep the burnish of vows made on Sunday gone and keep them bright 'til Sunday next. One Wednesday night Bailey felt like a walk and kept Thomas DeGrace company as he headed over to Pendleton Street to warm up his soul. When they got there, DeGrace tried to persuade him to come in. Bailey glanced at the sign to the right of the front door. FREE TRIP TO HEAVEN it read, SECOND FLOOR.

Nothin' free about any trip Dr. Willie's takin' you on, he said.

His cousin pursed his lips and lifted his chin, pointing it high in the air with righteous defiance.

Church got to pay the rent, just like you and me. Dr. Willie got to eat and put clean clothes on too, he said.

Magnus put a hand up to the sky, gave him an amen to shut him up, and made to walk on toward the river, maybe pass L'il Red's just to torment himself, which he did often enough. Nights when a certain mood stole his good sense, he stood on the street opposite L'il Red's, hiding from the light of a gas lamp in a doorway. If the weather demanded the windows be closed, he could not hear the whores' laughter and shrieks, the piano man pounding out furious pleasure on the keyboard, or the whoops and bellows of the clientele within. So he watched them dance, embrace, and fight in pantomime and hoped for a glimpse of Minerva Fishbein passing through the room to settle an argument or make a match. He never managed to spy her, but he kept on hoping. That night, as he quit Thomas's company and put up his collar against the night air, his head was turned by a sight that would stop a pack of rapine marauders in its tracks and wake the dead at the same time.

A woman crossed the street, the sight of her stopping traffic from every direction near or far. She was a large woman, a very large woman with skin as black as Bailey's own, evidence of an African heritage undiluted by the lust of white men. She stood half a head taller than he himself and was so wide at the hip and the breast he imagined she could bear twins and suckle triplets all at once. Her clothes were rich, her blouse a brilliant yellow silk ruffled at the neck and cuffs, her suit cut in the latest fashion to expose her legs from the calves down. Its plush gray wool was tailored against her frame in a way that confirmed she'd still a waist despite her girth and smooth, if enormous, thighs. She wore a great, broad-brimmed hat with a veil such as women rarely embraced after the Great War. Its netting came down to her neck and was tied by velvet ribbons at the back of her head. Its brim tilted slightly to the left so that it resembled wings in flight. The crown was studded with ropes of pearls entwined with feathers and topped by a pair of hum-mingbirds so artfully stuffed they looked about to burst into song. Beneath that remarkable hat, a mountain of thick black hair was piled up, secured by a dozen pins whose knobby heads were also of pearl. At the distance from which Bailey first saw her, it was impossible to see her face, but her size, her dress, the confident, almost military, strength of her stride—all of it created a tableau of spectacular feminine power and beauty. He wondered who she was, why she was in Orange Mound. If she'd strolled the streets of his neighborhood at any time before the flood, he'd know her. He'd have to. She would not go unnoticed or forgotten anywhere. He guessed she was a voodoo queen visiting out of New Orleans or an heiress through a lover to a vast sugar plantation somewhere in the islands. But what, he continued to wonder, was she doing here?

She walked directly toward him. A thrill enlivened his blood. He straightened his back and widened his smile, prepared to bow his head and kiss her hand when she got near. He could not believe his luck and thought, Ahhh. Big rich woman comin' right at me. My money troubles are over.

Then she walked directly past him to the door Thomas DeGrace held open and ascended the stairs for her free trip to heaven.

Thomas made to follow her, but Magnus Bailey's hand on his sleeve pulled him back.

Who is that woman, Thomas? She is surely the most curious lady I have ever seen.

Thomas jerked his head back and looked at him with surprise.

Why, you know her. I'm sure of it.

I could not forget such a creature. Tell me. Who is she?

Why it's Aurora Mae Stanton, Thomas said. From those Missouri Stantons I know you spoke of when you first got back home.

Magnus Bailey thought he was beyond astonishment in life, but the identification of that woman as Aurora Mae Stanton stunned. He could not imagine how she'd come by such physical transformation except through either the greatest misfortune or the greatest effort. When last he'd seen her, she was a lean and languid country marvel. There was a virginal succulence about her that dried every man's mouth with desire. Now she struck him as an epic goddess of sensual energy. Her copious flesh evoked both the fertile sustenance and the deadly menace of the Delta itself. Her material transformation was a deeper mystery. Then he remembered Mags Preacher McCallum's story about the night riders and Aurora Mae's escape from a life of the most vile servitude thanks to Minerva Fishbein. He remembered more. He remembered that after the flood, she'd returned to the family farm with money, lots of it, the origins of which were secret, no doubt connected to a crime of blood. His mind whirred and clicked like the gears of the slickest engine.

Perhaps I've been hasty in judging your Dr. Willie, he told Thomas, taking him by the elbow to enter with him the Miracle Church of God's People. He summoned his most irresistible smile. Let us ascend to the gates of paradise together, he said.

Thomas was excited, thinking he'd finally made a dent in his cousin's resistance to deliverance. When they got upstairs to the room Dr. Willie had consecrated, Bailey took note of a plain hall with rows of folding chairs, a plywood platform with a pulpit flanked by pots of lilies, and a modest homemade cross hanging on the wall. DeGrace said, Let me introduce you to the great man. Oh, you're gonna be impressed, I promise you.

But the great man was preoccupied.

Dr. Willie sat on a stool pulled up opposite a front-row chair occupied to overflowing by Aurora Mae Stanton. Magnus put a hand out to stop Thomas from approaching him. He wanted to step back and observe the man he suspected would be his chief competition for access to the woman's sizable purse. Dr. Willie was a short, stocky, bald man in parson's black. His hands were folded over a sizeable stomach round and hard as a barrel. He tapped his fingertips against his belly while talking nonstop, unless he paused to nod and smile, nod and smile whenever Aurora Mae Stanton managed to get a few words in edgewise. His eyes raised themselves toward the ceiling often, presumably whenever he called upon Jesus to make a point. He had small feet in shiny black shoes that jigged against the floor from time to time. Magnus thought maybe he was loosening them up for the prayer service. He surely looked the type that pranced back and forth, up and down, filled with the spirit, he'd say, although to Magnus's mind, Dr. Willie looked more likely to be filled with impatience for supper. Aurora Mae appeared fascinated by him. As their conversation drew to its close, Dr. Willie rose, bowed a little, dipped his head, and all but clicked his heels, like an actor in a picture show. Magnus critiqued the gesture as superfluous since the woman already had her hand in her purse to withdraw the inevitable envelope. Besides which, that particular piece of hoity-toity flair never worked its best magic without a monocle. Sloppy, he judged his rival, envying the fat little man of God who'd staked an early claim on territory properly his. An amateur.

The preacher stuffed the envelope inside his vest, checked his pocket watch, and moved to greet the other worshippers just entering the room. He blessed them profusely, claiming the day as one blessed by the Lord. Magnus Bailey sidled up to Aurora Mae and took the seat next to hers. He did not acknowledge her but sat with his eyes straight ahead, holding his hat in his lap, gripping its sides tightly as if anxious for the service to begin. He breathed deeply, slowly, and waited, waited for her eyes, still obscured from his observance by the veil, to sneak a look at him.

Up in front of the pulpit, Dr. Willie Smalls pitched his Jesus rant with a clap of hands and a rat-a-tat-tat of toes against the plywood floor. Oh, I am so delighted to see you all ready to praise the Lord, he started out with clarion voice in a rhythm that approached song. He who is the only Place where His children shall find respite from this valley of sorrows known as life and the Mississippi!

Amen, Aurora Mae Stanton murmured. And Magnus Bailey echoed her. Amen.

And who is that Lord I'm talkin' about? Dr. Willie continued.

From the back came a single uninhibited voice. Jesus! it said with conviction, although the rest of the people murmured indistinctly as they were not yet fired up.

You are His children! His darlin' baby girls and boys! Dr. Willie said. Don't you know your Daddy's name?

Then, Jesus! Jesus! cried out the whole congregation, all twenty-five of them, including Magnus Bailey and Aurora Mae Stanton, who found themselves speaking the holy name in concert, which excited them both. Each time they responded Jesus! Jesus! together under Dr. Willie's baton they could feel the heat rising from the other's flesh, and so a heady bond was formed between them. Dr. Willie went on to quote scripture from Noah and his flood, from the trials of Israelites in bondage, and at last, he preached salvation through King Jesus, then knit everything together in a convincing line of entreaty that culminated in a passed collection plate. Making an investment not in the Miracle Church of God's People but in the mind of the woman beside him, Magnus Bailey reached inside his pocket and withdrew three dollar bills for the plate before passing it to the row behind. His movements gave him the opportunity to look her square in the face, feign a great but not excessive surprise, and exclaim:

Why, Aurora Mae Stanton. Is that you? Is it even possible? Under all that net and feathers?

The lady in question made a deep trilling sound that came from somewhere between her mighty bosom and her strong, thick neck. She raised her arms and untied her veil, lifting it so that it folded artfully over the magnificent hat's brim like a cloud of spun sugar. Her face revealed, she tilted her head and gave him the wry look of a woman of the world, not that of the gangly wood witch of years before. The look said, or so he thought, Why'd you hold back so long, honey?

Yes, it's me. And you are Magnus Bailey, late of East St. Louis, are you not?

He rose and bowed before her in a quiet, graceful manner, with none of the ostentation of Dr. Willie Smalls.

At your service, he said.

They looked at each other for a moment or two, assessing the changes time and the flood had brought. He was relieved to see that despite the obvious ravages to her figure, her face was as handsome as ever. She put a hand on his shoulder and rose.

Life has not been kind to either of us, has it, she said.

He sighed then opened his arms and shrugged, a gesture he'd learned from the saddest man in the world.

Life is never kind to anyone for much of a stretch, my dear. How is your brother?

She took his arm and said, Why, he's well but settled in another town after the flood. Why don't you walk me home, and I'll tell you all about him.

Just like that, they left together and thereafter began working nearly every day side by side, as it turned out Aurora Mae was as much in need of a capable man as Magnus Bailey was in need of her money. She was building a house from which she hoped to operate a business in healing herbs and liquid remedies and having an awful time of managing her carpenters and plumbers, who were unaccustomed to listening to a woman on the job. All I do is throw money at the place and nothing much gets done, she told him. Magnus promised to help and help he did with a great and abounding joy as the money she threw at him in payment brought him closer and closer to his goal.

It didn't take more than a couple of weeks for Dr. Willie to understand he'd been replaced, that he should seek more fertile rows to hoe than Aurora Mae Stanton, which did not please him. He vowed revenge against the usurper Magnus Bailey. He was a small enemy, to be sure, but a large enemy can be turned to friendship when mutual gain is at stake, while a small enemy festers everlastingly looking for his chance.

XI

THEY TOOK TO HAVING supper together. It was a convenient time to go over the day's progress on the house, and they were both lonely, although neither would admit to such a pitiable state. Bailey didn't know very much about the construction of homes with storefronts, but he knew enough to spot a goldbricker, which was all Aurora Mae required. She liked going with him to the worksite to watch him harass the men who'd been milking her. It gave her a sense of power to stand behind Magnus Bailey while he delivered invective and ultimatum. He might have been a sword or a gun she held in her hand, directing the slash and fire. When it was over, it pleased her to know the workmen who'd previously dismissed her concerns bowed to her retreating figure as she marched away, Bailey at the rear holding high over her head the pom-pommed parasol that kept the punishing rays of the Memphis sun from her proud, unvanquished brow.

One night, while they lingered over their coffee, taken in the lobby of Mama's Morning Star Boarding House, where Aurora Mae had established herself while she awaited completion of her home, she made mention of her feelings.

It was different when my brother Horace and I worked together, she said. I had the things I did, he had his, and combined we made a life. But nowadays I'm doin' things I never dreamed of havin' to do before, and it's been a world of help to have you. You're somethin' like a partner. I never had one of those.

Her words seared the inside of his chest like a hot iron pressed against the soft, sweet tissue of his lungs. This was the moment, the moment he'd been working toward from the git-go, the one that signaled his achievement of an inroad to the core of her fortune if only he played her right. Beyond that immediate goal, he saw before him the glittering path he might walk upon toward a confrontation with Minnie Fishbein, which would end in the emancipation of their eternal souls. Not for a heartbeat did it occur to him that the road to release from the sins of the past should be paved with only the smoothest, purest stones. That idea came later to his mind, and Aurora Mae's sterling influence had not a little to do with its arrival. For the moment, what mattered was that he got where he wanted to go, not how he got there.

Even then, Magnus Bailey was not a monster. He admired Aurora Mae. He knew enough of her sad history to feel a warm compassion for her. She never spoke on the bits Mags Preacher McCallum told him about her past degradation. He could only guess about most of it. Her silence confirmed for him how deep her wounds went. Often, he wanted to ask her how she'd wound up at L'il Red's that time and what his Minnie did to save her. There were nights, when he was alone in his bed, staring at the ceiling, grieving his mama, the Fishbeins, and times gone, that he would give his life's blood to imagine Minnie in such a heroic role, yet he knew to press Aurora

Mae for details would only hurt her and push her away. There was no advantage for him in being anything but helpful to her. At the same time, he was not above bending her will that he might win from her everything he could.

He took her hand.

Darlin', he said. A partner is a very good thing to have in life.

He flashed his most seductive smile, hoping that the firelight of the lobby's hearth would glint off his gold tooth and dazzle her.

She laughed from the depths of her considerable belly.

Oh my Lord, Magnus Bailey, she said. You are the very devil, aren't you?

He shrugged but did not give up.

Why do you laugh? I may not be the man who strides up to your house in the woods with a bouquet of wildflowers and a worshipful air, but you've had that, haven't you? And where did it lead?

He was singing in the dark, but the shadow that covered Aurora Mae's features told him he'd struck his mark. He continued.

There's been love gone wrong in my life too, he said. I have my regrets. They are big and heavy and blight me.

He slapped the tabletop. The boardinghouse cups and silver-ware jumped. Aurora Mae, whose head hung low in contemplation, snapped to. She raised her chin and studied him with an expression that was startled, querulous, and hopeful.

I am not suggestin' that you and I traipse off into the sunset together, holding hands and whistling a song, he said. But we might keep each other company, you know, and help each other forget what needs forgettin', and make right what needs to be made right.

I have so much of both, she said, and her great black eyes grew distant.

Though Bailey did not know the exact provenance of her sadness, sorrow was something he understood well enough. He spoke softly, wistfully, to give their hearts a place of convergence.

I do too, darlin', he said. I do too.

He said it so earnestly, he convinced even himself her purse had nothing to do with his empathy. Aurora Mae put her hand over his fist, squeezed, then kept her hand there warming his. He knew they'd struck some kind of deal.

When the house was finished, he helped her settle in. They bought furniture together and set up the shelves and display tables of her shop, The Lenaka. The final day, the day before her opening, Aurora Mae was exhilarated, happy for the first time she could remember since long before the flood. She stood in the middle of her shop and regarded its appointments. Three walls of shelves were covered with bottles of liquid remedies in various sizes. The tables supported honeycombs of open wooden boxes in which fragrant herbs released their perfumes, making the air heady and thick. A glass case with a cash register on its countertop displayed rows of vials filled with powders, along with packets of bandages in a rainbow of colors. To the rear of the store was the entry to the living quarters, a curtain made of strung glass beads that cast prisms over the walls. Its valance was made of dangling chicken bones knit together with multicolored yarn.

It's perfect, isn't it? she said. Oh! but where is the sign? Do you have the sign?

Why, yes, I do. I put it up this morning while you were settin' up in here.

They went out through the front door to inspect his handiwork. The little brass bell he'd installed in the door's frame to warn her when a customer entered tinkled merrily. Aurora Mae squealed with delight. The sign hung from a short iron post just outside the front gate and read THE LENAKA, just as it should. As an aid to those who could not read, a variegated leaf dangling above a mortar and pestle was painted underneath the script. Behind the yard's picket fence and to the left of the house were boxes planted with herb seedlings.

In the back, rows of root vegetables were planted and a chicken coop constructed so that Aurora Mae might have access to some of her most common stock. A hothouse next to the chicken coop finished the place off. She was beside herself with joy. When she spoke, her voice was thick with sentiment.

Come inside, Bailey, she said. I'm going to make you one of my special teas to celebrate.

He had no idea what was in the brew she served him, but it made his head light. Soon they were laughing over next to nothing together. Aurora Mae sang his praises and her gratitude. Then she said, Look. You've helped me so much, let me help you. Why don't you move in here, to the spare bedroom.

His green eyes went large and round.

Now, now, Miss Aurora Mae. Whatever would the neighbors say? he asked, and they both laughed, knocking into each other on the couch where they sat, drinking tea.

All at once, she grabbed his arm.

I'm serious, she said. I want to help you. I need to help you. Isn't there some little business of your own you'd like to start up? I can be your partner. Isn't that what you wanted? That we be partners? Don't worry about the money. I swear I have so much money I don't know what to do with it. It burdens me. Sometimes I want to just give it all away. Why shouldn't I start with you, who has been helpful to me?

Magnus Bailey did what came naturally, for him, anyway, if not Mags Preacher McCallum. He asked her how she got so rich.

Where'd your money come from, Aurora Mae? How is it there's so much of it, with times bein' hard and all?

She shrugged, looked at him steady straight in the eyes without a blink.

I found it, she said. It came to me in the flood like a chick to the roost.

He didn't believe her, but he didn't press her on it. Aurora Mae was entitled to her secrets as he was entitled to his. He next made a show of refusing her help until she begged some more, and then he said yes.

Although by the time he left her it had begun to rain, he walked over to L'il Red's on his way back to Thomas DeGrace's place. He stood in his usual spot across the street, cloaked in shadow, his gaze fixed on the whorehouse. His eyes moved from one window to the next, floor to floor. It was raining, it was hopeless that he should see her, and yet there he stood for more than an hour, talking to her in his mind, telling her that what was past was past and what could be in the future if she could bring herself to forgive him for setting her down the road to ruin. When his heart filled with the picture of her response, weeping and grateful, leaving with him, hand in hand, toward their bright paradise, he quit his hiding place to go pack up. The rain came down now in blinding sheets. He turned his collar up and ventured through the rain with his head up and his chest thrust out like a boy imagining high adventure.

At first, Magnus and Aurora Mae lived together as brother and sister. They shared their meals, their daily troubles and triumphs. At night, they sat together in the parlor listening to the radio or the phonograph. They grew close and fond. Every once in a while, Aurora Mae would forget herself and call him Horace.

Using her seed money, Magnus started up a business as a bail bondsman, a venture he'd found lucrative back in East St. Louis when his partner was old Fishbein. His clientele were crooks of every description and color, but his bread and butter were white boys who'd drunk themselves into a pile of trouble of a weekday night and needed to get sprung from jail before their daddies noticed they weren't where they should be, boys who couldn't call Daddy's lawyer and depend on his discretion. He loved those boys, because none caused him a wakeful minute wondering if they'd skip. They gave him tips on the cotton and lumber markets where their daddies made their fortunes. Following up, Magnus Bailey doubled and sometimes tripled his money. The remainder of his clients he chose carefully for their roots in the community or the depth of their felonious pockets. His choices paid off. He lived modestly and banked most of his money. Come 1929, he figured he was just one more year from achieving the stake he needed, and then the crash came. His stocks floundered, and his bank failed.

The day it all fell apart, Aurora Mae came home from the market to the sight of Magnus Bailey weeping on the couch with a glass of neat bourbon in one hand and a revolver in the other. His collar was undone, his suit rumpled, his hair mussed. He talked to himself. His lips trembled. He didn't notice she'd entered. Quietly, slowly, she went to his side. Locked as he was in the miseries, he did not so much as lift his head. She knelt before him and put her hands on his thighs. He stared straight ahead, as if her considerable presence were invisible, and muttered.

It's over. All over. Can't do it now. Couldn't do it then. Three times now, I lost it all. I am cursed for my sins. Might as well die.

The hand that held the gun went up and pointed the weapon at his temple, but he had the shakes so bad Aurora Mae took it from him easily. As she got up to put it down far away from his grasp, she saw the bank paper on the mantelpiece and understood what had happened. Without hesitation, she sat down beside him and put her arms around him and drew him to her, cradling his head against the broad shelf of her chest, rocking him back and forth like her very own baby boy.

This all about money, Magnus? What a foolish thing to despair over. I have money. I told you. Don't you remember? I have so much money I don't know what to do with it. You'll be alright. I'll give you more. Look. Here's some.

She got up, went to a floorboard he never knew was loose, and pried it up with the fireplace poker, then with the strength of two hands dragged a good-sized metal box from the space underneath. She opened it and scooped up a double handful of gold coin. She knelt at his feet and poured treasure into his lap. It made a clinkity-clink-clink as it fell, and light from the parlor windows made it shine. Magnus looked stunned at first, and then he started to laugh in a high voice, like a woman or a child.

Oh 'Rora, oh 'Rora Mae, was all he could manage to vocalize, so he clasped her in his arms while relief flooded his veins like wine, and perhaps because he was that grateful, perhaps because he was that drunk, perhaps because he finally knew where she stored her money, he took her to his bed, where she accommodated his desires half out of pity and half out of affection.

By dawn, Magnus Bailey found his fortunes restored and his life significantly complicated. Luckily, Aurora Mae did not make further carnal demands upon him straightaway. Under the implacable glare of morning's light, not to mention sobriety and the restoration of his hopes, his fondness for her had settled back to its usual fraternal warmth, which harbored little erotic heat. This was no fault of her own, just the way of things with a man whose heart yearned in another direction. He got up, made her breakfast, served her in bed for a surprise, kissed the crown of her head as if he were her daddy instead of her lover, and went to his office where he had nothing special to do early on but where he could be alone to ponder the night's events.

Leaning back in his chair with his feet on the desk, a ribbon of sunlight glancing off his cheek and bow tie, he convinced himself that the change in his relations with Aurora Mae was a good thing, despite the responsibilities that commonly accompanied their new status. His first emotions toward her were anxious but deeply thankful. If she hadn't come home when she did to offer him an escape from mortal melancholy, he might likely be dead. The insight made his head feel oddly light. It floated above his thoughts, remembering the gun and how close he'd come. He put his hands on the top of his scalp and pushed down, hard, as if stuffing realization back under his skull. Next, he acknowledged he'd been heading in the direction of intimacy with Aurora Mae all along. A man and a woman living together can't help but come to it sooner or later. Still, he wondered who it was on her mind in the heat of the previous night, as it was obvious to him she was no more fully present than he was. That perception was probably the most comforting idea he had, one he'd repeat over and over to himself as time went by. She loves another, he thought, same as me. Like every deceiver, he sought justification for himself, and here is where he found it. To know that he was not the love of her life reconciled his conscience about his intent to leave her once he had enough money put by to rescue Minerva Fishbein.

Why, just as Minnie had rescued her! he realized suddenly. His feet swung off the desktop and hit the floor, raising a cloud of dust. Why, exactly like that! How could Aurora Mae blame him at the end of the day? The day she awoke to find him gone and knew with whom he fled, whenever that day came, would represent a balancing of the scales of justice. Now, wouldn't it just? he thought. I will be merely the instrument of divine correction.

He convinced himself of all this in a single morning, in the hours after dawn and before the opening of the courtrooms he haunted daily, seeking caged men desperate to be free.

When he returned home that night, he found Aurora Mae had moved his belongings to her bedroom and set up a table on the side of the bed opposite hers for his convenience. Her efforts touched him. He praised her for taking the trouble to make him comfortable, to which she responded, I need the other room for family company, should any ever arrive.

Even with Aurora Mae's seed money, the rebuilding of Magnus Bailey's savings was slow. Times were hard and grew harder every day. People were broke all over. Rich white boys drank moonshine at home. Criminals took a short sentence in jail for the three squares. One season passed into another, and he crawled toward his purpose when all his heart longed to sprint. In despair, he suggested to Aurora Mae that if she blended alcohol into her medicines, alcohol he'd acquire from contacts in the backwoods, folk'd beat down the door, but she was having none of that. That's the trouble, he realized, with a woman of independent means. They did things out of principle rather than need, which robbed a man like him of leverage. After a great deal of thought, he realized he too possessed a measure of integrity, one that would prevent him from soaking Aurora Mae any more than he already had. She was a good woman, they'd grown quite fond. He couldn't rob her.

He needed to branch out. He determined he must go see Minerva's father and propose they work on a new venture. First, he took up his post outside L'il Red's in the dead of night to tell the door and the windows and the balcony above the first floor porch what he was going to do and why.

You see, darlin' Minnie, he told the brick and glass and wrought iron, I can't imagine your daddy's fortunes been doin' any better than mine these days. Last I walked by, the old house was lookin' awful raggedy. We always worked well together. I can go places he can't and vice versa, that's part of it. Also, we both got the mind for business. Maybe what we require is each other. If he's strapped these days, I can put what I got on the table. I don't know how I'll approach askin' him about you. I might just leave it alone and see if he brings you up. I don't want to hurt him like that. But if he does, I'm going to tell him my plan to get you outta there and someplace safe. With me. Whether Gay Paree or anywhere similar you please.

He walked back to The Lenaka breathing deeply the crisp night air, his head high, redemption so close he could taste it. Although the night was clear and not a drop of rain nor veil of smog prevented him from awareness of his surroundings, he failed to notice, as he had so many times before, the short round man with little feet behind him, hugging brick and tree trunk, all along the way.

A Thousand Sacred Sweets

The Road to Ruin, 1931–1933

XII

————⋄❋⋄————

THAT MORNING AT AN hour verging on the impolite, a brisk knock on Fishbein's back door stirred him from his daily recitation of remorse to the Divine. Still in his slippers and robe, he adjusted the *kipah* on his head and shuffled to the kitchen, muttering, Who could it be? Who could it be? When he saw his old friend Magnus Bailey standing on the stairs in a three-piece pinstripe suit and silk bow tie, he was so startled he forgot the man's role in his daughter's dissolution and remembered only the best of their history. Ushering him into the kitchen quickly before the neighbors noted his excitement at finding a black dandy at his door, Fishbein then embraced him and clapped his back with two hands. Mr. Bailey, Mr. Bailey, he said, to see you again is like the air of springtime pushing through the window after a long winter. My heart is full.

Such warm welcome was a surprise to the other man, who expected the opprobrium of harsh questions and had prepared against them. Disarmed, he returned Fishbein's affection with his own, then pulled back and affected an air of ignorance about the fate of Minerva Fishbein.

I've been wonderin' how you all fared since the flood, he said. I am returned to Memphis some time now, and you must forgive me for not callin' earlier.

Forgive? There is nothing to forgive. Come to the parlor. We'll have tea.

Bailey was relieved to find that the disrepair evident outside the home had not extended in full to its interior. Much that he remembered was as it used to be, from the dark paintings of mountain stags and waterfalls to the silver moldings of birds and forest creatures lining the mantel although there seemed to be fewer of them. He sat on a couch similar to the one from which Minnie had once poured him tea so appealingly he was provoked enough to warn her of the facts of life and, all unwitting, propelled their fates into darkness instead. Finding himself in these surrounds produced in him a sentimental vulnerability. Tears of regret pressed against the backs of his eyes and clogged the back of his throat. He coughed to get a hold of his emotions. Fishbein took his time preparing the tea. Bailey distracted himself by poking idly about his desk, looking for hints of what business he might be up to but found only correspondence in Hebrew letters he could not decipher. On the breakfront against the wall opposite the fireplace, there were framed photographs of men and women young in the last century. The men wore satin caftans and tall hats, the women were severely attired and did not smile, the children—small and barely of an age to stand—were in dresses regardless of gender. Bailey could not recall seeing such portraits in days gone, although perhaps they hadn't interested him. There were no photographs of Minerva.

A rattling in the hallway announced the return of Fishbein. Bailey rushed to relieve him of the heavy tray he carried and set it on a table between two ancient Morris chairs that faced each other. They sat. Fishbein poured, and then sighed. With a sudden, sharp movement of the head, he lifted his mournful gaze from the cups to Bailey's face. Bailey saw that the man's eyes, melancholy on the happiest of occasions, were newly ringed in a deep crimson that made his eyes look yet sadder than before, if such a thing were possible.

Well, Magnus told himself, that's what happens when a man's precious child goes to be a whore. He lowered his own gaze, unable to meet that of Fishbein without repeated stabs of shame.

Why is it you are here, Magnus Bailey? his host asked as his flight of nostalgia had ended, and the man's presence confounded him.

To be honest, I thought we might do some business together, Magnus said. Fishbein accepted the explanation, inquired of his ideas, and soon the two found themselves on territory so familiar their conversation flowed without reserve. Bailey mentioned a vacant storefront in Orange Mound, which had been a grocer's for a hundred years before the flood, and a furniture store on one of Memphis's swankest streets that had not been replaced after the same disaster drove its owners away.

The way I see it, Magnus said, even poor folk got to eat, and rich folk want their gewgaws and fancy cupboards in bad times as in good, maybe even more. We can reopen those joints with stock goin' beggin'. If we price it right, Depression or no, folk will buy.

He further outlined his ideas about pricing and profit margin, including a plan to grab real estate fallen to historic lows in value. He became more and more animated, encouraged by the way Fishbein listened, pursing his lips, nodding his head, signaling interest and agreement at every turn. He felt they were that close to a deal when Fishbein suddenly slapped his knees.

Oy! I forgot the cookies. Goldele, will you brings in the cookies please?

A small voice answered him, as if the person to whom it belonged had been just out of sight, waiting all along for this cue. Yes, Zaydee, it said.

Had Bailey known as much about Jews as he thought he did, he would have known by that word what or who was coming around the corner bearing a glass dish of powdered pastries. Instead, he suffered a shock unlike any he'd suffered before. A bolt of ice shot through his veins, his scalp shivered, his hands jumped, and tea spilled from cup to saucer as he watched a slight young colored girl set down the plate of dainties next to the silver tray, then stand with her little hand on Fishbein's shoulder as she leaned against his wiry thighs, looking at Bailey quizzically, wondering what was wrong with the man or why her zaydee found him so important. She was perhaps nine years of age, with butterscotch skin, green eyes, kinky black hair, and every facial feature shaped as if in determined imitation of Minerva Fishbein's. Bailey put down his cup and flailed his hands about in startled confusion. He stumbled over his words, in disbelief of the sight before him. Who? What? When? rumbled through his brain like cannon fire but issued from his mouth in a whisper.

Fishbein introduced the two.

This is Golde. Golde, this is an old friend of mine from before you was born.

The girl curtsied. Bailey acknowledged her pretty gesture with a stiff nod. He noticed Fishbein had not told the child his name. He realized the omission was for discretion's sake, the need for which alarmed him on many counts.

Now, let us speak alone, *mine shepsele,* Fishbein said, and she was gone again, as swiftly as a waking dream. Fishbein stood. He paced in circles about the room with his head lowered and his hands clasped behind his back.

I am sorry to surprise you, Magnus Bailey, he said, but I had to be certain if you were knowing already of Golde's existence. *Nu.* I see you were not.

He continued to pace while he spoke.

But you are knowing what my Minerva is doing nowadays? Of course you are. Everyone knows. And Golde. She is not yours, then? I always wondered.

He snapped his head in Bailey's direction and just as suddenly, extended his arm, its hand with forefinger pointed at him as if in angry accusation. The gesture was an imbalanced accent to his words, which were pronounced softly, thoughtfully as if he talked to himself alone, a discordance that added to Bailey's sense of being drunk or otherwise launched into a world where nothing made sense.

The eyes, yes, the eyes are like yours, *nu*? But still she is not yours. Even to me, it seemed impossible. You were gone a year, maybe two, before she carried her. Of course, I knew what hell she had fallen into by then. Did you know that the men she chooses to debase herself with are all like you in some way? This I know already, because she tells me one day that she lives in a lake of pain and her only relief is from a hand that is like yours touching her, lips that are like yours kissing her, no matter to whom they belong or where she finds them.

He snapped his head and pointed at Bailey again.

If you knew how it tears my heart to hear these confessions from her! I wants to kill myself, but for Ha-Shem and the honor of my dead, I do not. Then Golde comes to my life, and she is so sweet, so smart, so much my little Minerva the way I always dream she would be if her family had not beens slaughtered before her young eyes, and by Gott! I resolve this child will not suffer as my Minerva did when she was *a kleine meydl*. This takes some work. Yes, yes, it does. First Golde is sick with the tuberculosis. Three years she spends in and out of the sanatorium. Poor child, poor child. She is not strong still. I take care of her when possible, but I am sure you are knowing what is for a child with a white mother and a black father in this world. A Jewish girl, no less, and a mother, alas, who is infamous. Golde can only be here in secret. I grow around the house a wall for her, a wall of weeds and broken steps, that no one sees her here. When she is not here, she is in the country in the home of a good woman Minerva finds. Her world, poor Golde, is tiny, like a shoebox. But she is safe in there, I thinks, and so far she knows little about her mother's life. O dear Gott, on this I pray I am right.

Fishbein took a handkerchief from the sleeve of his caftan and wiped his face, then sunk back into his chair and spread the cloth over his features like a towel in a barbershop. He raised a hand and wiggled his fingers, as if he had one more thing to tell, and then he told it.

Kosher, yes, we are raising her kosher. How could we not?

The room fell to such silence that the sound of Fishbein catching his breath and Magnus Bailey expelling his were as loud as competing bellows at an ironmongers' factory. Tears streamed down Bailey's face. Breaking the tortured quiet, he said, What can I do about this? What?

Slowly, Fishbein pulled the cloth from his face.

You can do as I do. Bear the weight of your sins. Blame no one. Beg Gott's forgiveness every day of your life, morning, noon, and night. Do no harm and help where you can help wherever you see the needs of it.

He raised his shoulders and spread his arms, palms up. Despite the misery of his eyes, a smile fell upon his lips.

What else can a man do?

But Bailey had taken his own counsel. A fire was born in his gut at the sight of those green eyes set in the middle of Minnie's face. He, too, stood and paced the room, only there was purpose in his stride the old man lacked, determination and faith in his ability to create justice where God had not. His arms spread wide to embrace the world.

I have a plan to redeem myself and Minnie, too, he announced. I need more money, that is true, now that I see I must take not only Minnie and you under my wing, but also this child, this blessed Golde. You'll see. It will heal us all.

Fishbein sat forward, wondering what in the world he could mean.

Bailey told him what he had in mind, the idea he had refined and embellished in secret. Fishbein was astounded beyond measure. He murmured gratitude to the heavens, considering Bailey's sudden appearance and stratagem a certain message from Ha-Shem, although what that message might mean was a mystery, given the outlandish impossibilities the man described.

I've been putting away money wherever I can find it, Bailey continued. Oh, I've worked hard. Then everything was taken from me at the crash or otherwise Minnie would already be free and you and Golde, too, I swear it! But I'll get it all back, and when I do, this is what I intend.

I'll go to Minnie and tell her how wrong I was to run away from her, first to my sainted mama's, and then to the river. I'll tell her it's all my fault that she has suffered and degraded herself while on that—what was it?—that lake of pain. Believe me, I've been adrift on a sea of my own. Then I'll tell her she must put herself in my hands that I might cleanse us both and renew her and protect her for the rest of her life.

Bailey leaned forward seeking Fishbein's eyes, holding them fast with his own to see what his true reaction would be when he announced the details of his intentions.

From that day on, he said in the gravest possible tone, only my hands will touch her, only my lips kiss her, and no others. I'll take her away to where a man and a woman like us can walk in the sun together and be happy.

Warmth flooded Bailey's soul. His beloved's father showed not the slightest objection to what amounted to a capital crime in their little corner of the earth, despite the underworld where Minnie earned her daily bread. Then something else crossed the man's features, and Bailey pounced on it.

Ha! I see it in your face. You doubt there is such a place? Well, I have a list. A list of places in the world where no one will give us mind.

Fishbein's head moved side to side while his shoulders raised again and his eyes filled with tears. What are you even talking about, my friend? Where are these places?

Paree, for one! the other man pronounced emphatically, in triumph. Did you know that? Since the end of the last war, Paree is crawlin' with the likes of me! Magnus laughed and thumped his chest. Like me! And there's islands off Africa, Mozambique and Macau. There'd be Brazil, did you know that? They don't care who loves who in Brazil. I'm still lookin' into how things might be in the Caribbean. I know how to get us where we need to go, too. That took some study, but I got it figured. I'll let her pick the spot. I don't much care where we go as long as Minnie and I can live without fear of torture and death for the great sin of love.

He sat down all at once, his heavy frame near flattening the chair cushions. He panted, he beamed, overwhelmed by the excitement his vision inspired in his own heart and the unexpected, devastating pleasure of finally describing his paradise to another human being and his Minnie's daddy, to boot.

Taken aback by his outburst, Fishbein stared at the man in front of him, measuring what it made sense to tell him. When any man is in a fever like this, he thought, a fever of delusion, it's dangerous to argue with him. Better to chip away at his madness bit by bit. After a while, he said, I'm not so sure about Europe, the place where is Paree. You don't know what is like for Jews there, my friend.

Bailey ignored him. I want Minnie to leave all her dirty money behind, he said. We will do this with what we've earned honestly by the sweat of our brows and the quickness of our wits or not at all. It's the only way.

Then he asked if Fishbein could help, financially, telling him now that there was also Golde to worry about, they should pool their resources and fulfillment of his noble aims would come quicker. The Garden of Eden would be but a step away for all of them.

Fishbein sighed. My fortunes is gone, Magnus. The Depression ruins me with everyone else. I have enough to keep the roof over my head and to put a little food on my table, but that is all.

Then we'll be patient, Bailey said. I'll work harder.

Fishbein studied him with narrowed eyes and pursed lips. You knows you are sounding meshugga. Nothing is easier than to dream a life of perfection, my friend, and nothings is more impossible than to live one. There will be many obstacles, terrible dangers, in your path, ones you cannot imagine now in this state of mind. Listen to me, I know whats I am speaking of. *Vez mir!* Obstacles! The first one will be Minerva. Trust me.

It would have been easier to convince a man stabbed through the heart that the red stuff on his shirt was not blood but strawberry syrup. Bailey struggled not to laugh at the other's caution. Fishbein's a sad case, he thought, with no optimism left in him. He smiled, nodded his head, raised his palms level to his chest and patted the air as if soothing all fears.

I ain't no stranger to peril, sir, and if your daughter will listen to anyone in the wide world, it's me. Don't you worry. I can bring her 'round.

He quickly gathered himself together to leave, telling Fishbein he would be back soon.

You can help me even without money, Bailey said. There're places you can go, people you can talk to I cannot. Let me set a few meetings up. And you'll see. You'll see how easy seizing perfection can be!

Fishbein nodded. He saw no point in bursting the man's bubble. That would happen soon enough without his help. Have it your own way, he said.

Magnus Bailey asked to see Golde again before he left. Fishbein summoned her. She entered the room this time more shyly than before, hugging a wall, her head down.

Sweet child, Bailey said, cupping her little brown chin in his great black hand, we are to become great friends, you'll see. Next time I visit I'll bring you a present. Is there something you'd like?

Her green eyes opened wide and lifted themselves to him. She chewed her lips then said, Peppermints would be very nice, sir. I surely love peppermints.

Warmed by the modesty of her wishes, Bailey laughed and said, Peppermints! Peppermints it is!

He left the house by the back door. His old swagger was back. He pranced lightly down the steps with an idiot's grin on his face, tapping his head with a forefinger as new plots and schemes raced through it.

Watching him, Fishbein thought, Sometimes a dream is all that keeps a man alive. And once more he sighed, then turned to prayer.

During his walk home, Bailey considered that no matter what else happened in the future, Providence had given him fresh purpose at which he would not—he could not—fail. Now in his hot imaginings, a new face, that of the child, his Minnie's child, rose up and shone brighter than his desires for the welfare of either her mother or grandfather. Oh, that darling Golde! he thought, that bright beacon of a life not yet spoiled by the violence of others, a life it was his duty to cherish, to protect, to help prosper. If he wasn't her father in the flesh, he was her father in spirit, and that mattered.

No wonder Aurora Mae found him changed.

Look at you, she said a week later, how you bound out of bed these days. Ready to take on the world, are you?

He laughed. It was a robust sound from deep in his belly, where the flame of his sacred purpose dwelt, warming, energizing every aspect of his being. He snapped the suspenders he pulled up over his shoulders, grabbed his jacket off the hanger in the closet, then bent and squeezed her bare foot, which peeked out from the covers of the bed where she lounged thinking about getting up.

The world, the moon, the stars! Magnus Bailey joked. There's coffee on the stove, 'Rora Mae. I'll drop by the store later on today, see if you need anything.

And he was gone.

Aurora Mae wondered if he'd fallen in love with someone. That's how he acted lately. Like a man in love. He'd sung hymns in the yard Saturday when he mowed the grass. He whistled while he shaved. He was more tender toward her, sweeter of tongue to the customers he met at The Lenaka when he chose to stop by and help out. She tried to determine how she'd feel if indeed it was the truth, that Magnus Bailey had another life, another woman, which would mean that sooner or later they'd come to a tipping point, possibly a parting of ways.

It was not a simple matter. Just as Bailey suspected, tucked away in her heart was a man from the past, a love born among the fields and woodlands back home, a virginal love that spent its honeyed passion in lingering looks and unspoken vows of ineffable delight until the night riders came, stole her away, and ripped her up. After that, she'd renounced the thought of enduring affection from any source. She was no longer capable of true pleasure. There were places in her that hurt every day of her life, not so much physically but in her mind, side effects of the wounds she'd suffered that night and in the months that followed, those oozing injuries that would never heal no matter how many potions she brewed or how much time passed. Why, she thought, would Magnus Bailey or any other man consider her maimed and damaged vessel a place to lay his own weary heart?

Aurora Mae Stanton was an honest woman. She enjoyed living with Bailey. His company kept her worst memories at the fringe of her consciousness, which was the best place she could hope to store them. He made her laugh. She could depend on him. Still, she would never love him the way a man ought to be loved, and it would be wrong, she decided, to hold him back from whatever love he managed to find elsewhere. But she was not going to press him on it.

That morning, she got going at a leisurely pace, lingering over her toilette, especially the pinning of her long, thick hair. She had a tendency to open her shop when she felt like it and close it under the same conditions unless someone banged at the door relentlessly, which signaled an emergency. Before unlocking the door that morning, she checked on her stock in the storeroom and went to the backyard to pick some mustard greens and licorice root. The dahlias in the hothouse looked peaked, so she set to nursing them on her knees. It was close to noon before she was ready to open her door to business, and when she did, the slumped form of a young woman fell across her threshold and into her arms. Aurora Mae gasped, thinking her dead. She examined her chest to determine if the heart beat, the lungs breathed. They did, but barely.

Aurora Mae put the woman's arms around her neck and lifted her, lay her down on top of a display case, then rushed to close the door. There was an ashen tint to the woman's cocoa skin, which was very warm. Her nail beds were turning blue, her hair soaked through with sweat. She wore a red dress heavy with the damp of her fever, and beneath it a corset of black lace. Long glass earbobs dangled down her neck and bangles draped her wrist. She had high-heeled shoes with worn-down soles. There was no doubt in the root woman's mind that here was a whore come to die in her shop, and she would die quickly if Aurora Mae could not find something in a hurry to prevent her. First, she put a funnel in her mouth, lifted the girl's head to a propitious angle, and slowly poured into her a tincture of foxglove to wake up her heart. After that, she administered a tea of powdered mistletoe, white willow, and hawthorn in case the foxglove failed. The patient's head lolled. She moaned. In the next instant, she bolted upright and had a coughing fit. Aurora Mae put two arms around her and steadied her just before the poor gal fell back against Aurora Mae's chest and passed out.

Aurora Mae had no idea what else to do for her except watch and wait. At times like these, she regretted her choice to practice her medicine for the folk of Orange Mound. If one went by the reputation she'd acquired and the sheer number of people who came to her shop, she had a successful business. There was only one alternative in town, the single medical doctor who accepted Negro patients. He kept evening hours for coloreds once a week. Everyone had to wait a very long time to be seen. By the end of the night, many were sent home and told to return the next week. He charged them what he'd charge a white man who walked into his surgery without an appointment in the middle of the day. Naturally, folk preferred to go to the always-available Aurora Mae, who saw the sick on credit she did not expect to collect. She excelled in ameliorating childhood illnesses, the cleaning and treatment of wounds, and the banishment of infections, but for those on the brink of death, she could offer only ease of pain and the promise of a swifter end. There was no hospital in Memphis or anywhere else she knew that would do any better for a whore in extremis than whatever she could offer. She carried the woman to the bedroom where Magnus first slept, the room she designed for visiting family, who never came. She stripped her and wrapped her in cold, wet towels. Several hours passed. Happily, the woman's fever broke. Praising Jesus, Aurora Mae sponged her down, then dressed her in one of Magnus Bailey's nightshirts and left her to sleep. When her man showed up at dusk, Aurora Mae was at the stove, stirring a potent soup to feed the whore when she awoke. She told him of the day's extraordinary events and gave him instructions.

I need you to go 'round Beale Street and see if you can figure where she belongs. I know her name is Pearl, but that's 'bout it. You might start at L'il Red's. You know, Minerva Fishbein's place. If she don't use this gal, she'll likely know who does.

It was the first time during their cohabitation that Minnie's name had passed between them. The five syllables shot through Magnus's heart like bullets from a Thompson gun. He put a hand on the kitchen table to steady himself. Fortunately, his lover had her back to him as she leaned over her pot, scraping at the bottom, turning down the heat. She noticed nothing. He swallowed his emotion and played along.

Sure. That'd be off on Mulberry, no?

No. South Third.

South Third it is, then.

Suddenly, Aurora Mae turned around, pointing a wooden spoon at him.

You ever see those two anymore? Li'l Red or her daddy? I recall you were close in St. Lou.

No, no, no, he lied. We went our separate ways almost afore I got 'em to Memphis.

She turned back to the stove.

I recall how sweet she was on you as a child. Oh, it was scandalous. Remember how jealous of your company she was at Mags's wedding and that time you all spent the night at the big house with Horace and me? So bold she was! Maybe we all should've guessed how she'd turn out. Funny how time fulfills inclination.

Alright, I'm off then, Magnus said before he broke down and told her everything.

He went to the river walk. It was a warm night, but the river was cool and a mist arose from it. He walked with his head down, deliberating if he should go on to Minnie's establishment. He could always lie later and say he did. It wasn't the best time for him to present himself. He wasn't half ready. On the other hand, maybe it wouldn't be the worst time either. Now that he'd bitten the bullet and contacted her father, he'd no doubt she'd know soon enough that he was back in Memphis. Not that Fishbein would say anything, but Golde was bound to mention to her mama the black man she'd met with eyes green as her own and she'd know, she'd know straightaway it was him. Rather than let her stew on the thought, it made sense to seize the moment and make his call. Bailey lifted his gaze. The mist coalesced to take the ghostly shape of Golde's face, which was also that of her mother. Alright, he said to the river, you don't got to beat me over the head. I'll go.

He knew from the many nights he watched over L'il Red's which hours belonged to white whoremongers and which to colored. It was white man's time when Aurora Mae sent him out, so he went to the back door. He stood on the stoop and took a minute to work up his nerve. As it was, his heart pounded so hard, his mouth went dry, and he feared he would not be able to talk. He clenched and unclenched his balled fists, calming himself by thinking, It's a good day. This moment was writ large in our fates from the beginning of time. I'd feel like dyin' whether it came on this good day or on one of my choosin', a day still comin', when I'd have the money and even the paperwork in order. But now will do, it's a very good day.

He rang the bell.

A burly black man with a face crisscrossed in scars, one thick and running all the way down his neck, answered the door. Blue tobacco smoke surrounded his head in thin, forked trails giving him the look of a demon straight from the womb of hell. Bailey stared at him, helpless as a child.

You wan' sumtin'? the brute asked in a jaggedy voice that suited his appearance.

It took a bit of a while, a period during which the brute looked as if he'd take a blackjack to him any moment, but at last Bailey said, I'd like to speak to Miss Minnie.

Why?

It's a private matter.

Then go to hell, the man said, making to shut the door when Bailey saw, coming down the service stairs that gave into the kitchen, a pair of sensible shoes and two white legs encased in dark silk, disappearing up a navy blue skirt of modest length, and a voice he knew well, a voice that had echoed repeatedly through his mind while he was on the Mississippi, on the railroad, in Little Rock, Dallas, Wichita, and Des Moines, rang in his ears.

Wait, John!

It took an eternity and then some, but slowly the sensible shoes descended the rest of the stairs. Each step revealed more of Minerva Fishbein to the view of Magnus Bailey, and more of Magnus Bailey to the view of Minerva Fishbein, until at last the two were face-to-face with only the brute between them. Their chests heaved, their life's blood rose then dissolved in their veins while their heads swam in clouds of sweet, thick air. Each moved forward half-faint with emotion while the brute, seeing the gravity of their reunion, stepped aside, enabling them to fall, gloriously, into each other's arms.

XIII

MINERVA TOOK HIS BIG hand in her own two small ones to lead him upstairs. The vulgar harmony of squeals, yelps, groans, thumps, riotous piano scales, and a single aching horn accompanied them. Smoke, cheap perfume blended with whiskey, and the sour stench of masculine desire saturated the air. Like a knight errant assailed by a gauntlet of temptation, Bailey closed his senses to all of it and focused on the slender back of the woman he persisted in thinking his sweet young gal, the wretched victim of his cowardice, for whom he had much to make whole. They achieved the landing. She released him, unlocked a door. They entered her suite, the office first with the dressing room and bedroom beyond.

They stood, shoulder to shoulder, looking around. He took in the room carefully, trying to measure what each square foot meant about his Minnie, at how she had changed or not changed. She moved her head with his to trace his gaze. What he saw was the order and precision that had impressed Thomas DeGrace when Fishbein sent him to fetch Minerva all those years ago. Every object was pristine, set in its place with care. There was nothing superfluous, nothing without purpose. It reminded him of her childhood habits, when all hell broke loose if the maid or her tutor dared to move the slightest object and so disrupt the calm that order gave her stormy soul.

It broke his heart.

She put her hands on him and turned him to face her. They stood flushed and open and shy as if no time had passed, as if she were yet at the dawning blush of maturity and he the unscarred dandy of cocksure step and rippling palaver. The hardness of jaw, the lines of suspicion writ around the eyes, the thin set of skeptical lips vanished from their features in favor of a soft, liquid longing. They kissed, at first sweetly and then with a yawning, hungry wrench of mind and heart and soul that propelled them, stumbling, to the bed.

Magnus had few cogent thoughts during the next quarter hour. It was his life's first intimacy with a white woman. The wonder and beauty of their skins' contrast spurred him to a state of marvel quickly followed by the stark recognition that the pale, blue-veined woman he caressed so tenderly had had many black men, who knew how many. A lust for complete possession of her rose from his gut to sear his hands and his mouth and his sex with a fire that battered against her flesh in a chorus of moans that pled and demanded at once.

Minerva was in ecstasy.

Afterward, they were both oddly embarrassed and, lying side by side, pulled the sheets up to their chins. Magnus spoke first.

What just happened here, Minnie?

I don't know.

What we just did could get me killed.

Not in this house, Magnus.

She propped herself up on an elbow and leaned against his chest. The mention of her business stabbed at him unexpectedly, and he frowned. She put a finger against his lips before he could speak.

This is a house where all things are possible, she said. If you knew who comes here at what hour under cover of daylight as much as night, through the front door, through the back, in company or on their own and each one lookin' only to soothe an urge impossible to satisfy anywhere else, you'd be amazed.

She got up and slipped into a silk robe embroidered with tiny blue flowers that lay draped over a chair next to the bed and went to the dresser to open her cigarette box, picking one out, lighting it with her back to him, then turning swiftly so that her red hair lifted and stole his breath.

Amazed, I tell you! She pointed at him with the smoldering cigarette. Amazed!

She plopped down at the foot of the bed and put her free hand on his right shin, which she stroked while a big, brazen smile played over her lips. I've waited so long for this moment, her smile said. I regret nothing, it said, if everything I have done has brought you here.

Magnus Bailey was horrified. Where had his sweet girl gone? Was there none of her left? Confusion addled him. He could not think what next to do, what next to say.

She seized upon his hesitation. Squinting one eye and pursing her mouth, she asked, And what has brought you to my door, Magnus? After all these years.

He swallowed hard to find his voice. I was sent to find out if you knew a whore named Pearl.

At the name, she lifted her chin to a sharp, mistrustful angle. Her spine straightened. She snorted.

Pearl. Gal with a fever, maybe? Run off from here just two days ago?

Maybe.

L'il Red's face went hard as he ever hoped to see it. Any harder and it'd shatter like glass.

That bitch. Look, if you know her, you tell her to get her skinny ass back here pronto. I got a heap of complaints about her we need to settle. I suspect she is more damn thief than whore. A l'il ole fever ain't goin' to get her off the hook. Huh. Pearl.

She spit out the last word like a curse. Magnus shivered.

Are you cold, darlin'? Minerva asked. I could light the fire.

Mercifully, there was a knock on the door, an insistent one, and the voice of the brute who'd answered the kitchen door earlier.

Red, Red! We need you downstairs. There's a ruckus gettin' started.

Giving Magnus an apologetic shrug, she yelled back to the man that she'd be right down. She got dressed in thirty seconds flat, patted her hair, stuck on shoes, and squared her shoulders, ready for whatever battle summoned her. She did it so swiftly, so calmly, she might have been a milliner called by her manager to reprimand the young girl who sewed flowers on her hatbands.

Don't go nowhere, now, she said. I won't be long.

No, I should be gettin' on, he said. For his sanity, he needed to be away from there, onto the street, where the air did not oppress, where his head might not ache from too many ideas all at once driving the sense clear out of it.

You can't leave. I won't let you.

He started to dress, only he fumbled with sleeves and pant legs and buttons and suspenders until his cheeks went hot. He spoke without looking at her. We both need to take in what happened here tonight, he said. I'll come back tomorrow. In the early afternoon. It's quiet here then?

She studied him without expression. Pretty much, she answered. Most days.

Alright, the afternoon then. We'll sit and talk. There's lots of talkin' we got to do.

Red! Red! came the brute's voice again, only from farther away.

Frowning, Minerva looked from the door to Magnus Bailey and back again. There was the sound of crashing glass downstairs. A half dozen voices, male and female both, shouted, screamed, or wailed. Red! The brute's voice rose above them all, Red! Red!

She threw open the door and stood at the landing with her hands on her hips.

If any of you bastards broke my French gilt mirror, there'll be hell to pay, she shouted down. Without a backward glance at her prized, long-awaited lover, she marched down the stairs, sturdy afoot as a rough rider descended from his mount.

The sight of her sent Bailey into a sweat. He could not get out of there fast enough. Soon as his shoes were laced, he bounded down the service-entrance stairs and out the back door, around the corner to the front of the house and to his usual position across the street. There he stood in his customary doorway, panting, his eyes wet, his throat sore, his gaze directed at the first floor of L'il Red's, where, according to the riot of movement and color he witnessed, pandemonium broke out, and his mind said, Minnie! What's happened to you! Oh, Christ Almighty, I know what's happened to you, but can it not be erased? I have my plan. I have Paree. Oh, please God, let there be a place you might go to heal our souls or I don't know what will happen to me. Or your daddy. Or that darlin' girl, Golde.

His head, his heart, his very skin hurt. Misery and horror at the block of ice his sweet gal had become conflicted in his thoughts with the smoldering memory of how they had joined. Perfect it was, indelible it was. Never, he thought, would he be able to match the experience of that transcendent moment when two felt the rise of one, and all the world had melted into obscurity.

The front door of L'il Red's swung open. The brute held a scrawny white man covered in plaster dust by the scruff of his neck. He swung the man back and then tossed him out. His victim groaned, struggling to get up. He was unsteady, drunk as a lord. After looking up and down the street as if for witnesses, the brute gave the drunk's backside a boot, and the man crumbled again. He folded his arms over his head. He begged for mercy. Under the pale green light of a gas lamp flickering over the whorehouse entrance, the brute's face was visceral, pure in its uncloaked pleasure at battering his victim. Kick, kick, kick. There was vengeance in his zeal as the drunk took the punishment of generations of like treatment in reversed color. Bailey thought he might kill him. He was about to step forward out of decency and save the cracker when the brute stopped, bent, went through the white man's pockets, and took whatever money he had, stuffing it swiftly in his shirt before returning to the whorehouse parlor.

Bailey darted out from his doorway. Are you alright? he asked the drunk, who'd landed at the last thrust against a lamppost.

The drunk waved Bailey away then pulled himself up the post with two hands. Once standing, he looked into Bailey's face while a naked panic crossed over his own. With the sudden mobility to which fear and alcohol alone can spur a man, he lurched into the middle of the street and then staggered forward, zigged, zagged, reached a corner, turned, and was gone.

Shaken, Bailey made his way home deep in thought. There was so much on his mind to discuss with Minnie the next day that he had trouble ordering it all. Despite a deep reluctance, he began to understand why Fishbein had warned him that the first obstacle to enacting his grand plan would be Minnie herself. Her corruption was more profound than he'd dared to imagine. Her depravity would not wash away in an afternoon, a week, a month, or even years. How could he expect to cut the rot from her? She loved him still. He saw that in her face, in the way she'd studied him softly, unblinking, while he held her, in all the startling ways she'd moved to please him, to give him pleasure. He lost himself reliving those fifteen minutes of rapture, and hope was reborn in him.

When he entered The Lenaka, he did not pause to wonder why the door was unlocked although the hour had grown late. Such banal concerns were beneath his lofty, difficult reflections on wrenching light out of darkness, purity from filth. With his head down, his lips moving as he recited to himself the arguments he might try on Minerva Fishbein the next day, he walked through the beaded curtain that led to the kitchen at the back of the shop and then, untying his tie, he continued to the parlor when Aurora Mae's voice muttering in a language he did not know came to him. He lifted his gaze to the sight of a most curious tableau.

Lying on the carpet tightly wound from ankles to clavicle in a white sheet, her eyes closed, her arms crossed over her chest, and holding a sprig of lavender between her hands was what looked like a dead, laid-out whore named Pearl. On the couch facing her sat Aurora Mae, dressed in the tasseled robe of many colors she wore for special occasions. Her hair was wrapped up in a scarf that came together at her brow in a starched fan. She balanced an unlit brazier filled with herbs and spices in her broad lap. Beside her was a dish that held pieces of broken blue glass, and next to that was the round, black-suited, white-collared bald man with tiny feet, Dr. Willie Smalls.

What on earth? . . .

So intense was the concentration of the participants that Aurora Mae and Dr. Willie jumped in a start while the whore named Pearl took in a sudden, deep breath but managed to keep her eyes closed and her hands still. At least she's not dead yet, thought Bailey. My goodness, my goodness.

Magnus, Aurora Mae said in a whisper, please don't say another word. You'll break the spell. Just leave the room or sit down over there by the window and hush up. I'll explain when we're done.

She lit the brazier and swung it over the whore from her head to her toes and then crosswise, too, while chanting a phrase that to Bailey's ear sounded like the half-African talk coastal coloreds used. At the same time, Dr. Willie knelt next to the whore's head holding a large crucifix over her while he called out in English to his Lord and Savior Jesus Christ.

Jee-sus! Save this poor child and cast from her the evil one that chains her soul! he said. I cast you out, evil one! In Jee-sus' name!

The reverend commenced with a lot of malaka-malaka-maloo, what Bailey suspected was a variety of the speaking in tongues he'd heard now and again at revivals up and down the river during his childhood and again during his bargeman days. A piece of showmanship on every occasion, he was sure, but he had to admit old Willie carried it off pretty well. Swallowing his disdain, he watched while Aurora Mae placed bits of blue glass all around the gal's body. The two officiants joined hands, spoke over her some more, and then they were done. Sweat dripped from both their brows, landing in drops on the gal's shoulder and hip respectively. The whore Pearl fluttered her eyelids and then sat up.

Water, she croaked.

They gave her water from a pitcher sitting at the ready on an end table.

Is the spirit gone now, gal? Dr. Willie asked, his hands holding the crucifix at arm's length, pointing it at her like a weapon.

She brushed her forehead with a limp and trembling wrist.

I do believe so. I do believe I feel a removal of the pressure.

Where from?

From between my eyes. And, she added, as if the ritual had resurrected in her a long-gone modesty, you know, down there.

Aurora Mae and Dr. Willie sighed in unison, then turned and grinned at each other in shared triumph.

Praise the Lord, Dr. Willie said. Praise the Lord.

There were tears and hugs all 'round. Some Praise Jee-suses and better get your strength back firsts. Dr. Willie left, proud as punch, walking out the door on the tips of his toes, it seemed, as he was assuredly taller than he'd been half an hour before. Aurora Mae put the whore Pearl to bed and tucked her in with cooing song and lilting promise. When she returned to the parlor, Bailey said, Do you mind tellin' me what zackly all that was about? What zackly were you and that old rogue up to with that gal?

She explained that after he'd gone off to L'il Red's, Pearl got out of bed and wandered around the house, singing psalms like a madwoman in screeching tones and unnatural rhythms. She'd scared the bejesus out of Aurora Mae, who feared she was possessed. The gal foamed at the mouth next, then bellowed in the voice of a man. Aurora Mae knew a few rites from her grandmamma, who'd cured more than one cousin of shivering fits and torturesome visions over the years. Her first thought was to employ them, but she'd never practiced such herself, so it was only prudent she call upon the single man of the cloth she knew well enough to ask for help. She used the new telephone to track Dr. Willie down and begged him to come over to try to exorcise the whore's bedevilment. Having just come from the hellhole that spawned poor Pearl, Magnus Bailey wanted to say he had a very good idea what bedeviled her, thank you very much, and it weren't no restless spirit, but likely the accumulated and sundry lusts of men for which the gal had likely met the limits of her tolerance. But that might open up a field of questioning he'd just as soon delay as long as possible, or at the least until he'd had a solid night's sleep, so he kept mum.

Aurora Mae was agitated from the events of the day. She wanted to talk alright, but what she wanted to talk about was the queer, damn well unearthly behavior of the whore Pearl, how her cries and singing—if you could call it that—made every hair on Aurora Mae's head stand on end, and how the summons and prompt arrival of Dr. Willie Smalls helped her to save the day.

He hurled a gentle barb at her in a dry, silken voice. You don't say, he said. Old Willie, the hero of whore and priestess alike.

She didn't notice his sarcasm. Yes, indeed, she said.

He tried again. And your hair stood on end? Bailey asked. Every strand of it?

Yes. Yes, I swear it did.

Must have been quite the sight.

They were lying in bed by this time, side by side. Aurora Mae gave him a punch in his ribs and, given the size of her, he said, Oof.

When I walked in she looked pretty quiet, he said. Had you all been at it long?

Some, anyway. First I gave her one of my teas to calm her down while we waited for Dr. Willie. We're very lucky I didn't kill her, don't you know. For a while there, I thought maybe it was me brought on her fit. I was just guessin' when I tried to bring her fever down. I put everything I could think of in her. Maybe what I gave her didn't mix right. But that Dr. Willie took one look at the situation and told me no, no, this was most assuredly a case of demonic mischief. That's why he asked her to play dead, to fool the spirit that was plaguing her. Helps bring 'em to the surface, or so he said.

Did he.

Yes. I'm sure I still don't know what was goin' on inside that gal, but all I can say is I followed his directions, and they worked. She's in the next room sleepin' like a baby, isn't she. Did you figure where she came from?

No, he said, no luck there.

In the morning, he snuck out before either Pearl or Aurora Mae was awake. He would have felt guilty for that, but he knew Aurora

Mae was capable of taking care of whatever came up when the whore opened her eyes. She'd look for him, then shrug and do whatever was necessary. He had to admire that and thank God for it too. Given the hours of her business, he doubted Minnie was awake either. He went to his bondsman's office and made himself a pot of coffee over the sterno. He sat at his desk, trying to make a list of what he needed to impress on Minnie, but there was so much, listing was impossible. Numbers one, two, three, and four were followed by a flood of words with no sense or order. The more coffee he drank, the more diffuse the list got, until he glanced at his paperwork and thought, This is the work of a madman, and despaired.

He leaned back in his chair and rubbed his eyes. As he did so, an unexpected apparition appeared beneath his lids. It was Aurora Mae, lying in their bed, punching him in the ribs. He saw her as something natural, fine, wholesome to which he should cling, and when he envisioned his Minnie, he saw something terrible and dangerous and worth fleeing. Yet it was for Minerva Fishbein that his heart, his body yearned. Nothing could explain this conundrum. He felt hopeless, lost, paralyzed. When the tiny chime of his pocket watch told him it was one in the afternoon, he managed to stand up and flatfoot it over to L'il Red's.

XIV

⸺◈⸺

MINERVA FISHBEIN WAS READY for him early. Rather than let her tired whores sleep in, she put them to work. She burst into their bedrooms at seven thirty in the morning. Most hadn't been to sleep before four, but still she bullied them, pulling their blankets off, tugging their hair. Get up! Get up, my fat lazy cats! she cried out in full voice. How often does your old ma have a visitor she wants to impress?

It was true enough L'il Red rarely entertained a gent. The thought was intriguing enough to get the women roused and bustling before they took breakfast. By nine, there were fresh flowers in the office and in the bedroom, where the sheets were pressed and perfumed. Behind Minerva's desk in the little ice chest she kept disguised as a table under a long cloth, dainty sandwiches nested on a fancy plate next to a bottle of bootleg Champagne. Sparkling glasses and crisp napkins bound by a band of gold plate lay poised for action on the tabletop. Minerva spent considerable time and effort on her toilette. She took a bubble bath and dusted herself with a powder puff as big as her fist. One of her gals finger-waved her hair at the crown, then swept up the rest and fastened it with blue porcelain barrettes. She put on her best French chemise, then a white silk blouse with satin buttons and a dove-gray skirt. She put on pearls, then took them off and pinned a Wedgwood cameo over her uppermost blouse button. Because it was Bailey she dressed for, she wore spectators, remembering how he'd favored them in times gone. When she ran out of preparations, she tried to get a little work done before he arrived.

At ten past eleven, she rose from her desk where she attempted to count the previous night's receipts and went to a window to see if she might spy Magnus Bailey on his approach. She figured if he were half as anxious as she was, he'd be early. Why would he wait 'til afternoon? While she watched the street, lustful, sentimental thoughts filled her head, and soon, her breath came hard. She twisted her fingers together in a pose that resembled a good Christian woman at prayer. When her clock chimed the half hour and he had not come, she shook herself, irritated by her vulnerability. What a sap that man makes me, she muttered, and marched back to her desk to commence recounting bills.

An hour later, she got up again, stared out a window, returned to her desk, forgot where she'd left off in her accounting, and started over. How does he do this? she asked herself. How does he manage to make me a flutterbug of a girl again just from the thought of him?

By the time Bailey arrived at one seventeen, she was frustrated, her stomach was in knots, and the soft rap of his knuckles against her door came to her as three loud cracks. Come in! she barked, thinking it one of her flunkies with some fresh annoyance on his mind.

But it wasn't.

Seeing the handsome hulk of him standing there next to a bowl of cut camellias, fedora in hand, his mouth working to form words that did not come, drove ill temper from her in an instant. He stared down at his shoes—spectators, she saw, a lover's coincidence that felt a sign of divine pronouncement—then looked up at her shyly, a boy's ardent plea in his green eyes, long thick lashes beating to keep emotion at bay. Her cheeks warmed; she rose and walked to him with less grace than she wished, bumping into a corner of the desk on her way. She stuck out a shoe to touch the toe of one of his.

A matched set, aren't we? she said softly.

Hardly, my darlin' girl, he said just as softly, and although he thought it dangerous to be intimate with her before they had their talk, he bent and kissed her lips. A sweet kiss it was, just a small, dear pressure against the mouth, but it led in a heartbeat to a place where no coherent, rational thought could enter. Once again, they found themselves locked in an uproar of limbs and orifice, this time in such a rush of need they didn't make it to the bedroom but coupled, half-dressed, on the floor.

My Lord, she said afterward. We are ridiculous, aren't we?

He got up, then extended a hand and helped her to her feet. He pulled his pants up and buttoned his shirt while she put her blouse back on, smoothed her skirt, and searched for the cameo, which at some point had flown across the room.

Ridiculous? I'm sure that's just the beginnin' of it. We are also doomed fools, for one thing, unless you listen to me.

It seemed their lovemaking had taken the edge off his anxieties while fueling his imagination at the same time. He sat in her desk chair. He took her hand and pulled her onto his lap. Then he started to talk, and all his previously disordered arguments spun themselves into a gorgeous web of seduction and persuasion, leaping mature and mellifluous from his tongue as if they were part of some old and practiced spiel he could recite by rote in the younger days to a pack of dock rats itching to burn their money and hold on to it at the same time. Just as he'd stretch out his hand and their dollars and coin would drop into his palm like rainfall, he felt her will melt into his, to bind there, close, hot, indivisible.

First, he spoke of their destiny. As all destinies have a beginning that shapes them, he spoke of their past, of her childhood, of the ways he knew her better than anyone else in the world, better even than old Fishbein. He slipped in and out of his critical act of cowardice with such slick finesse, she kissed his brow forgivingly. He surged on. He spoke of their shared ruin in its aftermath without putting too fine a point on her downfall, and then absolved the lion's share of culpability on both their accounts by railing against the society that had denied the natural expression of their affection that might have occurred had not fear of its cruel law and custom blocked the way.

What right, he asked, does this world we live in have to deny us our free and willing love?

None! she said, sinking onto his chest as if laying all the weight of her troubles against it.

Exactly right. Well, I have news for you, my dear. There are places we can live together under the sun where no one will harm us, no one will think we are anything more than a passing curiosity, and everyone will wish us well.

He told her about couples like them who lived hidden in the backwoods of West Virginia and the mountains thereabouts, earning from her a scornful little laugh, as he thought he might. Then he trotted out Uganda, Mozambique, and Brazil. She pulled away from him and made a face. He was unsure if she was mocking him or rejecting these venues as places so out of the realm of her experience as to be unthinkable. Alright, he thought, that's alright, as he was holding back the big hook.

And then, my dear, there is Paree. . . .

Minnie's back straightened, her mouth fell open.

Ha, ha! How she jumps at the bait, he thought, delighted and proud. He told her how hundreds of colored soldiers found happiness in Paris at the end of the Great War and returned to France rather than suffer the indignities of America once they were free of Uncle Sam's whims and regulations. He told her about Eugene Bullard, Josephine Baker, Henry O. Tanner, Florence Embry, Langston Hughes, and Leon Crutcher, omitting the sadder aspects of their marriages and love affairs across color lines, touting only their acceptance in the land of wine and joie de vivre. This was not deception, he decided. Marriages and love affairs ended every day for reasons that had nothing to do with color.

Then he went for the mother lode.

I know about Golde, he said. I visited your daddy a bit ago, and there she was. Oh, she's a fine child, Minnie. But she needs to grow up out of Jim Crow's arms. Here's my plan. We'll take your daddy and daughter with us. Then, my dear, we will all be happy evermore.

Before he was finished, everything unraveled. At the very mention of Golde, she turned her head from him, got up. She paced to the window and back, scowling. He could feel the heat of her anxiety from several feet away. He hadn't expected such a reaction. He knew it was a surprise to her that he'd met the girl, but why would the mere mention of Golde derail her so? He held his breath, waiting for explanation while a hope that maternity had kept even the tiniest corner of her soul uncorrupted rose, burning bright, from his chest into his throat.

No one knows about her, she said at last in a hoarse whisper, and she can never know about me.

She raised her arms and made wide circles to indicate the whole of their surrounds, upstairs and downstairs both.

About this.

Of course not, Minnie.

She had the need to explain how Golde came to be then, giving him the reasons her father had divulged along with details he could have lived his whole life without ever having to hear. But he listened. He owed her that. There were unexpected tears and hot embraces. He told her he didn't care about Golde's daddy. He would love and protect the child as if she were his own flesh.

She told him Fishbein would never go back to Europe, and how could she leave him? She might not be much in the way of a dutiful daughter, but she'd disappointed him quite enough already. Abandonment would be the final blow. If they took Golde away from him, it would kill him.

Let me talk to him, Bailey said. I always had my ways to get to him.

She agreed to let him try.

They ate the dainties and drank Champagne, made love again, and darkness fell. Their talk fell to the blissful chatter of lovers about the charms of each other's bodies and other nonsense. The piano man downstairs ran through scales, warming up, while slippered feet ran up and down the stairs outside Minnie's door as the girls got ready for the night's business. Spats broke out. The brute named John was heard calming things down with a word or a slap. Magnus Bailey could no longer suspend his knowledge of where he was and his lover's role as boss over the sordid mess that was L'il Red's. He told Minnie he had to leave and would be back, same time, next day.

There a woman somewhere you need to go home to? she asked.

I got a livin' to make, he replied, evading that conversation until another time.

She raised her chin, gave him a prideful smile.

I got enough for us both, she said.

He took her by the shoulders and squared her up to him so that she'd listen hard.

I know you don't believe me yet, he said. But someday soon, you're going to give all this up, and we're going to go far, far away and on my dime. We're going to start out fresh and pretty as a day in spring and leave all the past behind. That includes your money. It's the only way.

Her lips moved playfully as if she were choking back a great joke, but she raised up on her toes and kissed him. Well, you're the man here, aren't you?

Yes, I am.

He hugged her close, kissed her head, and made to leave.

Wait.

He stopped with his hand on the doorknob and twisted around. She stood strong, insolent, with her arms crossed, a hip jutted out to the side. An unlit cigarette dangled from her lip. The look in her narrowed eyes made a little worm of fear squirm inside him.

There's somethin' on my mind you made me forget.

What's that?

Why did you come here yesternight lookin' for that Pearl? Who's she to you? What you got to do with a piece of work like that?

He tried to come as close to the truth as he dared so that he'd sound honest and sincere.

A friend of mine found her near dead in the street and asked me to check around, he said. His voice cracked on 'around.' He hoped she didn't notice.

Alright, she said. Her face was impassive, sizing him up.

I can go now?

Yes.

He blew her a kiss and whistled his way down the stairs to give her the impression he was unaware she had her doubts about his veracity, but his feet had not left the landing when he heard her tell herself, On his dime! and break into a brittle laughter.

That slowed him down and hushed him up. He moved more

deliberately, head low, while he contemplated whether she'd meant for him to hear her derision. When he reached the door, he near rammed into one of Minnie's gals, who stood in his way. She was big and black as night like him. Her hair was bobbed, tamed, and rolled under. A scent of mineral oil and beeswax wafted through it. She had long fingernails painted the color of blood run cold and her eyelids were smudged with a silver grease. Her dress was short, thin, boldly cut, and she wore nothing to speak of underneath.

What's a bull of a man like you doin' with our skinny L'il Red? she asked him. You need more 'n that bag of pale bones to keep you warm, I am surely sure. Why don't you come by me sometime? I got a whole lot of fire.

Before he could think up what to say, a sniggering erupted behind him. He glanced over his shoulder and saw a clutch of whores made up and attired similarly to the one blocking his way to freedom. They leaned against the walls and one another, whispering, tittering, gawking at his discomfort and finding great sport in it. He filled his chest with air, flashed them every one of his square white teeth along with the gold one, and said, Ladies, I am certain you have much more profitable activities in store for you tonight and so I leave you to them. He pushed his way past the whore and escaped.

He stopped at a five and dime for peppermints and went double-speed to Fishbein's house straight after. When the old man answered his back door, Bailey just about fell into the house, he was that tired and distraught. Fishbein helped him to a chair at the kitchen table and fetched him water. Bailey drank it down and asked for more and drank that, too, while his lungs burned. Fishbein hovered over him, silent, his red eyes full of concern, his lips tight, their corners turned south in a mournful arc. Gasping, Magnus Bailey plunked down his bag of candy on the table.

I said I'd bring the child sweeties, and there they are, he said. His voice was hoarse and wavered. His eyes had in them a beggar's despair, as if the man before him were the last soul on earth who might offer him bread.

I've seen Minnie, he said. We are reunited, but I cannot fathom zackly what's happened to her. I knew it was bad, but it's worse than ever I thought. When I'm in her presence, I find one of my feet is in heaven and the other stuck in the tar pits of hell. Surely it was more than misfortune and a broken heart that changed her. She was smarter than that. What happened to her? What happened to our Minnie?

America happens to her, Fishbein said.

I don't understand.

This is a country where a person can toss out his past like yesterday's garbage. For a Jew, once the past is gone, there is nothing left. But America gives you plenty to fill the void. In America, you can takes your pick of all the apples in the tree. I think that's what Minerva does. When her heart is too sore for her to bear, she needs get rid of it. She grabs too much America, too many apples.

Fishbein shrugged and clapped his hands together in a gesture of finality as Magnus Bailey stared off into nothingness, considering his words. The America that Fishbein described was certainly not his America. If the colored man in America could cast off his past like that, why, he'd do it without so much as a backward glance. But the hard, ugly truth of the Negro's past in America kept him locked eternally in a trap of deprivation and anger he never planned or desired but simply had to learn to manage as stealthily as he could. Last time Bailey looked, there were no apples dangling in the air above his head, ripe for the taking. Every apple he ever bit into, he'd paid a high price for.

And that's it, the old man finished. *Nu?*

The telephone rang. Fishbein shuffled to the foyer, where his telephone sat on a small mahogany table. Bailey could hear his conversation from the kitchen.

Yes, *mine kind,* yes, I told him. I know. I know. But, *mine kind,* it is Bailey! Magnus Bailey, I tell. Not some *shmendrick* from the street.

He was silent for what felt a very long time, a period where even from the kitchen Bailey could hear the static screech of a feminine voice haranguing him at a furious pitch. This went on and on until at last, the old man interrupted.

Oy, enough already, Fishbein said. *Nu,* I am sorry, *mine kind.* I am very sorry. But now the cat is loose from the bag. It is not a terrible thing, believe me.

When he returned to the kitchen, he shook his head and rolled his eyes upward to beseech his inscrutable God. Some things, he said, never change.

He offered Bailey schnapps and was accepted. The two men repaired to the living room, where they sat in the same chairs they'd sat in before. Fishbein poured the liquor into shot glasses and downed his own in one swallow. Is good, no? he asked Bailey, who sipped his then smiled in spite of himself.

Yes, Fishbein said, smiling also. I confess it's the kind I like— peppermint! The taste of our little Goldele is all in the family!

The child, he told him, was not there. She was his only from Thursday night to Sunday night. The rest of the time she lived upriver at the farm of that good woman who also taught her lessons, as Minerva was afraid to have her in a public school. On Sundays, she had Hebrew lessons and Torah lessons from her zaydee. She could *bench licht* and knew her Shabbos prayers. On Friday nights and the holidays, Minerva came and stayed with them. Golde believed that her mother was a nurse with many urgent responsibilities at a hospital and that she spent as much time with her as humanly possible. I don't know, Fishbein said, how long she will keep to believe that.

Bailey promised again to rescue them all. Without mentioning Europe, he promised he would get the child and her mother, and

Fishbein, too, to another, safer world before Golde had a chance to learn the truth. He promised with such fervor, Fishbein was gentle with him.

And the money to finance this great escape, my friend? Where it comes from?

Bailey reached for the bottle and poured them both more schnapps. This time it was he who downed the drink in a single swallow. I'll get it, he said. Don't you worry. I'll get it.

Okey-dokey, you'll get it.

One more shot and Bailey felt the room enclose him in a warm embrace of hope and enthusiasm for the future. In the strangest way, he felt as if this very room was where he belonged more than any other place on earth. The Lord works in mysterious ways, he heard the voice of his long-dead mama say, and her tone prompted him to scriptural thoughts.

I'll work for her, he told Fishbein. I'll work for her as hard as Jacob worked for Rachel.

Fishbein held up a finger and wagged it at him playfully.

But will there be a Leah in between? he asked.

Aurora Mae was erased from his mind as easily as chalk on a blackboard.

No! Bailey laughed.

So then we are talkings seven years? Fishbein said, playing along.

Seven years is too long! It'll be less! Far less! Bailey swore.

He left Fishbein's that day a bit drunk. He hadn't wanted to leave. He lingered as long as he could at the paternal home of his beloved, the home where all things felt possible, where images of his own youth as well as Minnie's surrounded him like friendly ghosts. But duty called through the dam of peppermint schnapps, and he walked into the night to make his way home.

Aurora Mae informed him that the whore Pearl would be staying on awhile. She was going to take lessons from Dr. Willie. When she'd taken enough, she'd be baptized and renamed Sister Pearl to become, if everything went alright, a handmaiden of the Miracle Church of God's People over to Pendleton Street.

I know you don't like Dr. Willie, Aurora Mae said.

You'd be right about that.

And I know too it'll irritate you when he's around. But whatever else he is, he surely knows how to talk to a gal. Pearl came here sufferin' and wantin' just to live. Now she wants to be reborn too. She wants to be washed clean in the livin' stream of Jesus' love. Lord knows, she got plenty of muck on that soul of hers after workin' so long at Minerva Fishbein's, which by the way, is where she told me today she come from. Can you beat that? You don't mind we keep her awhile, do you?

Magnus Bailey, feeling softhearted as drunk, guilt-ridden deceivers are wont to do, was touched that Aurora Mae thought he had a vote in the matter. Of course I don't, he said, thinking the more distractions Aurora Mae piled up around herself, the easier he'd have it visiting Minnie and working for their future. He felt a twinge of guilt for the deceptions he'd committed already and for those he planned for the morrow. He reminded himself that he'd never made a vow of fidelity to Aurora Mae, nor she to him. They'd only ever sworn loving friendship, not eternal love, and that knowledge comforted his conscience. If old Willie kept her company for a time, he'd just have to live with it. Maybe having the preacher hanging around was a good thing. If he was going to leave Aurora Mae someday, she'd need a new man to fill in the gap. She'd do better than Willie anon, he judged, but he'd be serviceable for a while. He laughed at himself. Funny how his opinion of Dr. Willie had softened now that he needed him.

Bailey considered how lucky he was that Pearl landed on their doorstep before he'd ever been inside L'il Red's, or she'd know him by now and his particular jig would be up and fried for breakfast.

As he laid his weary head down on the pillow to the left of Aurora Mae Stanton's, his last thought was, Wouldn't it be a wonder if bringing Minerva Fishbein to Jesus would erase the hardness from her soul the way it was about to do for the whore Pearl? Now, wouldn't it? Then the room began to swim about, and he thought no more.

Fairer Worlds on High

1934–1936

XV

IT WAS A PLEASANT Saturday morning in March. Fishbein walked to shul with his head down, his mind full of worries, unaware of his surroundings. Sweet notes of spring buoyed the air if not his thoughts. Now and again winter's last gasp came up off the river in a bracing draft that shot up the sleeves of his coat and threatened to sweep the hat off his head. He barely noticed.

When he'd left the house, Golde was asleep. Magnus climbed the steps by the back door and Minerva bustled about the kitchen putting out plates of food from the ice chest and the bread box. She had a burnish about her, that glow of happy domesticity women in love acquire. She seemed younger, innocent even, an impossibility that caused her father a shudder of alarm. Where could all this lead but into a world of danger and pain? Magnus spoke of golden exile, but Fishbein knew better. There was no such thing. Exile was a ripping up, a tearing away, a flight from one set of evils to another. The new place might feel benign, but that was always a lie, or at best a misapprehension. Evil in a different tongue, while incomprehensible at first, disguised in layers of superficial impression, was still unequivocally evil. Look what had happened to him and Minerva in America, once their wonderland of tolerance compared to Europe. Look what happened every day to Magnus Bailey's people whose chains of iron had been loosed but never removed. The human heart is a comedian, he thought, making fools of every man who nurtures hope there like a disease no therapy can excise.

Did any life escape pain and loss? Inconceivable, he thought. Yet, without fear of contradiction, such was the constant object of his prayers. *Mine Gott, mine Gott,* he muttered in the morning, in the afternoon, and in the night while tears sprung forth unbidden. Grant our Golde a little miracle! Grant our darling girl a life of joy!

Hope for Golde was the only reason Fishbein could find in his poor fool's heart for encouraging the insanity of Minerva and Magnus. For two years now they hurtled along a primrose path strewn with brambles sharp as arrow tips, studded with insurmountable boulders, crisscrossed by poison streams. Those two lived with switches inside their brains, he decided. Switches that with a single flick could erase the past and blur the present so that neither of them had to admit the truth of how they lived when they were apart. Flick! they were together. Flick! the hour would come when they'd bid good-bye and return to their outside lives. Flick! they would commit their duties in that other sphere with efficiency and aplomb, their shadow selves in perfect repose, a daydream or two their only sustenance until the next assignation. How many times, he wondered, did they approach each other after a spell apart full of doubt, shame, regret, even a resolve to end this madness when, flick! The first glance, the slightest touch dissolved all but their hours together and that idiotic notion of the future they nurtured between themselves. It was the worst nonsense. There could be no happy resolution. But Minerva and Magnus were adults, free to enhance or ruin their lives as they saw fit.

Golde was another story. The child grew older every day. Fishbein was tormented by concern for her welfare. Although she was a good child, an obedient child, her lack of a proper home ate at her more with each passing year. How often she complained to him out of Minerva's earshot that she longed desperately for a life where her mother and grandfather—Bailey, too, and oh! if God were kind, two or three brothers or sisters—lived with her under one harmonious roof. I'm so lonely, she'd cry with her big green eyes brimming. He bought her a bird in a cage, a cat, even a turtle to keep her company, but while she loved and cared for them, she whined to him, I want a family! And if I can't have that, a real friend! A playmate! Only this too her mother forbade even in the country, lest some thoughtless child reveal the truth of Golde's origins. Minerva's web of rules and subterfuge had protected the child so far, but it was futile to try to contain her body or her mind much longer. It was only a matter of time before she rebelled.

Fishbein's deepest fear was that she discover her mother's business at the worst possible moment, when she was at puberty, and this event fast approached. For the moment, she was a good child, and what's more, a good Jewish child, Fishbein's hopeful response to the Divine who had severely challenged her mother from the time she was three when she arrived, naked and bathed in blood, in a stranger's doorway. However corrupt Minerva had become, Fishbein forgave her on account of that moment thirty years before. With such a beginning, how could even Ha-Shem expect her to turn out any differently? But Golde. Golde was another story. Of fragile health from the start, beautiful, delicate, quick, and bright, the child filled his heart daily with a melting affection and terror both.

On days when fear for her innocence consumed him, the fool Fishbein found himself longing for the fulfillment of Magnus Bailey's promises. Yet for all that man chased after every dime he could squirrel away, the times were mean, and after these two years his purse was not half large enough. It was likely Minerva didn't care. Fishbein suspected that her support of her lover's efforts was whimsical. It seemed to him that in her heart she did not believe Bailey would ever have enough of a stake to carry out his plans. He certainly didn't see any signs that she would soon give up her livelihood in favor of dependence on him. Like every human before her engaged in a disaster about to happen, Minerva deluded herself, thinking she could protect Golde from the truth forever.

That Friday night while her mother put the child to bed, Bailey and Fishbein drank a digestif and mused together.

I can puts up this house, wreck though it is, Fishbein said. Maybe that will get us sooner to the promised land.

It would help, Bailey said. As he looked up at his friend, his eyes softened in gratitude.

Fishbein pounced upon his sentiment.

You know, I am thinking even so that Paree is exactly the wrong place to go. Maybe you have heard of this German Bund? It is a harbinger, I tell you. Things are not so good for Jews wherever the Bund blinks its eyes. I know, I know, they are German not French, but, my friend, you cannots know how Europe is, how an idea spreads from one place to another like a fire that comes wild to a dry forest.

Minerva came down the stairs just then. With his head turned toward her in delirious devotion, Bailey ceased to listen to him.

Nu, thought Fishbein as he kissed the mezuzah of the Baron Hirsch Synagogue, if we are doomed, we are doomed. It is the way our people have always been, living with hatred outside the door, in the backyard, down the street, but, *baruch Ha-Shem*, living, and so we get used to things the way they are. What was it Minerva said to him the last time he tried to talk her away from Europe? When he warned her of the animus he feared would rise up there and also here, in America?

Papa, she said, so people hate Jews. This is new?

She laughed in a sad but resolute manner, and then she shrugged.

Oy, oy, oy, he repeated, shaking his head. I have never been able to affect her behavior. Why do I think I can now?

He pulled open the heavy door of the synagogue and commended himself not into the hands of Minerva and Magnus Bailey but into the hands of God.

As always, he was early, arriving before the beginning of services. To his surprise, the shul was bustling. The patriarchs Loeb and Goldsmith were on the bimah, pacing to the wings and back, carrying papers of some importance it would seem for the way they cradled them tenderly as Torahs in their arms. The leaders of the congregation milled about in an excited cluster just beyond them. Their voices were steady and rushed, like an ocean tide, rising, crashing, receding, rising yet again. Behind them lesser lights pushed and shoved to be closest to whatever it was that animated them. Anshel, the gabbai, rushed by. Fishbein touched his elbow and asked, What is goings on? To which Anshel, a plain man not given to detailed response, said, We have a guest speaker.

Hoo-hee, thought Fishbein, must be some special guest. He stood on his tiptoes to look above the crowd, but he could not see through the throng to someone new. He might have done better had he joined them, but he determined that if the guest was as honored as it appeared, either that rich or that learned or that holy, the father of the most infamous member of the Jewish community of Memphis, Tennessee, was the last person anyone wanted him to meet. Fishbein was a pitiable pariah of sorts at Baron Hirsch Synagogue. Though once a respected newcomer at the shul, feted and celebrated as a pious man as well as a man of means, when Minerva fell from grace, so did he in the eyes of his fellow congregants. Why he did not disown her, rip his sleeve, declare her as one dead confounded them. In their view, Fishbein was weak, culpable, enslaved by love for his daughter, and so, unable to rebuke her. He forgave them their harsh judgment. They'd never known the bloody child who'd cried out, terrified at his door, her yawning need for order, the way she'd perched, since childhood, like a trembling bird on a high wire, her balance ever precarious, fighting for a slim chance at happiness, and in the end undone by a gale of wind that took the name of Magnus Bailey.

Taking his usual spot in the back of the synagogue, Fishbein uttered the blessing before putting on a talis, swung the garment over his shoulders, its fringes fluttering, and steeped himself in prayer and meditation. As always, the more he prayed, the sadder he became, thinking of his long lost ones: his mother, his father, his beloved wife, and the child she'd carried, the entire Jewish quarter of his city in the old country, Minerva, of course, who was as lost as any of them, no matter what Magnus Bailey planned, and George McCallum, too. As he davened, he sighed and moaned. When the congregational service began, he was unaware at first, too busy with his sways and dips, with repeating the phrases of Kaddish over and over. No one looked at him, wondering who had died of his people. Everyone knew this was his habit and vow, to perpetually pray for his dead both during *yarhzeit* and every day that was not *yarhzeit* besides.

The *parsha* that day was Ki-Tisa, which makes mention of God's instructions to Moses on taking a census of the people with him in the desert. It relates also the story of the Golden Calf and the destruction of the first tablets of the law. Fishbein closely followed the reader as he recited the text. Not only was the *parsha* the corner-stone of every service, a sacred obligation to fulfill, but the honored guest was surely a speaker coming to exhort the congregation for some purpose or other and would just as surely use the *parsha* as an inspiration for his talk.

After the service, Anshel announced in his large, plain voice that everyone should stay to listen to their guest, who had important news. As always after the prayer that more or less concluded every service, the final Kaddish, the mourner's Kaddish, Fishbein was immersed in sorrow, and it took some time for him to come back to himself. He did not catch the speaker's name or where he was from, but up on the bimah was a big, broad-shouldered man with a black beard and blacker eyes, ruddy cheeks, and skin darker than Golde's. He opened his mouth and boomed in a voice that was enormous even in comparison to Anshel's. It was like thunderclaps resounding between mountaintops, and the census of the *parsha* was the focus of his words.

Shema-Yisroel! he boomed in the accents of the East. You citizens of Memphis, recall that other Memphis where your fathers were enslaved! Once again, the Lord God commands an accounting of your numbers and a tax that will mean atonement of your sins!

They were close to Pesach. Fishbein assumed they would listen to a jeremiad about bondage to the world of the flesh and redemption from it, which was freedom, freedom to choose another bondage, a better bondage, one to a book of Law and priestly obligation in return for which Ha-Shem would embrace them. It was a pleasant theme, one of renewal. The open windows of the synagogue filled the air with the fresh, budding world outside. For the first time that day, Fishbein inhaled the scent of regeneration and was nearly consoled. Then the orator took a turn he did not expect.

Far from here, the man said, far from this fat land with its pretty snares and stealthy traps that enslave the righteous, lies a world struggling to be reborn! It is Eretz Israel, the land of your fathers, and she calls to you, she calls to you in the morning, she calls to you in the afternoon, she calls to you in the night! You must make ready your souls to receive her! She will save you and hold you at her bosom, for nowhere else in the world will you be safe, and nowhere else in the world will you be free!

Look to Germany, he said, where Leviathan licks his lips and sharpens his teeth! How long shall the children of Moses recline there, sleek and satisfied upon their couches before they find them full of nails and sharpest knives? Look to your own New York, where Germany's handmaidens gather to set the stage for your condemnation! And here! Even here! Where you are used to riding your river in comfort, holding the hands of gentiles, who pretend not to despise you as you drift along, without purpose, without the guidance of the Lord! Here in the mountains to your east, is the devil William Dudley Pelley and his forgeries, the Benjamin Franklin Prophecy. Ah! You do not know him? He is a brother of the heart to the German Chancellor Hitler and in the mountains of North Carolina, he gathers his army, his Silver Shirts, who long for your blood and, failing that, your expulsion! There he gathers his people around him to teach them the vilest lies and pretend they have come from the mouth of your Franklin. Not since the Protocols of the Elders of Zion has such filth been received so lovingly by our neighbors! Hear the alarm, O Israel, hear it!

The orator paused. He wiped his big, shining face with a white handkerchief the size of a dishtowel. For a moment, he seemed to collapse inward. His shoulders caved in toward his chest, his neck bowed 'til his beard touched his belt. Then, as if a tight coil had sprung inside him, he popped himself open, stretching his arms to the heavens. His face tilted upward and his chest filled with air as his conclusion boomed forth.

Come home, O Israel! Today the census of the people in our homeland reaches 350,000, although the tax Ha-Shem levies upon his people is steep in blood and sweat. But the arms of one's mother are always sweet, even in the most troubled times. In Jerusalem, where yes! our people were slaughtered just five years ago for the great sin of praying at our Wall, we did not abandon her. From days of old they have tried to wipe us out, and yet we stay, and our numbers grow and grow. Come home, O Israel. Make aliyah! We will welcome you with bread and salt, with milk and honey. It is said that when a righteous Jew enters Jerusalem, even the stones dance. Listen to their music and come home!

The assembled applauded. Loeb and Goldsmith rushed over to shake the speaker's hand. Then Loeb made an appeal for the World Zionist Organization and oral pledges were made. Even Fishbein was moved to pledge twenty dollars he could not spare. He left the synagogue inspired, resolved to present Minerva and Magnus with a new idea. Aliyah.

When he entered his home, he could not determine if the two lovers were flushed and breathing deeply because he had surprised them in an intimate moment or if they'd been arguing. They stood at opposite ends of the living room. What's more, they looked in opposite directions, as if distracted by petty pursuits, although everything about their postures suggested this attitude was a deception. He heard Golde playing with the cat upstairs.

My darlings, he said to the other two, I have a solution to all our troubles.

They picked their heads up and regarded him with veiled looks. But what did they hide? Sorrow? Anger? No matter, his solution would distract from whatever ailed them.

Eretz Israel! he said. This is where we should go. To Jerusalem, City of Gold!

Blank expressions greeted his revelation. He went to Minerva first, grabbing her hands in his and speaking most passionately to her.

I am sorry, my child, that we did not go there straightaway when you was small. It's where we belong. It is our home. Of course, if we had gone all those years ago, we would not have dear Magnus and our darling Golde in our lives, so maybe I'm only a little sorry.

He laughed in his strange, ragged manner so that the mirth that issued from him resembled a halting sob. He crossed the room to

Magnus. He put his hands on the man's shoulders and looked him square in the eyes.

I met a man today from Eretz Israel. He was darker than Golde. You know, in the East there are many Jews like him. And Africans who also live and prosper there. You will be as free as in Paree, I am sure.

He turned and stood with arms outstretched, one toward Minerva, the other toward Magnus.

So, what do you think? he asked.

He wiggled his fingers, expecting them to rush into his arms from blissful excitement. Magnus looked at his lover with his eyebrows raised, soliciting her assent before he made a move. When she spoke, her voice was as dry as Sinai sand.

Oh, Papa. You've gone meshugga.

Magnus intervened.

I don't know, Minnie, he said. I wouldn't mind walkin' the steps my Lord walked.

Fishbein started. Here was a new kettle of fish, he thought. His Lord. When did Magnus become a Jesus man? Well, they were all raised that way, he knew, but never in all the years he'd known him had Magnus Bailey ever uttered anything like this 'my Lord' that just rolled from his lips as if that phrase of devotion was common to the core of him.

Minerva spoke up before he could follow his thoughts on where the complication of Magnus Bailey's beliefs, should they prove just and deep, might take them all. She held out her arms much as her father did and lifted her shoulders.

Papa. Magnus. Do I look like a pioneer to you?

The men stared at her. Her shoulders dropped.

I didn't think so.

Golde came down the stairs, the orange cat under her arm with its neck stretched out, its feet dangling. Why the cat didn't struggle for release was a mystery. When she achieved the foyer, she put the creature down. It ran and hid somewhere. The child saw her grandfather and went to him and wrapped her arms around his waist. He bent his head to kiss her cheek.

Zaydee, she whispered in an available ear, is it safe yet?

Whats you mean, *mine shepsele*?

Her long green eyes narrowed and directed themselves toward her mother, whose hands were on her hips, whose mouth was pinched.

Oh, nothing, Zaydee! she said with her gaze yet on her mother. Her grip on her grandfather tightened.

Then Magnus came and took her from him, scooped her high up in his arms, which pleased her so that she laughed and put her head on his neck to kiss him in three wet little smacks.

Come, little brat, he said, and I'll read with you. We'll take the Good Book and act out parts. You can choose the chapter and verse.

She chose David's escape from Saul's wrath. They settled in a corner of the room with Golde perched on top of a couch, her hand shielding her eyes as she made believe she was at a tower window peering out over the realm of Israel. At first, Magnus was on all fours pretending he was a sheep in a rocky field under her gaze, then he used a thin, reedy voice and was Michal lying to her father. By the time Golde pretended to descend the tower wall by a rope of twisted bed sheets, they were all laughing, including the child who made her laughter a part of the play as an exultant cry of freedom from David's mouth.

Fishbein had collapsed in a chair, entirely distracted and charmed by the tableau. Not until everyone settled down and Minerva went to the kitchen to lay out their lunch with Golde behind her wanting to help, dragging Magnus along with her small hand around his large one as she did not want to be separated from either of them even for a moment, did Fishbein consider the child's whisper to him, its odd urgency, the look that passed between mother and child. He pondered the mood of the room when he'd returned from shul and regretted he'd been so enthused with the idea of aliyah that he'd brushed his observations aside. A moment lost, he thought, too late to decipher it now, but one I should not forget. Then Golde called him to the dining room for lunch.

After lunch, Fishbein took a long nap as was his habit. When he awoke, he found himself tangled in blankets and in a sweat. Snatches of a nightmare came to him. He tried to put the pieces he could recall together. The dream had started out benignly enough. He was on a ship, a sailing ship soon to arrive at port. Golde was with him and he held her up high in his arms. Her legs wrapped around his bony hips. Their hearts were light, joyous. Although it made no sense since Jerusalem is a landlocked place, with no coastline, he felt he was showing her the shining city of gold as he had once held Minerva to show her Lady Liberty. That part of the dream he found reasonable, given the day he'd had. But then he remembered there'd been a chain of iron attached to his waist. When he looked backward to see where the chain led, he saw Minerva fastened to the other end. She was bent over the reclining form of Magnus Bailey, who looked to have something very wrong with him. Whatever it was, the sight caused Fishbein to gasp within his dream and clutch the child closer to his vest. He'd opened his mouth to scream but no sound came out. After digesting these details, ones both startling and vague as the elements of dreams often are, Fishbein shook himself, washed his hands, and quickly said a blessing of protection.

He went downstairs and the four had dinner together. Minerva returned as usual to her business, but at the latest possible hour. She could not abandon her livelihood on a Saturday night no matter how Magnus and Golde begged her to stay a little longer. The child went to bed on her own, and Magnus left also, back to that life of his they knew so little about.

Sunday followed Saturday as it always did, and Fishbein felt a fresh veil of melancholy descend over him as it did every Sunday, because toward the end of the afternoon a car would come and take Golde away from him, back to her foster home in the country until the next Thursday night. The hour approached when her departure was near. He told her to pack up her things in the satchel she carried back and forth and to say good night to her animals. He heard her chatter to the cat, gurgle to the tortoise, and chirp at the bird, and then there was a knock on the back door.

What now, what now, he thought, thinking the child's car had come early as it sometimes did. He puttered to the door and opened it. There on the opposite side of the screen door was a short, round colored man, rocking back and forth on his small booted feet. His profession was obvious. He wore a black suit, a black fedora, and a round white collar. He clutched against his chest a white leather book with a big red cross on its front. Behind him was a pretty young colored woman in a long white dress covered by a kind of apron. She wore a white kerchief wrapped about her head and knotted at her crown. She looked like a nurse, but when the preacher made his introductions, he referred to her as Sister.

First, he lifted his hat. Reverend Dr. Willie Smalls, here, my friend, he said. And this is Sister Pearl. We have come to ask you if you've heard the Good News.

Vez mir, thought Fishbein. I hear plenty of news, good and bad, he said, moving to close the door. And I wish you goodwill buts good-bye. . .

The Rev. Dr. Willie Smalls stuck his foot past the threshold. His head shot forth like Golde's turtle's head when it poked out of its shell, with elongated neck and eyes darting all about the room. He's looking for something, thought Fishbein. Then his breath caught in his chest, and his heart thumped against his rib cage as he realized what, or who, the preacher sought. Stay upstairs! he tried to tell her silently. Is not safe!

It was too late. Is that Auntie Julie? Golde asked from the hallway as Auntie Julie was what she called her caretaker and teacher from the country. You're early, Auntie!

She came around the corner into the kitchen. Although she was behind him, Fishbein knew she was visible to the Rev. Dr. Willie Smalls for the way the man's eyes widened and lit up, the way a small, cruel smile played at the corners of his mouth.

Oh! Golde uttered, retreating immediately back around the corner, where she put her back against the wall, trying for all she was worth to flatten herself against it, into it even, if such had been possible, until she heard her grandfather use rude words in a brusque tone, none of which was like him at all, then the door slammed, and she heard the feet of the preacher and his companion retreat double-time away.

She crept back into the kitchen. Her grandfather sat in a chair at the kitchen table with his elbows on the table and his face in his hands. She went to him and gently touched his knee.

I'm sorry, Zaydee. I'm sorry. It wasn't safe, was it?

Old Fishbein sighed, thinking what a life they had given her, to fear for her safety constantly, without knowing why.

It's alright, *mine shepsele*. Nothing happens, did it? he said. You are here and I am here and puss and cheeps and the slow one? So it was safe in the end, yes? Wasn't it?

Alright, she said with a brave smile and upturned chin. I believe you, Zaydee.

But she crawled into his lap anyway and held on to him while he hummed her a song from the old country, rocking her sweetly in the fading light until Auntie Julie came and took her away.

XVI

THERE IS A RHYTHM to love affairs like the one that seared the lives of Minerva Fishbein and Magnus Bailey. The flames of lust burn too fast and too high to find sustenance in the heart, and whatever lies in their path suffocates. Charred bits of reason and care are strewn in their wake, opportunities lost forever. Weariness is thick as ash in the mouth. This did not happen to those two. Thanks to their history before the first embrace, from that day to their last they were joined together like iron soldered to copper. But the quick, sharp heat and inevitable cool was exactly what occurred between Dr. Willie Smalls and Sister Pearl of the Miracle Church of God's People, especially on the good reverend's side of things.

The gestation of the whore Pearl's spiritual rebirth was either inordinately long or preternaturally short, depending on who judged the process. Twice a week for half a year, Dr. Willie came by The Lenaka in the midafternoon to provide her instruction while the root woman tended her shop and gardens. Whenever Dr. Willie arrived at the shop, Pearl's demeanor changed. She stood straighter. She tamed her hair with her hands every other minute. Sometimes, she was unnaturally silent. Others, she talked nonstop. Aurora Mae put the girl's agitation down to zealous piety. Nights the two women were alone, Pearl shared with her tales of whorehouse degradation, vulgar tales weighted by great sadness and remorse. Such pitiful incidents were all too familiar to Aurora Mae, given her bondage to the men who'd stolen her from her family then sold her to L'il Red. She felt a queer guilt that the madam had set her free thanks to knowing her from days gone, but at the same time, L'il Red had been a cruel tyrant to the broken girl weeping in Aurora Mae's sitting room. The guilt blinded her where Pearl was concerned.

Most of the girl's sordid stories ended with the testament, Oh, I surely hope I never have to do that again! which led Aurora Mae to think they were both pretty much done with men. A life of shared affection without lust wasn't so bad, she tried to tell her. Not for the damaged ones like you and me. It never occurred to Aurora Mae that the preacher ravished Pearl daily while she trimmed her vines and ground her pestle.

It started when his hand brushed against Pearl's thigh in seeming accident as the two knelt together in prayer. On Pearl's side of things, an unnatural shock went through her from that small and fleeting touch. It was as if a lightning bolt had entered her flesh, struck a dry place, and started up a conflagration inside. Dr. Willie was a man of God. The men she'd known before were demons of spit and sweat and darkness. Not one had ever made her feel anything but numb. In her eyes, Dr. Willie was day to their night. Where the others had been links in the shackles that bound her, Dr. Willie was her key to liberation. She purely loved how the preacher's hand would press her knee in sympathy when she spoke to him of her childhood as a sharecropper's daughter in a pile of seasons too dry or too wet with no food on the table half the time and the cold or the heat stealing up her legs and down her breasts every day of her life, so that her skin was always raw and aching from one thing or another. She loved how he stroked her back lightly when she spoke of her older siblings who worked like slaves at her daddy's side just to keep the family going. When she spoke of the babies younger than she, their illnesses, the tiny coffins, her tears would start, and Dr. Willie would clasp her to his bosom to still her grief, which pleased her as it made her feel some kind of loved, even though everything she told him was a pack of lies. She made up some of her best stories just for the burning warmth of him. They were half a sight better than those she made up for Aurora Mae.

There came a day when the preacher and his acolyte were parsing scripture together on the settee, and the story of Mary Magdalene came up.

How I wish my hair were long, Pearl suddenly announced, lifting her arms and running her hands through her short cornrowed mop for the way the gesture arched her back and lifted her breasts. She wore a modest gray shift, loosely yoked at her midriff. With her arms raised and her chest thrust forward, the shift tightened here and gaped there transforming its pious intent into a shameless invitation.

The reverend sat back and studied her with his eyes narrowed to keep the desire she provoked veiled. And why is that, child? he asked, his voice thick.

Quick as a bug, or maybe a lizard that skittles off a bench, she hopped up then knelt at his feet. Her hands on his ankles were hot. If it was, she said, I'd wash your feet with it.

She bent low and leaned forward. Her round, high backside came up so that he could not miss it no matter where he looked. She rubbed the side of her face against his shoes. It was too much. He took her by her elbows and pulled her up to him 'til she sat on his lap. He had her for the first time right there on the settee.

Now a conflagration had been lit inside Dr. Willie Smalls, too. Soon the only scripture read or psalms sung in the back rooms of The Lenaka were those committed in haste while Aurora Mae had yet to go to work and kept them bothersome company. They fondled each other even in her presence, the second her back was turned. Sometimes, while she waited on a customer an involuntary cry would issue from Pearl or Dr. Willie's mouth as the fire between them burned high and bright. My, but the Lord is praised mightily this noon, Aurora Mae would say, shaking her head and smiling with satisfaction that the poor whore had achieved such sanctity and joy.

One day, Dr. Willie was late for their lesson. Pearl fretted and paced. Maybe something happened to him, she said.

Aurora Mae soothed her. Don't be silly, Pearl. It could be so many different things keepin' him. A man like that has his plate piled high with responsibilities. You're not the only sheep in his flock, you know.

She'd meant to jolly the girl along, but in mentioning other sheep, she'd shoved a thorn deep in the whore's heart. By the time the good doctor arrived, Pearl was trembling with resentment and irritation.

Dr. Willie, his head down and shaking from side to side, waved his hands in the air as apology. I know I'm as late as springtime in a cursed year, he said, but a poor sufferin' child needed my counsel.

You see? Aurora Mae said before quitting the room. I told you so, Pearl. She's been troubled about you, Dr. Willie. Had you run over in the street by the milk wagon and the fire engine both.

Once she was gone, he might have wished he'd been run over a little bit rather than face Pearl's ire. Poor sufferin' child! she hissed at him. I know men. You all can't break a nasty habit unless another's taken its place. What lost little slut was that zackly who required your impious counsel?

He put his back straight and his chin up in the air. What has been related to me in the confidence installed by power of my collar, he said, is sacrosanct. I cannot help you find peace with my great sin of tardiness. You must look to your own soul for that. You are bein' both uncharitable and unreasonable. I see we have much prayin' to do together, my child. Much.

Prayin', she said. Oh yes, let us pray.

She got up close to him and pulled out from her bag of tricks a caress Dr. Willie found so perverse he thought he might die of sinful pleasure. If she would only do it again, he swore, he would gladly roast on the spits of hell forever in her name. So she did, that day and the next day and the day after that and every day until he grew bored, and then she opened her bag of tricks once more and pulled out a fresh manner of posing and poking and stroking and enflamed him all over again. This game of theirs continued long after her baptism until even a former whore as practiced and skilled as Pearl could find nothing new to intrigue him. She could only perk his desire by whispering wicked stories in his ear of the things they might do if they invited others to join them. He responded most favorably to fancies that employed the participation of Aurora Mae, which angered her although she kept her resentment locked in her heart. By this time, she figured she had Dr. Willie in her pocket, but if you asked him, he'd say he had her in his, and he'd tell you such with a world-weary sigh, like a man bound to a wife he no longer had use for.

That Sunday in March as they hurried away from Fishbein's home before he had a chance to call the police, she proved herself more cunning than Dr. Willie usually gave her credit for, which was a mistake in every case.

Oh, my sweet Jesus, she said. I been wonderin' why you wanted to try that house two days in a row. Never mind no one answered your knock yesterday.

Um, hmm, what?

That child peeping 'round the corner. She could be Magnus Bailey's, couldn't she?

Dr. Willie wasn't so sure. His heart had caught in his throat at just the glimpse of her, but it seemed too good to be true that the Lord would deliver in that moment in that time exactly what he needed to crush Magnus Bailey once and for all.

What makes you say that?

Why her eyes! They are zackly his, ain't they? Who is that old Jew anyway?

The preacher covered his excitement in vague mutterings, then hopped on a bus more to shut Pearl up than get anywhere fast. Elbow to elbow with a great press of colored folk stuffed in the back, he took to nodding his head and smiling at everyone as if he were greeting congregants at his ramshackle church just to avoid discussing the matter any further with her.

If there was any man alive Dr. Willie Smalls hated with all his heart, it was Magnus Bailey, who had poached from him the biggest, fattest calf he'd ever eyed toward sacrifice. If only she were his, Aurora Mae and her money could make the Miracle Church of God's People a cathedral. Colored folk would come from every county in the state to witness its glory and hear the wisdom of its preacher's word. He'd wear garments of silk and finest cotton, his Sunday suppers would never lack for meat, and he'd sleep in a fine feather bed of his very own rather than the miserable straw-filled one that cradled him nightly in the back of McCracken's Cash Groceries, where he worked daily as stock boy and nightly as watchman for the privilege of housing his congregation on the floor above. Such were his hopes for Aurora Mae Stanton when he'd met her, well-heeled but hard put to joy after the flood. Until Magnus Bailey came along and in the space of a Sunday how-dee-do stole her clean away.

He suspected Bailey hated him as much as he hated Bailey, which was why it was such a shock to have the man approach him not one week ago to ask of him a favor.

Dr. Willie was sitting in Aurora Mae's parlor waiting for Sister Pearl, who'd taken up permanent abode in the root woman's house. They were due to make the usual rounds of the Miracle Church of God's People's devotees, offering spiritual guidance, Dr. Willie called it. Sister Pearl referred to the exercise as goin' collectin' or the shearin' of the sheep. Bailey came in and removed his bowler hat as a sign of respect, which nearly knocked the preacher off his chair, such was his utter and complete surprise.

Dr. Willie, I've seen the good work you've done with Sister Pearl, Bailey said. She has transformed from a vile, wicked creature to a pious woman of great charity and cheer, and I'd like to applaud you for that.

Dr. Willie folded his arms over the shelf of his round belly, his hands tented as if in prayer. He smiled.

It's the Lord's doin', not mine, he said, raising his eyes to heaven. All praise to Him on high.

Amen.

Amen.

The two enemies sat in opposing chairs now, beaming falsely at each other. Dr. Willie was having the time of his life. Magnus Bailey looked about to swallow thistles. The reverend had known more than his share of desperate men seeking release. He could see this one had a most heavy burden to unload. He leaned forward, putting on his gravest empathetic expression while inside he was just about bursting with pleasure to see the man suffer.

What troubles you, son? he asked.

Then Bailey said the most remarkable, the most desired, thing.

I need your help.

Of course, whatever I can do.

Bailey got up and paced the room, leaning on the mantelpiece by the hearth, then quitting it almost instantly. He had a great restlessness inside. Oh, yes, thought Dr. Willie, how he suffers! It was hard, oh, it was exceeding hard for the reverend not to laugh out loud.

Bailey told him about an old associate of his, the Jew Fishbein, whom he'd known ever since that man got off the boat in St. Louis many a year ago. Much of the good fortune Bailey had had in life, he swore, he owed to two people: Fishbein and, of course, Aurora Mae. And it pained him, it pained him awful to see the sorrow of Fishbein, a man who'd never hurt a soul on earth, let alone a colored man, an unusual quality, Dr. Willie would have to agree, for a white man in their part of the world. The sorrow of Fishbein, it seemed, had a name and that name was infamous. It was the name L'il Red.

She's his daughter, you see, Bailey said. And if you could do for her what you've done for Sister Pearl, steering her away from the flesh, givin' her a brand-new soul, sweet to Jesus, a soul that'd help her start her miserable life all over fresh, maybe someplace outta here, where the misfortunes that drug her down started, then it would heal her father also, I am sure, and I would not rest until I had properly and completely thanked and rewarded you.

Magnus Bailey told him most of this with his head turned away, as if he were ashamed to face his gaze. When he finished, he looked him straight in the eye, so that Dr. Willie could see plain and simple that the man was the most desperate wretch alive in Memphis, Tennessee, in the year of our Lord nineteen hundred and thirty-four.

Praise Jesus, Dr. Willie thought, Bailey is stuck on the queen of whores at whose house I have watched him moon in a darkened doorway on many a night! I thought it might be one of the lesser lights of that palace of sin, but no, it is the Jezebel herself that he longs to clasp to his thumpin' chest! Praise Jesus! for mine enemy has given me all the weapons I need to destroy him!

Aloud he said, I'll surely do my best, son. But you know, these Jews are hard to win. They are more stubborn than any whore might be to the Word of God. It would appear you have charged me with the double whammy. This could take some time.

Bailey got up and walked around while he talked. Now, now, he said, I've pondered that part some. If I asked you to try for the daddy, well, then surely it'd be a fool's errand I'm sendin' you on. But this is the daughter. She got the habit but not the belief, so far's I can see. How could she believe and live like she does? Ain't nothin' in the Bible but condemnation of her kind. And her daddy, why, he might not like her takin' to Jesus at first, but when he sees her leavin' her old life behind, and behavin' in a wholesome way, like Sister Pearl, I think he might warm up. Of course, I realize this all could take a great deal of time. Please, then, start immediately.

Bailey took some bills out of his pocket and pressed them in Dr. Willie's hand.

I realize this will take you away from your usual pursuits, he said. This is for the church. With my gratitude.

The Rev. Dr. Willie Smalls waited until Bailey quit the room before he counted his take. Three sawbucks. Thirty dollars. When Sister Pearl found him, he grinned ear to ear, and as they were alone, he swept her in his arms and hummed a snippet of a tune while waltzing her around the room. Oh, ain't it just a great day? he said, and the former whore took his mood as she found it, without question for once, and agreed.

Now here he was, a week later with yet a new weapon in his arsenal against his enemy. There was a child. A l'il chocolate child, he chuckled to himself, imagining the day he'd oh so reluctantly relay the news to Aurora Mae Stanton that her man had a child with the whitest dirty whore in Memphis. But first he had to get to L'il Red. No need to rush on the root woman's account. Oh, she'd fall in his trap alright, no need to hurry there. But L'il Red. She's the one he had to take care of to twist Bailey on a spit. There was no doubt more money to quarry there than thirty dollars.

Such was his happy mood, he took Sister Pearl to a restaurant in Orange Mound, a hole in the wall that served up greens, biscuits, and stew for those without a proper family to visit for Sunday supper. It might have been the Ritz for the pride it brought her. She sat up straight, crooked her little finger as she utilized her spoon, and beamed meltingly at the five diners and chef who waited on them as if she were the lady of an old plantation. Watching her, Dr. Willie considered that it would be to his benefit to keep Pearl in a grand state of mind if he were to make the best use of her in a conversion of the likes of L'il Red. Who better to inform him of the madam's wiles and weaknesses? Who better to draw her out from the doors of her establishment to face him?

While he walked Sister Pearl back to Aurora Mae's, he plotted a campaign against Babylon. A dozen schemes played out inside his mind, each successively more elegant than the last. Always, his fancies ended in victory, with the weeping Jewess begging him for absolution of her uncountable, noxious sins. Ah, to have the paramour of his enemy kneeling at his feet where he would crush her also beneath his heel! Such sweet delight, he thought, such sweet delight!

When they reached The Lenaka, they found a note from Aurora Mae scrawled on a paper bag and tacked on the ice chest. Emergency with sick child, it read. Like to be gone all night.

Now, here's a piece of luck, Pearl purred at him, grabbing his lapels and leading him to her room.

Dr. Willie reprimanded her.

You would profit from a child's pain? he said while following her without protest.

Come on, my dear reverend. What's the worst could happen? That Aurora Mae could come back early and find us?

She then whispered to him in her throatiest the delicious events that might transpire if Aurora Mae could only witness his big, hard sex, which would cause her to fall panting into their outstretched arms, and the Rev. Dr. Willie Smalls found himself lost in reverie for the next eighteen minutes, a reverie of the impossible suddenly within his grasp.

XVII

L'IL RED WOKE UP and lolled about entertaining a daydream, one in which she had never chased after Magnus Bailey to find her ruination, because he'd never lied and left her to begin with. She could have kept on conjuring that paradisiacal world forever, but her reverie was disturbed by a commotion going on outside her rooms. She struggled out of bed in a foul mood, threw on a quilted robe, and opened her door to see what was going on. It was before noon, but half-naked gals charged up and down stairs and hallways at high speeds, jeering and cackling like deranged hens. Some carried slop buckets that they took to a landing window and, pushing their sisters out of the way, tossed swill outside. Cheers and claps erupted as whatever filth a whorehouse can find rained down on the street below.

Bailey's Minnie barked an order, and the wall of whores parted like the Red Sea. She went to the window and looked below. There, right next to whorehouse slops splattered in puddles along the side-walk, was a line of picketers, maybe twenty strong. Half a dozen carried homemade placards across which was hand-scrawled in bold black letters: *A Whore Shall Be Burned Alive, Lev. 21:9; Her House Is the Way to Hell, Prov. 7:27; Whoremongers and Adulterers the Lord Will Judge, Hebrews 13:4;* and the like. The leader of the picketers was a short, round man in a black suit with a round collar, who directed them in circles, blocking traffic, and more important, L'il Red's front door. Minerva Fishbein sought out a familiar face among them. She called out her chief enforcer. John! she demanded, wondering where the brute had gone to that he'd let this parade of Bible thumpers invade her territory. John!

He went for your man at the police, one of the whores said.

What for? Why didn't he just phone?

There's somethin' wrong with the line.

Now L'il Red was hopping mad. She stuck her head out the window and yelled to the man on the street she'd wanted John to fetch: Thomas DeGrace! Get in here! I want to talk to you!

The short, round man in a black suit went over to Thomas DeGrace and spoke in his ear. DeGrace handed off his placard to one of the others and stepped up to the front door of L'il Red's. He hesitated under the iron grate balcony flanked by gas lamps. Then he used the doorknocker.

Idiot! thought the madam as she charged back to her rooms and sat behind her desk. Who knocks at a whorehouse door? Only a weasel, afraid to face her. She smiled a hot, teeth-baring smile. Good, she thought, good. He should be.

One of the whores collected Thomas DeGrace and brought him to her office, where she wasted no time in castigating him. His left foot was barely over the threshold when she started in, remind-ing him of their long association, of the debt of gratitude he owed her father, and last but not least, the affection they both bore his cousin, Magnus Bailey. What will Magnus say when he hears how you have harassed me? she demanded, much as once long ago Thomas DeGrace had demanded of her what would Magnus say if he knew she solicited men from the back alleys of Beale Street. Her fist banged on top of her desk. Everything that was not under a heavy glass paperweight jumped. Why do you side with some jack-leg preacher against your own blood?

Up until that moment, Thomas DeGrace had no idea that Bailey and Minerva Fishbein were united or reunited or whatever it was she meant to indicate to him in her outrage. The revelation flummoxed his tongue. It was all he could do to frame a meager defense of his church and its founder.

The Reverend Dr. Smalls seeks only to bring the peace of Jesus to your heart, Miss Minnie, he said, but his head was down and he could not meet her eyes.

Jesus!

He dared a peek up. Minerva's features were knotted with the kind of dark emotion that DeGrace recalled sprung out of her whenever she had her temper tantrums back in the time he was old Fishbein's man.

I've been hearin' enough about Jesus of late! This Dr. Smalls. He the man been botherin' my papa's house?

I surely wouldn't know, Miss Minnie.

Sirens screeched outside. Both Minerva and Thomas DeGrace went in a rush to a window to watch the police in L'il Red's employ leap out of their cars and disperse the picketers by cracking a head or two under a nightstick. Thomas DeGrace was relieved to see that Dr. Willie's skull was not among them. In fact, he did not see Dr. Willie down there at all anymore, which was because the preacher's seasoned ear heard the sirens ahead of the rest. The reverend knew what was coming and fled in plenty of time, not that any of his congregants noticed, so occupied were they with either hurling Bible verses at the whorehouse windows or keeping their heads down to avoid slipping in puddled slops.

Once the police cleared the streets, they trooped into L'il Red's for their rewards, pecuniary and otherwise, which gave Thomas DeGrace a chance to steal outside and scurry off. It was in his mind to get over at once to the Miracle Church of God's People, where he was certain folk would be nursing their wounds while Dr. Willie praised them and Jesus both. Instead, he found himself at Magnus Bailey's bail bondsman office. When that man was not there, he walked over to The Lenaka to see if Aurora Mae knew his whereabouts.

Why, he's in the back, takin' his lunch, the root woman told him as she arranged herbs inside poultice wrappers, which she tied with string and placed neatly in a display case. As Thomas thanked her and hurried through the beaded curtain into the living quarters, she asked his back, What's gone on? Somethin' happen? DeGrace did not answer her.

Magnus Bailey sat at the kitchen table with his jacket and tie off, a great napkin tucked into his collar and anchored at the sides by his suspenders. He drank a broth in which pork knuckle swam with split peas and garlic. He gripped a spoon in one hand and a chunk of dark bread in the other.

Cousin, DeGrace said.

Bailey looked up. His visitor was fiercely agitated. He'd never had the habit of stopping by The Lenaka in the middle of the day for a social call. Bailey's first thought was someone had died. The two no longer had many people alive in common since the flood wiped out Tulips End.

What's the matter, Thomas? Please tell me it's not Alice.

Alice was Thomas's baby sister, who lived near Knoxville. She was the gem of the family and taught school to colored children of a dozen ages in a one-room shack in the woods on the side of a mountain known for its dense fog and windstorms. Magnus Bailey pictured the family pride swept off her perch by a maelstrom of nature and destroyed.

Oh, no, no. It ain't Alice.

Thank the Lord. But then what?

Thomas sat down at the square table across from Magnus. He gripped the sides with his hands and leaned his torso forward. It was an alarming posture, and alarmed is what Magnus Bailey felt regarding him.

It'd be you.

Me?

Last time Bailey checked, all his limbs and wits were intact. He started to chuckle, but Thomas DeGrace slammed his fist on the table with much the same passion that Minerva Fishbein had slammed her desk with hers. Listen to me! the fist said. You are in peril here!

I heard something today about you from a most curious source, and I must find out for myself if it be true.

Bailey nodded encouragement that his cousin might continue.

I heard, or I discovered, I should say, that you and Miss Minnie are . . . are . . . He could not find the word right away, so he looked up to the heavens and found it. That you and Miss Minnie are coupled.

It seemed to take a measure of life out of the man to say the words. He stopped and caught his breath, breathed in and out a few times noisily to recover his equilibrium. He continued.

It may interest you to know my spiritual leader, the Reverend Dr. Willie Smalls, has undertook to close down her establishment in the interest of the public morals. I found myself today demonstratin' outside her gates when she called me in to plead her case, I supposed. Instead, she invoked your name as her partner and protector, which means, Magnus, that not only are you a whoremonger but also a danged rascal who would pervert the goodwill of Miss Aurora Mae Stanton, a saint of our community, to his own ends. What is surely more, if Miss Minnie were not L'il Red but some common white gal out there lookin' for adventure, why this taste of yourn to cross the color line could make you quite dead and painfully so. Please, cousin, please tell me all'a that is a misunderstanding of mine and none of it's true.

Bailey didn't speak right away. First, he liberated the napkin from its restraints and wiped his mouth. He stood up, put on his jacket, and rearranged his bow tie. Taking his bowl and cutlery to the sink, he rinsed them out, laid them to rest in the dishpan with exaggerated care as if they were rare artifacts. He took so deep a breath his shoulders raised and his chest expanded beyond normal size, until his frame was that of a beast, a bear of some kind maybe or a mastiff on its hind legs, which cast a huge, beastly shadow on the wall. Then, without turning around, he admitted everything. With each word, his body came back to itself, almost hissing from its joints with the release of each syllable, collapsing inward bit by bit until he was himself again, only his shoulders were no longer squared but tilted inward toward his heart, perhaps in self-protection.

Yes, he said, it's true. We are coupled, if that's what you want to call it. I would say we've been truly coupled for more'n two year 'cept that maybe we've been coupled from the time the earth was made or before that when the heavens were made and then the briny deep. But I am no whoremonger. I've been tryin' to save her from her own mind as long as I can remember. Dr. Willie's been tryin' to close her down?

Thomas DeGrace tried to absorb everything the other man told him, but huge hunks of it battered up against his understanding. Yes was all he said, simply yes and quietly, too.

Magnus Bailey turned 'round to face him, to find out more about what had transpired that day. He was very much surprised that a man of the cloth would take to the streets when there were more peaceable tactics at hand. When he'd hired him on, so to speak, it was to exercise gentle persuasion, a rousing sermon or two of the kind he'd overheard him use while instructing Sister Pearl.

He considered that first Saturday a number of weeks back. Dr. Willie'd come to Minnie's daddy's door, and she'd made them hide from his knock rather than answer what was obviously a harmless call to salvation. They argued over her refusal to answer the door 'til Fishbein came home from synagogue, which ended the discussion. Afterward, Bailey assumed the preacher would call again and then again after that, until he wore down her resistance and captured her attention, maybe worked a miracle, the kind his church exclaimed aloud in its very name. He never expected he would gather his forces to ram the gates of perdition over there to L'il Red's. How had matters escalated? he wondered. When he turned to face his cousin, it was to ask him just that, as if the man might actually know. But instead of facing the distraught Thomas DeGrace, he found himself looking over that man's head and through a fringe of glass beads, confronting the startled, uncomprehending features of Aurora Mae.

Bailey moved toward her with his arms outstretched. 'Rora Mae, 'Rora Mae, let me explain, he said, but she brushed by him in a rustle of skirt and work apron. He followed her, still calling her name. 'Rora Mae, 'Rora Mae, he called out to the thin air, for she'd disappeared into her bedroom and quietly shut the door. There was no slam, the lock did not turn. He figured he yet had a chance at talking to her face-to-face. He continued to plead sweetly from the hallway.

Let me in, 'Rora Mae, he said outside the door. If you think things over, you'll see you're not so surprised as you may feel. I know I was wrong not to tell you, but I'd like you to know my reasons. Let not this be the way two friends end, friends who've been as dear as we.

A little time passed. The door creaked open. Magnus Bailey crossed over to meet the consequences of his duplicity and explain both the venalities and virtues of his heart. He closed the door behind him.

Aurora Mae sat on the bed, her head down as she twisted a handkerchief in her hands. When she raised her face to him, it was tear-stained, its expression both hurt and questioning. Why? her round, full eyes asked. Why? her lovely mouth, poised in a trembling O, echoed. What did I do to you?

Magnus Bailey knelt at her feet and held her hands in his, handkerchief and all.

I am a scoundrel and a wretch, he said, who has deceived you and who deserves your anger. I beg your forgiveness. I was lost in a storm of frustration and love for a woman whose sins I am responsible for.

She looked at him then with less pain than surprise. How is that? she asked, and he told her in some detail about young Minerva Fishbein, who'd had a passion for him, and who'd ruined herself chasing after him when he ran away rather than face her fierce affections.

I wronged that woman miserably long ago and have spent all my life since either in penance or tryin' to redeem her. Do you remember when we first got together? We admitted to each other that we had loved and lost before and that neither one of us would likely love again like that, ever. You remember that, 'Rora Mae? Well, I don't know who it was branded your heart, and I don't deserve to have you tell me. But it was my Minnie, the world's L'il Red, that I meant.

He told her he thought she'd known he had a shadow life. What else did she think could explain his absence for days sometimes and regular as clockwork on Friday night and Saturdays?

I thought it was the night courts keepin' you busy, she said.

His shame deepened. I don't blame you if you hate me, he said. All I ask is that you don't hate Minnie. She don't know about you. She knows I have another life, but she never asks the details.

He shrugged and frowned to indicate L'il Red's lack of interest in his time away from her was just another symptom of the corruption of her heart for which he felt ultimately responsible. Suddenly, Aurora Mae got up, disengaged herself from him, and walked to the other side of the bed that she might talk with the mattress between them as a buffer. Oh, she said, I could never hate Minerva Fishbein. If it were not for her, I would surely be dead.

The story she told him was a gift, manna from heaven for a tormented lover starved for the nourishment of hope that his beloved's damaged soul would ever be cured. Aurora Mae began at the beginning, with a halting description of her abduction by night riders a decade before. Magnus spared her. I know about that, he said. Mags told me somethin' of it.

Well, you can imagine, or maybe you can't, the hell I went through with those men. They kept me locked in a cabin deep in the woods and did me however they saw fit for weeks. Then, I guess, I dunno, they needed money more'n they needed me. One day, they chained me and put me in a wagon and took me here, to Memphis and L'il Red's. She bought me for ten dollar. Can you imagine that? Ten dollar. I was terrified what was goin' to happen to me next. She looked to change so much, I figured I did too and I didn't think she remembered me. I was afraid, frankly, to tell her I knew her from the younger days. You never know how a person is going to react when you hold the past up to 'em. You'll never guess what she did. She took me up to her rooms, and she washed me with her own two hands and put me to bed. She tucked me in like my own mama, and while she did, I said to her, Why you doin' all this for me, Miss Minnie? and she froze there by the side of the bed, lookin' at me hard. I knew then she knew who I was. She knew but all she said was, My name's L'il Red, and then she closed the door and left me in peace. I slept sound for the first time since I was taken. I slept like the dead.

In the mornin', she put me to the road, on horseback, with a man of hers, and we traveled to a big old plantation, owned by her partner in the whore trade, her moneyman. They say his people lived down the street by Mr. Fishbein when they was kids. Who knows how they run into each other later on. Anyway, I was put to work in the kitchen. I did alright there a couple of years. That kitchen was the salvation of me until it became a hell.

Bailey had never heard of Minnie's partner. A panic stabbed at his heart like a knife. How could there be a man that important to her life somewhere around and he not know it?

Where is this moneyman now? he asked, bracing himself for a revelation that would even the score between him and 'Rora Mae in the sharp, bitter way of fateful justice.

Oh, he's dead. Long dead. In the flood.

While all these revelations and consolations occurred, Thomas DeGrace was still in the kitchen, dimly wondering if he should leave or not, when the beads of the doorway curtain rattled again. He turned toward them, more or less anxious, wondering who would dare to enter through the empty shop, but it was only Sister Pearl.

What's goin' on? she asked him, her voice an intense, conspiratorial whisper. Where's Miss Stanton? Why are you here instead of, you know, on that street with him?

Did you know about them two? he asked her, remembering how she'd arrived in Aurora Mae's life, the route she'd taken through her to Dr. Willie's congregation.

What two?

Magnus Bailey! he said sharply, as he was irritated now by the abundant thickness of women. And L'il Red!

Sister Pearl sat down at the kitchen table. She was still, stunned. Her jaw had dropped but not much. Then she started to laugh in a soft manner no less manic for its quietude. She rocked back and forth, hit the table with the flat of her palm, and jigged her feet against the floor. To Thomas, she appeared plain crazy, so he left her there on her own. His day had been challenging enough without throwing crazy women into it. He left for the church.

A couple of hours later, Aurora Mae Stanton and Magnus Bailey emerged from the bedroom, both of them with tear-stained faces, both in postures weary with confession and regret. Aurora Mae carried a traveling bag of paisley cloth with oak handles. She went to the loose floorboard in the parlor, pried it up, and gathered handfuls of gold coin from her strongbox, depositing them into the bag. It looked to be a fortune she transferred, and yet the strongbox had barely a dent in its store.

I'd tell you take what you need, Aurora Mae said while she closed up the box and replaced the floorboard. But I'm not feelin' quite that forgivin' just yet.

Magnus held up his hands and waved them in a gesture of refusal.

I told you. The one thing I'm committed to here is that the money Minnie and I use for the new start be pure. If I wanted to use your money, I could've stolen it long time ago. You've given me too much already. I can't take no more.

She smiled in a grim way, the way folk smile at funerals, remembering the dead.

The funny thing is I believe you, she said. Listen, I'll go to Cousin Mags's for a bit to give you time to get your things out of here. But if you go in the meantime, as you hope, away with her, I ask you at least leave me a note and let me know.

I truly doubt there's much chance we'd leave so quick, but of course I'll leave you a note. You can bet on that.

They embraced, chastely, and on their cheeks the tears were now fully streaming again. When they left the house for the train station to put Aurora Mae aboard for St. Louis, they were barely aware of their surroundings. Neither of them noticed Sister Pearl hiding outside the parlor, hugging a wall, ready to leap out soon as the coast was clear and figure what floorboard it was exactly that covered up all that treasure.

Once she found it, she took up as much coin as her pockets could hold, and then she stuffed more into her underclothes. She chinked and tinkled when she walked, which made her giggle so she took out the coin. Using kitchen rags, she wrapped it in tight, noiseless bundles then packed these into her church whites, which she'd taken to wearing every day, not just on Sundays. She left to walk directly but slowly over to the Miracle Church of God's People. The weight of her stash kept her from hurry. By the time she got there, only the most severely wounded remained behind with Dr. Willie. He was happy to see her for the help she could give in nursing them. She signaled for him to meet her downstairs in his tiny room behind the grocer's, the room he shared with sacks of flour and rice and tins of fruit and fish and vegetables. He would have taken his time, being alone with her had lost so much luster he often dreaded it, but she was glistening all over with sweat, and her eyes had a fire in them. His curiosity was piqued, and he made haste.

When they were alone, she did not speak. Her eyes burning with triumph and malice, she removed the bundles of coin from her pockets and underclothes and undid them, spilling out their contents on the end table by his sleeping cot. She found the amazement on his face the most delicious experience of any they'd shared. She told him where she'd found it. The amazement in his face grew. She told him there was plenty more, more than he could think ever in his imaginings, and the amazement filled his face so much, she thought he might burst. Aurora Mae is gone, she said, with no plan to come home for a while.

That about did it. The Rev. Dr. Willie Smalls pursed his mouth into a round hole, and from it issued a deep sound like that a cow makes when it sees the hay coming. His amazement pushed out of him in a long, steady lowing. He plunked down on the edge of his cot, ran his hands over the gold, then stared at his shiny black preacher shoes, thinking. When he was done, he did not say you must bring this back. Instead, he asked, So there's more where this came from?

Oh yes, she said. Much more.

It wasn't much of a leap from there for Dr. Willie to decide he no longer needed Aurora Mae if he could so easily get his hands on her fortune. Already, he was planning his escape from Memphis to some new part of the South where he could build his cathedral and command his destined throng of followers. He pondered whether or not he'd need to take Sister Pearl with him or if he could set her out with a share of loot without fear she'd make up some story and turn him in to the authorities out of spite. The more he thought, the more he realized there was only one thing that kept him from fleeing immediately. He had not yet had proper revenge on Magnus Bailey. Maybe he should stick around Memphis a little while longer just to torment him.

XVIII

⊷ ◦ ⊶

IT'S BEEN GETTIN' REAL ugly out there, Minnie told Magnus. That rat bastard Dr. Willie comes back twice a week and with him now are the temperance ladies, who got some reason to think closin' me down's goin' to bring back Prohibition. And oh my lord, the labor unions too. Yesternight, I had fifty colored people on the street making such a racket my gals couldn't sleep, and don't you know there was nothing else for them to do. Who knows how long I can keep 'em. They had photographers from the newspaper, too! There's no man white or Negro in the state of Mississippi going to try to break that line. The nights they aren't there, cloggin' up my street, castigatin' folk that come within thirty yards of my door, business goes to a trickle. I fear there's houses of far less quality taking my regulars away. I don't know where he gets the money, but that rat bastard Dr. Willie must be paying my coppers twice as much as I can. Maybe it's the labor unions. Can't be those goddam wizened temperance types.

Despite the fact that Bailey's heart soared with hope at the reduction of her enterprise to such a pitiful condition, he also wondered how Dr. Willie financed his assault on L'il Red's. How could the preacher come up with and pay for his scheme of ruinous demonstration since he'd only paid him the once, three lousy sawbucks, and that was to proselytize her soul not destroy her livelihood. Although he could never tell Minnie, he wanted to clap the man on the back and praise his ingenuity.

Well, darlin', was what he said aloud. Those unions got a pile of money.

Why don't they go bother the ships at the dock? Why they botherin' poor whores?

Magnus Bailey pondered.

Religion, he said, they got religion.

Vez mir.

It was a Saturday just after noon. For once, Golde had run out of steam, told them she was tired, gone up to bed for a nap. The two sat on Fishbein's settee holding hands. Minnie sighed.

I don't know, Magnus. Maybe I wrung out of that chicken all I'm gonna get. Maybe its time to pack up and leave, just as you've been sayin'.

Minnie! Magnus nearly jumped off the couch to go down on one knee at her feet. Instead, he grabbed her with both arms and held her close to his heart.

Minnie! I swear I will prove you right to put your faith in me. You need never fear for any lack in your life. I will fill it up with love and protection.

When Fishbein returned from shul, they informed him that the corner had been turned, the book closed and a new one opened. The future lay before them bright and free. They spent the rest of the day in jubilation, telling Golde the family was on the verge of a great adventure and that she and her mother would soon never

be parted again. After three stars were out, Fishbein took his led-
gers and spread them on the dining table. Bailey sat with him and
reported orally where he had money and how much, which amounts
Fishbein duly recorded. They studied their columns together and
became dejected for a brief time. Fishbein made some phone calls.
He came up with a member of Baron Hirsch Synagogue, who dealt
in all manner of real estate and who offered cash for the house and
its furnishings. The price was far from what Fishbein had hoped. It
was clear the man intended to make a handy profit out of the seller's
urgency. But it was enough, and *Dayenu!* Fishbein declared, and
they were agreed. Minerva offered to supplement their shoestring
budget with the profits from her business plus the sale of the building known as L'il Red's. Her father frowned but was silent. Magnus
said, I have been clear all along on this. None of your money from
that place, none of it, will come with us. I do believe if we took it
along we would be cursed.

They argued a bit, especially after Fishbein computed the bottom line of their stake. It was ridiculous to Minnie that after all
these years she should not take the profit from her labors with her.
Her father told her she must give her possessions to charity for
the blessing it would bring, like a sin offering of old. She raised
her eyes upward and appeared to stand by her own wishes, but
in the end she demurred, thinking she could always secret cash
in her trunks and valises. The fiercer argument came when they
discussed where they would go, Paris or Jerusalem. At first, Magnus Bailey was in the middle and said he'd abstain from the vote.
He'd go wherever the other two wanted. After a back and forth
between father and daughter during which neither budged, Minnie gave Bailey melting looks. He got off the fence to throw his
weight behind her. It would be Paris, they decided, but all would
keep their minds open. If Paris didn't work out, they'd find a way
to Jerusalem later on.

Fishbein shrugged in a manner so elegant it might have been Gallic. He couldn't complain too much. That Minerva would soon quit her corrupt life was the best news he could imagine.

So, is Paree, then, he said. Who knows? Maybe they changed over there.

He shrugged again, which made the others laugh as it looked as if the saddest man in the world had just made a joke.

It was time for Golde to go to sleep for the night. She'd been yawning through the excitement of plans for the future, yawning and smiling ear to ear. At one point she asked her zaydee for toothpicks to keep her lids open, and they all laughed wondering where she'd got such an idea. Her mother took her upstairs to tuck her in. She was gone longer than she ought to have been, but the men didn't notice. They were much occupied with the price of train and steamer fares, how many compartments they should purchase for the crossing, whether or not the two men should share a room, with Magnus posing as Fishbein's valet. Minerva and Golde, they postured, could travel as lady and lady's maid in a pinch. But maybe it would be better to have Magnus and Golde pose as father and daughter? Minerva came back downstairs. She moved slowly with halting steps. Her men failed to notice. She cleared her throat to get their attention. They quit their chatter and looked up at her who was paused in mid-descent.

We're not a moment too early, she said. Golde's blood times have started.

Fishbein made the blessing for the arrival of new seasons and then tore his sleeve and said Kaddish.

Bailey, who knew enough of Jews to comprehend both the tearing and the prayer, asked his paramour, Why does he do that? Why pray for the dead?

Minerva moaned, a chorus to her father's mourning.

For Golde it's a kind of little death, she said. From now on, her innocence is in constant peril. She's going to grow up!

Bailey embraced her and offered comfort. Now, I'm pretty sure Golde her own self would like to grow up, he said in a sweet tone that made her smile in spite of herself. And since she's a colored child, she always was in peril more'n others 'round here. Don't worry too much. She'll be safer in Paree.

At the end of the evening, Bailey determined he would ride in the car with Minnie back to L'il Red's and spend the night, which he often did now that he'd left Aurora Mae's for Thomas DeGrace's cot by the stove. You might need muscle, he said, if Dr. Willie's gang is still there.

They left the house through the front door, Bailey walking a few paces behind. He got in the front seat of Minnie's car next to the driver, but once they were on their way, he half-turned and put his arm backward over the seat so she might lean forward to grasp his hand. He thought for a few minutes about telling her he was done with Aurora Mae, but then she'd never quite known about her. Minnie never asked questions about his life away from her anyway. And now that he had none, what would be the point of revealing past complications?

Let us out here, Joe, Minnie said when they were close to L'il Red's and could see that, for once, there were no crowds of reformers milling about. I'd like me some air.

Magnus Bailey waited on the sidewalk while she stuck her head in the driver's window to speak with the man Joe, who'd been with her a good seven years. His heart swelled in his chest, his blood ran warm as he heard her say, Joe, you've stuck with me through thick and thin. I want you to be the first to know. I'm giving up the business soon, and I want you to have this car. I'll not be needin' it anymore.

First thing that Monday, they went to her bank together. She asked the manager to draw up a check that would clear her accounts. She discussed with him how the bank might manage the sale of her building, what the price might be if she wanted to liquidate quickly. She understood times were hard, but she'd take any amount reasonable. All the while, Magnus Bailey stood behind her with his hands joined in front of him. His eyes stared into the space above the bank manager's head. He looked, like every good domestic, to be neither listening to nor comprehending white people's business.

As soon as they were back on the street, he walked behind her only very close. He told her how proud he was of her, how he loved her that moment more than ever, that his heart was so full it hurt. He asked her what charity she was going to give the bank check to, told how there was an orphanage he knew for little mixed babies who never hurt anyone. It's always going begging, he said, but he could not see the sly workings of her mouth as she tried to keep from smiling at the thought of giving away all that money she'd worked so hard for, given up so much for. Why wasn't handing the car off to Joe enough? she wondered.

The skies had turned dark. There was a storm brewing. The sensible thing would have been to hail a cab, but they wanted to walk down a certain street they knew, one that was always quiet, even in the middle of the day. It was a street without homes, only warehouses near the docks, and it was hard times, so most were abandoned. They'd taken to traveling that street when they were on foot together. They felt alone there and safe enough to hold hands for a minute or even embrace. It gave them a thrill to express their affections in the open air. Practice, Bailey called it, for Paree.

I think we need more practice, she said that morning after checking up and down the street to make sure no one would see.

Bailey stopped and she turned toward him and they held on to each other tight with their eyes closed, dreaming of Paris, feeling warm and cozy in each other's arms although the air had turned damp and cold. Suddenly there was the sound of scuffling feet all 'round them. Ice shot through their veins. Their eyes opened. Five rough white men, one holding a bat, the other a knife, three more with stevedore hooks stood around them in a circle. Their clothes were torn and filthy. They looked to be on the bum or something close to it.

That's her. That's the Jew whore. I seen her in the papers, the one with the knife said.

That ape muss be her jigaboo lover, another said.

Muss be.

There was no way out. They couldn't bolt. There were too many of them. There was no use even in trying to talk their way out of trouble. Had the thugs been of his own race, Bailey would have tried talk and maybe won their safe passage, but these boys, these boys were hurt and misery served up plain. Bailey was a big man. He thought he might be able to take down a couple of them, but no matter what, he saw straightaway that his life and maybe Minnie's too were most certainly over. With nothing else to do, he roared like a warrior from out of one of his mama's African tales. He roared so loud the earth shook under his feet, and the heavens opened, hurtling lightning and hail down upon them into that circle of death. He charged forth at the man with the knife, who seemed to be the leader and knocked the man down. Bailey fell on top of him and got stabbed in the gut. The man with the bat came up behind and swung hard at his skull and spine, two, three times until Bailey was bathed in blood. Then someone hauled him off the man with the knife, and through a fading eye Bailey saw that the last two held tight on to Minnie, who kicked and screamed while the hail fell and the lightning flashed. I'm sorry, darlin', he tried to say, I'm sorry I forgot how life can change on a dime, but a stevedore's hook ripped through his chest and another ripped through his face, and he was dead.

They let her go long enough to collapse sobbing onto Bailey's body, then they dragged her and the corpse into a warehouse and used her at their leisure, away from the storm outside. Minnie retreated into the still, dark place her mind had gone all those years ago when she'd spent the night in the bedroll of a bandit chief. By the time the men were done, it was late in the night. She was no longer conscious.

They found a sack big enough to hold them both, who knows what came in it once upon a time, could have been anything, potatoes or rice or cotton or cane. They broke Bailey's limbs first so they could fold him up. They decided she was small enough to leave whole. Then they stuffed the lovers inside the sack with a half hod of bricks even though they heard the cloth rip some. They got the sack into a wheelbarrow, hauled it by the river, and dumped the pair in. Bailey's Minnie had been unconscious all that time, but when she hit the water, she came to. At first she struggled and got the sack open more by the tear. It wasn't enough, and she took in water. Down she sank, down to the riverbed with her arms around Magnus Bailey, and a few minutes later she died too.

It's a small mystery how Minerva Fishbein's body broke free from that sack a couple of months later and floated to the surface near the spot downriver where Tulips End once stood. Her corpse was ruined, and no one was exactly certain who it was but for the red hair and the body's general size, along with the fact that old Fishbein had reported his daughter missing within a time frame that made it logical to decide the corpse was hers and hers alone. As there were no injuries the coroner could distinguish that might not be caused by watery decomposition and the postmortem bites of crabs, the scrapes of run-ins with branch and rock, her death was declared either accidental or suicidal, and she was planted on the outskirts of the Jewish cemetery where the wicked lay to ponder their fates eternally since neither Heaven nor Gehenna would have them.

Magnus Bailey never surfaced. If his Minnie left him somewhere near Tulips End, maybe the best thing was for him to rest there, near his people who departed the world in '27 that they might all unwilling save the lives of their neighbors 'cross river who'd got their hands on dynamite.

As it happened, when Aurora Mae Stanton arrived to the old family farm, she found Mags very ill, just starting up with the lung disease that would kill her within a few years. Her household was in chaos. Her boys ran wild. Her husband, Joe, neglected his fields from the taking care of her. Sara Kate was newly married to a St. Louis man and lived there with him, struggling to make ends meet. Each of them held down more than one menial job. Sara Kate was not able to come home and help out, even on the weekends. The bank where Mags kept her savings had failed with the others in '29. There wasn't much to eat except what Joe could catch and no money at all for medicines.

Aurora Mae took one look at all the trouble around Cousin Mags and rolled up her sleeves to take care. After several months, the Dunlap household was again in order, the boys tamed, and Joe back in his fields. Mags was strong enough that Aurora Mae thought to go home for a spell. When she got there, she found a locked store, a torn-up parlor floor, a nearly empty strongbox with just a few coins scattered on its bottom, and a letter from Sister Pearl. The letter said: Now that redheaded whore is dead, Magnus Bailey and I have fallen in love and run off. You will never see us again, and I'm willin' to guess you might not think that such a bad thing.

She was thrown into a state of confusion, anger, and grief and went to the Miracle Church of God's People to save her soul from darkness. Dr. Willie, she was told, had left town around the same time Sister Pearl took off, some said out of a broken heart, and no one'd heard from him since. Thomas DeGrace and a handful of others kept the place going. They showed Aurora Mae much sympathy, offering to pray with her. They would pray she'd find her way toward forgiving those who had harmed her, but instead she renounced religion after that. When she got home, she cut her hair off, buried it in the backyard, and turned her back on men once and for all.

Fishbein had mourned the loss of his daughter's virtue for so long, the loss of her life felt like one more knot in the string of his miseries, something he'd always expected to experience before his own soul escaped the curse of Adam's flesh. In other words, her death was a sorrow but not a surprise. He discovered that when a man thinks he has cried all of his tears, he has not, and wept more for Magnus Bailey, who was surely also dead. He had no delusions there. If it were not for Golde, he might have expired of grief. Just as her mother had rescued him from the ultimate despair when he was a young man, her child gave him cause to put one foot in front of the other in his ripe age. He kept her with him, seven days a week. The neighbors considered her his help, a girl he used for cleaning and such. When he went out for his shopping and to the minyan, he took her with him, leaning on her shoulder with one hand as his most recent sadness had made him ever more stooped. The neighbors saw this and gave her a new name, which was Golde Cane. At the synagogue, she left his side and prayed with the women in their section. Her Hebrew was accomplished, her sentiments sincere, and the ladies of Baron Hirsch Synagogue petted and cosseted her for the charming novelty of the dark-skinned serving girl who could pray.

He put off the sale of his home until after the mourning year. A month before her first *yarhzeit,* he put a marker on Minerva's grave. He had it engraved with her name, in English script and in Hebrew, and below that the date he'd guessed years before might be that of her birth followed by a date he made up for her death. He wanted some words, an epigraph of some kind. After much deliberation, he instructed the engraver to carve into the stone the words *Beloved Daughter and Mother* and below that *Nothing Is Certain Under the Sun.*

Around the time Germany readied for its Jew-free Olympics, he was on board a boat, a simple Greek fisherman's vessel. He stood at the prow with one arm around the slender shoulders of Golde Cane, whose slight frame and saddened looks mirrored his own. With his other arm outstretched, he gestured across the glittering blue bay to the massive stone walls of Jaffa, its ancient spires, and red clay roofs. Look, *mine meydl*, he said, look! Eretz Israel!

For the first time since her mother went missing, the girl cried out in pure, unbridled joy.

She raised her arms and lifted her palms toward the sky in a gesture familiar to every Baptist in the land of her birth.

Hallelujah! she said. Praise the Lord!

Fishbein looked from her to the coastline and back. Despite his promises to Magnus Bailey, he saw that Golde would be an odd duck wherever she went, even here.

Oh, *mine meydl*, what a dear, strange bird you will seem to the good Jews of Eretz Israel, he thought. Maybe me, too, after all these years. How can I tell? America puts the stamp on you without your knowing.

He searched for a term that everyone talked about in America these days, one he considered particularly apt for his musings. He found it.

Technicolor. Yes, America puts the stamp on you in Technicolor.

He studied again his Golde, her bright new smile, her green eyes set in a brown face that looked so much like Minerva's it stabbed his heart. He studied the azure sea, the cobalt sky, the red roofs, the sparkling stone that grabbed the sun and clasped it to itself like a garment. The stamp of Eretz Israel looked to be Technicolor too. He shrugged. It's alright, he thought, it's alright. Then he laughed and raised his palms upward like Kohanim about to give the priestly blessing.

Hallelujah! he said. The Hebrew felt good in his mouth. Hallelujah! We are home!

Acknowledgments

THERE WAS A POINT quite early on in the writing of *Marching to Zion* when I'd written a particularly dramatic scene and had no idea where to go next. I thought maybe what I had was a very long short story and that the novel I'd intended to write was stillborn. I nearly stopped working on it altogether. Enter my dear husband, Stephen K. Glickman, always my hero. He said, "Why don't you take your own advice? Aren't you the one who's always saying, 'Follow the voice, the voice never lies'?" So I did. And along the way, I discovered the plot and characters of *Marching to Zion*. Yet another reason to be eternally grateful to the sage I married.

Speaking of gratitude, I must grant my agent, Peter Riva, his due, which is mammoth. Peter is a brilliant man, as good as the game, and I am proud to be under his wing. Diane Reverand, my editor, must also take her bow, especially for her stamina in the face of my stubbornness.

Once again, for their expertise in shepherding my novels across all media, I am deeply indebted to the undeniable genius of Jane Friedman, Jeff Sharp, and Luke Parker Bowles; the shining wisdom of Tina Pohlman; the knife-sharp shrewdness of Rachel Chou; and the sundry and glittering talents of Danny Monico, Galen Glaze, Nicole Passage, Rachelle Mandik, Jason Gabbert, and of course, my own darling Laura De Silva. Thank you all. Your energy and commitment astound. Bravo.

About the Author

BORN ON THE SOUTH SHORE OF BOSTON, Mary Glickman studied at the Université de Lyon and Boston University. While she was raised in a strict Irish-Polish Catholic family, from an early age Glickman felt an affinity toward Judaism and converted to the faith when she married. After living in Boston for twenty years, she and her husband traveled to South Carolina and discovered a love for all things Southern. Glickman now lives in Seabrook Island, South Carolina, with her husband, cat, and until recently, her beloved horse, King of Harts, of blessed memory. Her first novel, *Home in the Morning*, has been optioned for film by Jim Kohlberg, director of *The Music Never Stopped* (Sundance 2011).

EBOOKS BY MARY GLICKMAN

FROM OPEN ROAD MEDIA

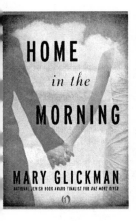
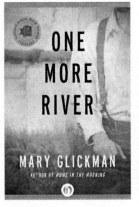
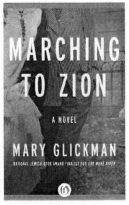

Available wherever ebooks are sold

OPEN ROAD

INTEGRATED MEDIA

Open Road Integrated Media is a digital publisher and multimedia content company. Open Road creates connections between authors and their audiences by marketing its ebooks through a new proprietary online platform, which uses premium video content and social media.

CPSIA information can be obtained at www.ICGtesting.com
Printed in the USA
BVOW07s2138161013

333961BV00002B/2/P

9 781480 435629